These Wicked Stars

Book One in the Nightfall Bazaar Series

Catelyn Wilson

To Katie, for everything.

THESE WICKED STARS

by Catelyn Wilson

DARIUS'S SOUK
GATES OF
THE BAZAAR
SASKIA'S TAVERN
THE BAZ

ZAIRE'S PALACE
THE ARENA
ENTRANCE TO THE UNDERWORLD
RUINS OF THE GODS

ONE

Darkness stalked me, clad in midnight robes. My breath plumed in front of my face, backlit by patches of weak winter sun. Something followed me. A formless whisper that flitted around every rock and tree of the island.

A flash of darkness swooped across the corner of my eye. I clutched my shawl tighter. They were here already, the monsters they warned all children of. The creatures that come from the sinful Bazaar that visits Veara Island at the Alignment of the planets. They were real, and one was here for me.

Stop. I clenched my jaw and stared hard into the forest nearby. There was nothing but creaking pine trees and rocky beaches. The frenzy in the air and buzz of gossip had addled my senses after weeks of chatter about the festival.

A cold breeze cleared my head. I shook off the ridiculous feeling of being watched by monsters and wrestled my long bronze hair from the grasp of the wind. With one last glimpse around, I hurried off the little lane that led back to my aunt and uncle's home, and headed towards the port.

The hulking profiles of ships braced against the cloudy sky. Sailors and merchants shouted and swirled around the docks, unloading supplies and passengers. I ducked under the arm of a lumbering sailor and wound through the maze. The tightness in my stomach and the chill on my neck eased as I dove deeper into the busy port.

I knew this sprawling array of salt and rotting wood better than anywhere else. Here I was almost normal, close to the sea and the promise of freedom, away from the vengeful eyes of my aunt and the whispers of gossip from respectable society.

Almost.

"Hazel." A rattling voice called my attention away from a vast ship, its sails emblazoned with a foreign kingdom's crest. "It's about time. What were you thinking, keeping an old woman out on the eve of the Alignment? I've been waiting all morning for you to pick up these silks!"

"Sorry," I murmured, and pulled my thoughts from the glory of the ships and the people arriving on the island. "Thank you for bringing them. It's impossible to get what Veronica wants from the mainland. Now she only talks about the western kingdom's fabric."

The old woman, Sigrid, looked more miffed than usual. Her skin, puckered and wrinkled around her eyes and mouth, was ashen. "You think I care? It cost me good coin to ship this in for your blasted cousin so close to the festival. If it weren't for your aunt and uncle's standing on the island, I wouldn't have given her request a second thought."

"Then let me pay you so I can get out of your hair," I grumbled, but she ignored me as usual. Sigrid, Veara's only merchant of fine fabrics, was also the island's most notorious gossip.

"Look at all these people." Sigrid curled her thin lip and spat at the ground near my boot. "Coming to celebrate something they don't understand."

I gingerly stepped further from range and fished out the gold coins Veronica had given me to pay for her new ball gown. The old woman snapped them up greedily before she glared at a group of young men disembarking from a stately-looking vessel.

"Thirty years since the last Alignment and all those deaths, and still people learn nothing. You know the governor's brother was taken by the Bazaar last time."

"I'm sure it will be alright, Sigrid," I said, placing the heavy bolts of crimson silk in my satchel. "Those stories about the festival and the Bazaar are just fairy tales meant to scare children."

And they certainly did.

"Bah!" Sigrid scoffed. "You're forgetting I was here for the last festival and its backwards catering to wide-eyed fools. You listen to me, girl. All this fuss over the seven planets lining up just so in the sky, granting entrance to a world of magic and treasure—it's blasphemy to the Fates. The festival is an abomination. If you step outside, you'll be snatched by devils and shadows, dragged straight to the old gods!"

My throat went dry. The dark flash I had seen on my way to the port nagged at my thoughts. A passing shadow. A bird overhead perhaps, or a whipping sail. Nothing more.

"I won't be going outside once night falls," I vowed, my skin curiously slick with cold sweat. "I'll be back next week with a new order for Veronica's winter wardrobe."

"Heed my words, Hazel. This festival will damn our island one day. Just you wait." Sigrid adjusted her deep black shawl and pushed past me, heading for her narrow offices near the main dock.

Streams of people from all over the Nederhølm Kingdom, and well beyond, filled the docks. They flooded towards town, looking for lodging. Some prepared wares to hawk to those who were foolish enough to celebrate in the thick of the night. Others spoke in hushed whispers in foreign tongues of the Bazaar and its secrets.

I breathed in deeply, letting the scent of pine, salt, and anonymity wrap around me like a blanket. I wanted to linger, maybe wander among the fisherman and hear their tales of mermaids and sirens. Maybe I would see Linus' ship docking and rush to meet him.

The thought sent a thrill of excitement down my spine and a rush of heat to my cheeks. It died just as quickly. I had to return to my cousin and finish her dress for the ball.

With my arm and shoulder already burning under the weight of the fabric, I turned towards the hilly path once more. A stiff wind whipped against my cheeks and cut through my simple homespun dress and tattered shawl. I braced against it, shoving my way through the clamoring crowds swarming the island, eager to see if the tales were true for themselves.

I hopped over a puddle of briny water and kicked aside a length of discarded rope. Just as I exited the gates, pushing by barrels of dried goods, something dark and cold shrouded my shoulder. The sensation of being watched trickled across my skin once again. Dread, unexplainable and icy, spooled in my belly.

A hand made of infinite darkness reached for me from within a nook of towering barrels and boxes. A finger crooked at me. Beckoning. My eyes stuck on a swirl of black robes, the flash of bronze skin and glinting metal. I staggered backwards, my lips parted, ready to fill my lungs with a scream. But then my back hit something firm and warm. A body.

"Linus!" I gasped. Relief flooded my veins, and I grinned up at him. It took all my willpower not to throw myself into his arms.

I glanced over my shoulder once. The barrels sat empty and unassuming. I swallowed back the urge to tell Linus. A trick of the light and clouds, that's all.

My fiancé looked just as surprised to see me. He pushed his sandy blonde hair out of his eyes. "Hazel, what are you doing here?"

"I could ask you the same question!" I laughed, my voice only a little tight. Three long months since I had seen him last. Relief rushed like champagne through my veins. "When did your ship get in? How did the trading go in the western kingdoms? I want to hear all about it."

Linus' suntanned face seemed to pale under the sky, darkening with a blanket of grey clouds. "We should get you home. It will be dark soon and you shouldn't be outside. We'll have time later to discuss things."

I was a little crestfallen that he didn't wrap me in an embrace—or better yet, a kiss—but I shoved my disappointment down. He couldn't risk being seen with me in public. Not yet. And I couldn't blame him.

But he'd never failed to regale me with stories of far-off ports and glittering shores. He knew how badly I wanted to escape the island and the painful past it held for me. Linus was my answer to it all. Between my marriage and the open water, I would finally be free.

"I know, but Veronica said the bustle for her dress was all wrong and demanded this ridiculous silk you can only get from Ishtar and—" I faltered.

Black robes, made from smoke and shadow, swirled around the gates of the port and billowed up the hill. A man. A monster.

My eyes stung as I blinked rapidly. I looked around, but no one, not even Linus, seemed to notice the apparition. My mouth went dry, the words I might say sticking in my throat. My fiancé looked at me strangely and that settled it.

I was imagining things. Shadows were not men. Monsters were not real.

"You should get back." Linus' eyes were a little hard and stared over my head. "The governor posted a notice that all islanders should be indoors by nightfall and can't leave until the Alignment is over in a week. Any who breaks his law will be punished severely."

He took my hand and guided me from the ports and crowds, back the way I had come. The small path seemed lonelier than when it was just me.

"Why doesn't the governor just ban the festival from our shores if he is so worried about it?" My voice caught, and I coughed to cover it up.

He shook his head and answered distractedly, "Stories about the festival and the Bazaar have reached the farthest corners of the world. Trying to stop something so ancient would be impossible. Every time the festival grows in popularity. Let the fools from foreign lands lose their coin and minds. It matters not to me."

The stories didn't seem so childish with the chill on my skin and the night closing in.

"Will you speak to my aunt and uncle at the ball? When you were here in the summer, and your letters, you said you would." I kept my voice light.

"I'll speak with them," he promised, but his voice sounded wrong. "Everything will be sorted. I'll make sure of it."

Not exactly the most romantic notion.

Linus had sworn he would tell everyone that we were engaged. It would raise me from the stain of my mother's name. We would travel on his ships, seeing every corner of the world and find a new home. The thought made my heart ache with longing. I'd waited so long and finally, *finally*, it was happening.

"Head home. I'll see you at your aunt's ball tonight," Linus said and squeezed my hand. He moved to the other path in the fork. One way led to town and the other back to the cold halls of the home I'd never been welcome in.

"Is everything all right?" I asked, squinting to take in his rumpled appearance.

His cream-colored suit was wrinkled, and his cheeks flushed. Why wasn't he more excited to see me? My heart slammed against my ribs. He couldn't possibly be rethinking our engagement, could he? Before he'd left three months ago, he had been radiant and happy and whispering his devotions to me on the beach.

"Everything is fine." He smiled faintly. "I'm just tired from the journey. I'll see you soon. Save a dance for me, will you?"

I checked for any sign of people, but a small copse of pine trees hid us from view of the main road. I threw my arms around his neck and kissed him. After three long, lonely months, I'd forgotten how good it felt to be held. His hands were warm on my shoulders and his lips tasted like salt and the promise of adventure.

He gently pushed me back, glancing over his shoulder like he was afraid we would be seen.

"I'll see you tonight," I said breathlessly, fighting off the hurt of his rejection. But there was a question behind my words. I didn't want to walk back alone, not today, not when I wanted to be with Linus more than anything.

He ran one finger along the chain of my necklace, where a ruby engagement ring dangled next to my mother's locket. His blue eyes looked stormy and troubled.

Linus nodded silently before he turned towards town and walked away.

Two

My aunt's house was cold and silent. The heels of my worn shoes clicked on the polished marble floors, leaving drops of water on the pristine tiles. I climbed the stairs to my cousin's room.

"There you are, Hazel. What took you so long? Mama will look for me soon to welcome guests to the ball. I'll have to take two coins from your commission." Veronica huffed from her seat at the vanity.

I bit back a retort and forced a pleasant smile to my lips, even though I wanted to hurl the bolts of fabric at the back of my cousin's head. "I have the silk for the bustle. Which do you prefer?"

Veronica stood and stalked to where I waited, three bolts of heavy fabric in my arms. Her small, pouting lips twisted as she scrutinized the material with a critical eye. She passed them between her fingers for a few moments and then compared them to her perfectly smooth complexion.

"This one." She flung the deep, blood-red crimson on the bed. "It will make my eyes stand out the most. And don't forget to add more than just two layers this time. I want to look as ravishing as possible tonight."

"Of course." I dipped my head and set to work pinning the new fabric in place on the gown hanging on the mannequin.

Veronica grinned as she watched, no doubt imagining the endless line of young men waiting for the chance to dance with her tonight. The bodice was tight enough to make anyone's eyes water, but the vibrant scarlet gathered in perfect pintucks around the waist. It was a perfect dress; even I could admit that about my work.

Once I'd secured the bustle, I slipped the dress free of the mannequin and buttoned my cousin in. I fastened every hook, clasp, and ribbon as Veronica stared into her large silver mirror.

"Don't be too put out if no one asks you to dance, Hazel. I'm sure you'll find someone one day." Veronica continued to admire herself and then snapped her fingers. "Oh, maybe the butcher's son, Radcliffe, I think is his name. He's ugly enough to not be picky."

I didn't even have time to scowl.

"There you are," Aunt Lilliana's voice startled us.

My heart flew in my chest and I set my hands behind the small of my back, not allowing my eyes to lift past the brocade stitched at my aunt's collar. She hated when I looked at her with what she described as my 'baleful and too-far apart eyes'.

"Oh, Mama, what do you think of my gown? Hazel has just finished it, isn't it lovely?" Veronica spun, allowing the flames from the gaslight to dance across the gold thread stitched into the bodice.

Lilliana's mouth barely turned up at the corners at her daughter's praise. "Quite," she agreed. "Even your cousin has some talents, I suppose."

I kept my lips together at the grudging praise. Aunt Lilliana paced forward, the heavy velvet of her dress trailing behind as she inspected me with a disdainful curl warping her thin mouth.

Finally, she sat at the vanity and turned her dark blue eyes on me. I fought the urge to squirm. It was as if the woman could see through my skin. Would she find an excuse to keep me from the ball tonight? Did she know her disgraced niece was planning on marrying far above her station?

"Will the Hale's be at the ball tonight, Mother?" Veronica spoke up, elbow deep in her jewelry chest, clearly unaware of the tension in the room.

"Of course. And Mr. Hale is bringing his son, Linus. I do not think we have had the chance to meet him yet. He has been off on the seas helping run his father's shipping company. It will be nice to have such a respectable young man on the island."

I turned away to smother my smile, pretending to organize the needles and thread. The thought of Linus, tall and striking, wandering the halls made my pulse jump. We would finally announce our love to our families. No more hiding or secrets. I'd leave this place and all the terrible memories for good.

"What are you smiling about?" Veronica huffed.

I whirled around, cheeks burning, pulled from the fantasy too soon. "Just thinking about the ball tonight and how I must thank you again, Aunt, for allowing me to go. It is such a kindness." I winced at the forced sweetness in my voice.

Aunt Lilliana's brow furrowed. She detected displeasure as easily as a hound could locate its prey.

"I invited your sister to the celebrations. She and her father will stay for the entire week," Lilliana said, ignoring my attempt at flattery. "You will be on your best behavior while he is here. Do you understand?"

The blood drained from my face. I was happy to see my sister, but I hated her father. He haunted my dreams more than I cared to admit.

"I will," I promised, my throat tightening as Lilliana stepped forward, towering over me in her heeled boots.

"Be sure that you do. That man is a saint for staying with your mother after what she did to him. Any other man would have divorced an adulteress and sent the ungodly results far away. If you so much as breathe a word to him, I will find out. Mark my words."

She let the veil of the threat hang over me like a pall. Despite years of experience, I flinched. Flashes of the few years I'd spent in the household of that man flickered through my mind. Though he had never laid a hand on my mother for her sins, he certainly not hesitated to lash me with a belt or the back of his hand for the smallest of mistakes.

"And do something about your hair," Lilliana growled. "That widow's peak is far too obvious when you pull it back like that. Do you want everyone to be reminded of my sister's immoral ways?"

My fingers unconsciously moved to my forehead. My bronze hair was just like my mother's, but the prominent widow's peak was decidedly not. The pad of my thumb brushed the scar from where I'd tried to shave it off years ago.

Yet another reminder I was not the daughter of Jorgen Rhodes.

It was bad enough my eyes were the wrong color for the cold climes of the North Sea. Everyone else had blue or green eyes, but I bore the burden of dark brown ones. Like pools of mud, Aunt always said.

There was no hiding who I was: the bastard of a nameless sailor who had abandoned my mother only a few months into their affair.

"Make sure you wear something presentable," Lilliana sniffed.

With the flick of her wrist, I was dismissed.

I ducked from the room, stifling with tension and unspoken insults, and dashed for my quarters. The wind howled in from the sea as dark clouds threatened a storm that would no doubt last for days. The halls were empty, and I rubbed my arms against the chill.

Casting a glance over my shoulder, I paused near the ballroom. I could imagine myself and Linus dancing there in just a few hours. We would swirl across the floor, all eyes on us as guests whispered about our engagement. About how respectable my fiancé was. Maybe they would admit they were wrong to treat me so badly all these years. To shun and mock a blameless bastard. If Linus loved me, I must be worthy of their respect.

I squeezed my eyes shut for a moment, committing the fantasy to memory.

A flash of lightning bathed the ballroom in bluish light. A shadow stretched long across the checkered floor, reaching for me. I turned towards the windows.

No.

In the depths of the trees and rocks beyond the window, a man with bronze skin and dark eyes glared back at me. Shadows clung to his shoulders, curling off of him like smoke. A glint of wickedly sharp metal hung at his side. My lungs seized around a silent cry for help.

I stumbled until my back collided with a low table. A vase crashed to the floor. The sting of porcelain shards against my ankles felt distant, like it was happening to someone else. The man moved closer; the lower half of his face bathed in darkness. I closed my fingers around a shard of broken pottery.

Another flash of lightning webbed across the sky, and thunder roared overhead.

The man looked right at me, held a finger to his lips, and disappeared. Like smoke in the wind.

Night One

THREE

Thoughts of swords and ghostly men frayed my nerves. Anxiety gripped my stomach tightly as I headed for the ballroom a few hours later. Night had fallen over our island, and I didn't dare breathe until I heard voices.

Servants filed through the manor, pulling curtains and drapes tightly shut. I brushed my hair back, letting it fall down my shoulders. With one last glance in a mirror to make sure my hair swept over my forehead and covered my widow's peak, I stepped into the light.

Scrubbing my palms over the gathered satin of my dress, I prayed my hands wouldn't leave any sweat marks. I had spent weeks on my gown, pilfering scraps of fabric from my aunt and Veronica whenever I could. Tiny faux pearls lined the bodice and the deep emerald and black complimented my eyes in a way none of the light pastels and dingy browns I'd always worn could.

Voices buzzed in the grand foyer. Footmen and maids swirled about, hands laden down with silver trays and precariously stacked glasses. I paused at the threshold of the ballroom, scanning the swirl of bodies. Flashes from the morning flitted through my mind. Swords and dark eyes and black robes. I clutched at my skirt with rigid fingers.

I hadn't imagined the man following me. Something was wrong.

Maybe he knew my mother. I bit down on my lip, scanning the corners. A roar of laughter from a group of men blazed throughout the room. Whatever the shadow man wanted, he would not find it here with a bastard.

I took a deep, calming breath. Warm lamplight chased away the dull throb of fear, and I entered the party.

Drapes of white gauzy fabric draped the ceilings. Towers of floral arrangements braced against the walls. The checkered marble floors gleamed in the lamplight and jewelry shimmered with every move. My hand crawled to my throat, and I rubbed my fingers along my mother's locket and Linus' ring before I tucked the necklace back into the top of my gown.

"There you are, Jorgen." Aunt Lilliana's crisp voice trickled to my ears, sending a jolt of dread down my spine. "And Adelaide, so good of you to come. We have you in the very best of our suites and are so honored you chose to spend the festival at our humble gathering."

"Come now, Lilly," Jorgen's gruff voice sent me flying into the shadows of a column, "your parties are always magnificent, even during this miserable season."

Lilliana laughed, throwing her head back and parting her dark red lips in an exaggerated smile. I peeked around the column, swallowing my fear.

"Hazel!" Adelaide's soft voice tugged me from my hiding spot. I winced and took a few steps closer. "What are you doing over there? You look so lovely!" My sister pulled me to her chest in a hug.

Though she was only twenty and a year my elder, Adelaide always seemed far more mature and grown. She had a feminine form, soft curves, and bright blue eyes. She was what most men wanted in a wife: the perfect daughter of a respectable marriage. Her father's name had been the only thing that saved her from the shame of our mother.

I had not been so lucky.

"What's the matter? You look like you've seen a ghost," she asked.

I shuddered against the memories of that man, the one following me. But I took in a shaky breath to steady my nerves. Linus would be here soon. No one could hurt me if he was by my side.

"I'm just nervous. Let's go over to the orchestra." I tugged her hand, clad to the elbow in a long white glove. Jorgen's narrowed eyes followed us the whole way across the room. I didn't let go until we were half-hidden behind the instruments.

"Is it really going to happen tonight?" Adelaide whispered. Soft music floated from the strings of the band. Heat crept up my neck, but I nodded, keeping myself from watching Jorgen and his disapproving glower.

"Linus said he'd tell them tonight. Have you seen him yet? I don't know if I can breathe," I said, hands pressed to my chest.

Adelaide squealed and pulled me to her side. Her face split in a wide, excited smile. "I've only just arrived, but the last of the carriages were behind us. It's almost dark, so no one will be outside at this point. I'm sure he's here."

"And you swear you have told no one, even by mistake?" I grabbed her arm.

Adelaide huffed and dropped her shoulders, rolling her eyes towards the chandelier glimmering overhead. "Of course not."

"You know your father. If he even suspected something, he and Lilliana would conspire a thousand ways to throw me into the sea."

"Don't be so dramatic." Adelaide waved her hand dismissively.

I couldn't help myself. I stood on my toes and craned my neck to scan the crowd. Gowns swirled across my vision and laughter pealed over the crowd. A blur crossed the back of the room, dodging between the columns.

I froze, refusing to blink. Russet skin. A sword curved like a fang. My ribs constricted even as a familiar trickle of recognition dawned on me. I fell back against a column, my shoes slipping out from underneath me.

The partygoers laughing near the columns didn't even notice the armed man towering behind them.

I threw my gaze to Adelaide, wondering if she had seen him too, but a drunken man bumped into her and slurred an apology, stealing her attention. I pressed myself further into the wall. My stomach dropped to my toes as I twisted. The man dressed in black was gone.

Had I imagined it again? A symptom of nerves and exhaustion. It had to be. I hoped to the Fates it was true.

Adelaide gasped and turned me by the shoulders towards the main doors, forcing the vision of the black-clad man from my mind in an instant. "Look, there he is!"

A familiar head of sandy blonde hair, tanned skin, and soft blue eyes entered the room. I couldn't hear the words that came from my sister's mouth. Linus' smile was blinding, like the break of dawn over a calm sea. His gaze found me and his smile faded to something softer, more secret.

My skin flooded with heat when he took a graceful step forward, just as the other guests lined up for the opening dance. What had I been worrying about again? I didn't care.

"Hazel." His voice smoothed over my ears as he bowed deeply and kissed my hand. "Would you give me the honor of the first dance?"

"Yes, she'd love to," Adelaide blurted, shoving me forward. I didn't bother to give her a glare. My heart was too busy fluttering in my chest.

Linus' firm hand guided me to the dance floor, in front of the entire town. My mouth went dry. It was happening.

Whispers followed us as the music began, the first strains falling sweetly to my ears. I tried to focus on Linus, his warm hands, and his perfectly tailored coat. We were a few steps into the dance when I looked into his eyes.

There were smears below his lashes. His usually tan skin was sallow. Normally, he would whisper soft things into my ears, telling me how excited he was to marry me. But he was silent, like at the port. Something was wrong. He hardly looked at me while he guided us through the steps, twirling me under his arm in a swirl of silk and lace and confusion.

"What is it?" I asked. He guided me away from his arms, and I had to let go of his hands to catch those of another girl as we exchanged partners briefly. Linus shook his head once as if to say he couldn't discuss it yet.

When we met once again in the middle, Linus appeared even more tired, his expression drawn as if he dreaded something. Could he dread the thought of marrying someone like me? Did seeing me in this dress, pretending to be what I wasn't, give him his first real idea of the damage I would do to his reputation? A rock settled in my stomach.

"Linus, please, what is the matter with you? What have I done?" I pleaded.

The music reached its crescendo, the soft melody of the violins gave way to high-pitched trills as musicians manipulated the strings with greedy fingers. He shook his head like he couldn't get the words out, and yet he pulled me close for a moment, his warm breath brushing my cheek.

"You know I care for you, Hazel. No matter what, that will not change."

"What are you talking about?" I asked, softer than a whisper. He opened his mouth to speak again, but the applause of the crowd drowned out any hope of further explanation. He withdrew his hands from my waist gently. It felt like he had shoved me away.

"Wonderful!" My uncle's voice carried over the crowd of excited revelers. "We are so pleased you could all come as our guests. While we are here to celebrate the festival of the Alignment and the blessings the Fates have been so kind to grant us, we have another reason for gathering so many of our friends and family."

"Linus—" I caught his sleeve, trying to push through the crowd to reach him. But he pulled away, recoiling like I was rancid water. "Won't you tell me what it is I've done? I thought you knew what it could mean to be seen with me in public. I thought you understood."

"Please, Hazel. Just know that this isn't what I intended." Linus adjusted his waistcoat.

"What did you intend? What do you mean?" But then the speech I had been ignoring slammed into me like the gale raging outside. The blood rushed from my limbs, burning me as it traveled to my seizing heart.

"Lillianna and I are so pleased to celebrate the engagement of our daughter, Veronica, to Linus Hale."

I felt the ground rushing up to meet me.

Linus looked past me, no, straight *through* me. The crowd parted for him as a round of gasps and applause erupted over the gathering. My vision tinged with black and I stumbled back a step. Linus climbed the stairs to stand next to Veronica. I nearly retched when she pulled him closer for a kiss.

"Hazel!" Adelaide's voice hardly breached my thoughts as she grabbed my hand. "What is going on? How is this possible?"

"I don't—It can't be." Icy dread spread through my scalp and settled in my chest.

Adelaide pulled me from the center of the room as well-wishers crowded about, pushing to congratulate my cousin—and the man who used to be my fiancé. My knees buckled, and I stumbled into the hall, my face flushed with shame.

"Of all the awful things our cousin has done to you, this has to be the worst!" Adelaide hurled a growling curse at the ballroom. She stomped into the hall; shoulders bunched around her ears.

I collapsed on the cool marble floor, leaning my head against the wall, and gasped for air. My bodice strangled my lungs, my heart. I couldn't breathe, couldn't think.

"Talk to me, Hazel! You can't let this happen!"

"She couldn't have known. You were the only one who knew about me and Linus."

I had to close my eyes. Flashes of memories, now tinged in a painful red, swarmed me. Linus kissing me for the first time by the sea. The memory of him pulling me into his arms as he whispered how we would go far away. They felt more like a nightmare than the dream they'd been only moments ago.

"Veronica had to have known! She loves to torture you and do anything she can to make you miserable. Linus wouldn't have—"

"But he did, Adelaide. I can't believe I thought even for a moment that someone would want to be with me. I'm a disgrace. I'd do nothing but pull him down to my level," I said hollowly.

"I wish you wouldn't say such things. It isn't your fault what Mother did." Adelaide set her jaw.

My fingers wound around the golden chain and I tugged out the locket, prying the brass apart with my thumbnail. It was all I had of my father, a tiny token with a dent in the side. Mother hadn't told me much about him besides that he had given her the locket as a symbol of his affection, promising to rescue her from a callous, loveless marriage.

But he never came back.

"I can't blame him," I said, my voice small. "How could I?"

Adelaide's face crumpled; her mouth opened to protest, but no words came out. Even my sister, as much as she wanted, could not defend the logic. I was worthless in the eyes of our society. The product of an affair that was blatant and cruel. Linus had finally come to his senses.

She sat down and pulled my hand into hers. I kept my other fist closed around the locket, pressing until it left a round imprint in my skin. The music began again as we sat there in the low light. Voices and cheers echoed across the halls.

It should have been me in there, dancing and basking in congratulations. Linus was supposed to be my salvation, my way of redeeming my birth. But now...

"She doesn't want to talk to you," Adelaide snarled.

I jolted to my feet, eyes stinging. I don't know how long we'd sat there while I cried and the revelry continued unbidden in the ballroom. My backside ached and my legs stung with thousands of invisible needles.

"Please, at least let me explain myself," Linus said tightly. Hope tugged at the bits of my shattered heart. Perhaps he was coming to apologize, to admit it was a misunderstanding or mistake.

I wiped beneath my eyes with the heel of my hand. Adelaide stood beside me, hands planted on her hips and eyes snapping with fury. I wished I felt angry. Instead, looking at Linus in his well-tailored waistcoat and perfectly tied cravat, I felt irrevocably broken.

"It's okay," I said, squeezing Adelaide's hand.

She looked at me in disbelief. I knew Adelaide would have slapped him if I had given her the signal. Finally, she grunted and stepped back, folding her arms and skewering my ex-fiancé with a glare hot enough to scald.

"I thought you'd left," Linus said after a moment of insufferable silence. My eyes lifted past his collar to his face. His mouth was stained red with Veronica's lip paint. I looked away, my stomach twisting.

"There's nowhere I can go during the festival." My voice trembled and my traitorous heart flipped in my chest.

Adelaide retreated a few more steps as if sensing the need for privacy.

But she remained close by, offering me her unwavering strength. I wished I could possess a single iota of it myself.

But I was weak, so very weak when I met his stunning blue eyes.

"I'm sorry, Hazel. This isn't how I wanted you to find out. I wanted to tell you earlier and explain everything else."

"You're engaged to Veronica, not me. What else is there?" I wanted the words to sound biting, but they were flat, accepting. Why couldn't I be angry?

Linus sighed and pressed his fingers to his temples. "I love you, Hazel, believe me."

"Stop," I pleaded, a tear leaking from my eye. "Don't say that if you don't mean it. How could you?"

"But I mean it. I swear this isn't what I wanted."

"Why didn't you tell me at the port? Why wait until now?"

Linus raked his fingers through his hair and let out a frustrated sound. "I didn't want to hurt you. There's too much to explain, and I didn't want you to be outside so late."

A bitter laugh caught in my throat. "You could have written. A thousand chances you've had, and you waited until now?"

"Hazel, I couldn't. You know how much you mean to me." Linus shook his head.

"I understand, really." I took a small step back, desperate for distance. "You don't want to marry me, to be tied to my name. Veronica is... she will allow you to be respected."

Linus' mouth formed a hard line and his hair fell across his forehead. He looked towards the open doors of the ballroom and closed the distance between us. I sucked in a breath, wondering for a moment if he would kiss me. But his hands merely skimmed my arms before coming to grasp my fingers.

"It's my father. He lost all of our fortune in some horrible deals. That is why I was sailing the new fleet to the western kingdoms to trade personally. We needed the money. But it won't last for long. He insisted I marry Veronica. Her dowry is enough to settle our debts, and then some."

"Did he know about us?" I whispered.

Linus blanched a little. "No, he doesn't. He can't. If I am going to save my family, I have to have the money that marrying Veronica would bring. Do you understand?"

"So, you are ashamed of me, then?" My voice trembled. Somehow, the answer to that question was more important than anything else. Had he ever loved me? Was I merely a distraction or a means to an end?

He hesitated, blinking rapidly. "Of course not."

I studied his face, the contours of his cheekbones to his aquiline nose. Such a noble face. But for a terrifying moment, I couldn't tell if the face I thought I loved was lying.

"How could you not have told me? We can figure something out; this isn't what needs to happen. I'm sure of it," I begged, my fingers tightening around his.

"I don't see how. The money you make from sewing dresses is hardly enough to cover thousands in debt." He dropped my hand.

My heart twisted as his eyes fell.

"There you are, my love!" Veronica stumbled out of the ballroom, one sleeve slipping down her shoulder, a flute of champagne clasped between her fingers. "What are you doing over here?"

Linus stepped away swiftly. It felt like pulling a thorn from every nerve. Veronica's eyes narrowed as she looked between us, to the tears staining my face and the blush creeping up her fiancé's neck.

"What is going on? What are you doing, Linus?" Veronica's sultry voice changed to poison. Linus looked at me, the skin around his eyes tight, pleading with me to keep the secret.

I felt hollow, like the pain had rooted out every part of my being that he had touched.

"Nothing, dear. Shall we dance?" Linus pressed his hand into Veronica's lower back, trying to guide her back to the party.

I tore my eyes away, wiping at my damp lashes once more. The lamplight glinted fiercely off the diamond on her finger. It made the simple ruby ring around my neck look pitiful.

"Why are you looking at him like that? What is the meaning of this?" Veronica shook him off, red creeping from her dress and into her face. Her shouting drew stares and whispers from within the threshold of the ballroom.

"It's nothing," I said, but my voice quivered.

"You've had too much to drink, Veronica." Adelaide stepped between us, her arms reaching to stop our cousin from coming closer.

"Apparently so, because it looks as if your rotten, disgraceful sister is attempting to ensnare *my* fiancé!" Veronica shouted, the flush in her cheeks spreading to her chest. I flinched away, stepping on my skirts.

"Please, you don't know what you're talking about," Linus hissed.

But it was too late. The crowd turned its attention from the dancing to us. I wanted to run, to flee, and hide my face in shame. Accusing eyes turned on me like knives. Gossip flitted through the air like fireflies.

"It isn't enough that your mother threw herself at any sailor that wandered onto shore, now you have to go after the man who is to marry me?" Veronica stalked forward, pushing Linus away. "I let you sew my clothes, I give what little money you have, and you repay me by trying to seduce Linus?"

"You don't understand." I held up my hand, desperate for her to stop speaking so loudly. "It isn't like that, I swear it."

"Girls, what is the matter?" Lillianna materialized from the crowd pressing at the doors, eager to hear the next words. She kept her face serene, her shoulders back, but her eyes blazed.

"The apple doesn't fall far from the tree, Mama." Veronica stomped her foot and pointed at me. "I caught her here in the dark trying to lure Linus to her room!"

"That is not true!" I shouted, my eyes flying to Linus and his mortified expression. Lillianna held up her hands, silencing me quicker than if she had raised a belt.

"You will not make a scene here, girl. Go to your room and we will deal with the consequences of your actions later," she threatened.

A scream burned in my throat. How did everything turn against me so quickly? Blood roared in my ears. Veronica's sneer broke something in me, snapping it in half.

"It's not what you think," I said before I could stop myself. "I was not luring or seducing him!"

"And I am to believe that?" Lillianna scoffed, her eyes darting to the crowd pressing in around us.

"Yes, you should." My voice was firmer than it had ever been. Heat licked up my neck and buzzed at the base of my skull. Veronica's venomous glare and the pure vitriol my aunt heaped upon me were too much to bear. I couldn't do it any longer.

My aunt's expression slipped a fraction, but it was enough. "You are nothing," Lillianna hissed, glancing at the crowd of her guests pressing closer. "You are the bastard of a horrible woman. Your mother's death was a blessing on this family. She got what she deserved."

I heard Adelaide's sharp inhale, Veronica's choking gasp, and felt the slap of skin as my hand collided with my aunt's cheek. My chest rose and fell, my breath burned my lungs.

Silence.

Lillianna's stony face seemed to crumble and rearrange into planes and angles sharp enough to kill. She grabbed me by the hair and wrenched me forward. Gasps rippled across the crowd as she threw me at the door.

What had I done?

"Your mother deserves no respect or the idiotic reverence you heap upon her memory," Lillianna seethed. "You are a disgrace, a stain on our family. You think you can flaunt yourself around, try to break up a marriage before it's even begun?"

My jaw clicked together, and my muscles tightened with years of anger and pain. Years of being passed from relative to relative when Mother died. Years of being told I was ugly, sinful, and useless. I straightened up to my full height, even as Lillianna bore down on me with the wild look of a blood-drunk soldier.

"I've been engaged to Linus for six months." The words bubbled up from somewhere deep inside, falling from my mouth without control. "How does your precious daughter feel about being second choice to a bastard?"

Lilliana breathed in sharply, eyes wide with disbelief.

Veronica's face turned even redder than her scarlet dress. Linus looked at his feet but did not deny it. For that, I was grateful, at least. I was not totally worthy of his shame.

Aunt Lillianna wiped the shock from her expression and stepped towards me, an accusing finger forcing my back against the carved wood of the imposing double doors.

"As if anyone would tie themselves to you," she snarled. "As if anyone would willingly take a scandal into their home unless the law demanded it."

She flung the door open and the crowd of shocked onlookers fell away from the rain and shattered moonlight as if it were poisonous. My heart stuttered to a stop. No one was to go outside during the eve of the Alignment. It was dangerous, deadly even.

"What are you doing?" Linus took a half step forward before Veronica yanked him back by the coat. He hardly spared her a glance though, his eyes fixated on the open door.

Lilliana snarled; her thin lips transformed with the cruelty I knew so well. "My years of charity to you, and you spit in my face. You are a spoiled, horrible, ungrateful child! You will leave his house and never return. If I ever see your face again, I will make sure the constable knows you are an adulterating thief."

"No!" Adelaide wailed, pushing through the crowd to fling herself between me and the yawning mouth of the door open to the night. "Please, Aunt. At least let her stay until the first night is over. You can't throw her out now!"

"I will not allow her in my house for a moment longer. She has disgraced me for the last time. Seducing an engaged man, striking her own family—I'll not abide by it." Lillianna's face contorted, red with anger. With shame and years of simmering resent.

"Aunt, please—" I stammered when she pushed me closer to the freezing night air. All of my bravado dissipated with the heat leaching from my skin, stolen by the chill in the air.

I would die out there. That is what all the stories said.

Strange people and creatures of fantasy and myth roamed during the eve of the Alignment, searching for those who would give in to their whisperings and temptations. Hungry from decades of separation from the mortal world, they would force me to that horrible Bazaar the stories spoke of. The one where you can buy any sin.

"Please!" Adelaide clung to my dress as if she could keep me inside with sheer force of will. "Don't do this."

"Get away from her, Adelaide," Jorgen demanded, his voice sending shivers of fear through me. "Do not touch her. She is worse than even your mother."

Those words were worse than a curse tumbling from a set of pure lips. Jorgen was the only one who despised me more than my aunt. He was finally making good on the same threat he always had, to keep me away from my sister. I could see it in the disgust that distorted his face.

I cast my eyes around the crowd, searching for a face that knew reason. But they all looked at me as if I were being condemned to the noose like a common thief.

Hard stares, warped scowls, and hissing words.

No.

"The festival is made for people like her. I don't doubt she will fit in amongst the other abominations." Lillianna grinned wickedly.

The man in shadows would find me if she threw me outside. The planets would align, opening the Bazaar. He would drag me to it. Feast on my heart. My skin turned to ice. The only thing that kept me from falling apart was the red mark on her cheek. Part of me refused to feel bad for it, relished in it even.

"Hazel," Linus spoke, reaching for me. But then his hand fell away and his eyes lowered. He looked crossed somewhere between pity and fear. Was the fear for himself or for me?

"Do not," Veronica hissed, moving to stand between us, her chest heaving with angry breaths.

"I'll be alright. I promise to find a way." I hoped he knew what I meant, that I would find a way for us to be together somehow.

He glanced at Veronica, who glowered down at me with death in her eyes. Linus nodded slightly, almost imperceptibly; our eyes locked.

"Get out," Lillianna snarled, pushing me.

I staggered, one foot crossing the threshold. And then she pushed once more until I was completely outside. Freezing rain stung my skin and soaked through my dress immediately. I gasped at the cold, my bare arms erupting into goosebumps.

The last thing I saw before the doors shut and locked against the terrors of the night was Adelaide's horrified face. And behind her, a strange man dressed in black, the shadows clinging to him like he wasn't even there at all.

FOUR

I stood in the dark and waited for something terrible to happen. I don't remember for how long. At some point, the freezing cold and bitter wind must have pushed me to walk. Instinct driving me to get the blood flowing to my numbed fingers and toes.

Moonlight shifted through gaps in the clouds as the rain slowly eased. My shoes slipped over the cobblestoned streets while I wandered aimlessly, trying not to freeze to death. My skirts were heavy and soaked, making every step a water-logged nightmare.

I tried to keep my thoughts from Linus marrying someone else, or to the fact that I was now homeless. Or the certain death that awaited a lone woman on the eve of the Alignment. Every shadow seemed sinister, like the talons of monsters waiting to drag me into the trees.

Gritting my teeth, I wrapped my arms tighter around my middle. I needed to get somewhere warm and dry or I would not live long enough to find a way to be with Linus again.

I turned towards town at the south end of the island. The inns would be full of tourists and revelers wandering the festival. I could sneak in unnoticed and find somewhere to stay, for a while at least.

Thoughts of warmth and purpose drove me down the steep hill towards the glittering lights of the town. Low-slung stone buildings and skinny wooden houses grew in frequency until the thick forest gave way to sharp cliffs and then the dark sand beaches near the port.

My jaw ached from my teeth clenching together. My fingers looked nearly blue and burned with cold. I sniffed, passing my hand beneath my nose, and finally entered the city streets. Violent shivers wracked my body, so hard my vision blurred.

Fires burned on the beaches as people danced and celebrated despite the cold. The silhouettes of gargantuan ships and small schooners looked menacing against the midnight sky. The streets were thick with tourists. People selling trinkets and food. I didn't recognize a single face.

I was the only islander foolish enough to be trapped outside.

The blazing windows of an inn beckoned across the square. I held my sopping skirts in one hand and raced to the door, opening it slowly. The buzz of voices collided with my ears as the warmth of the raging fire slapped my skin.

I kept to the shadows, sliding along the wall in my dripping gown. The innkeeper did not look up, far too busy counting the gold in his hands as drunk patrons laughed and enjoyed themselves.

I sat by an enormous stone fireplace and sank to the rough wooden floor. My fingers ached, and I held back a hiss as the flames warmed them. The room was thick with patrons, and enough coats and skirts obscured my hunched figure that I felt safe enough to stay for a while.

Slowly, the heat from the fire burned through the chain of my necklace, singeing my skin. I flinched and pulled it away from my neck. The chain slipped through my fingers until Linus' ring and my mother's locket rested in my palm.

Perhaps the cold and the fear had kept me from feeling the full effect of the events of the night, because there, shivering and alone with nowhere to go, it was as if someone had kicked me in the stomach.

A tear slipped down my cheek, burning hotter than the flames licking at the logs of the fireplace. The ruby glittered in the light. I traced it with my fingertip, wishing the night had not gone so horribly wrong. Another tear, and then another, leaked from the corners of my eyes. I wiped them away angrily, but the dam had broken.

I had been so hopeful. The two of us were going to leave the island. We would travel far and wide together. That dream had been crushed the moment they had thrown me to the wolves with nothing but my dress and a broken engagement. I hiccupped and buried my face in my knees.

There had to be a way to solve Linus' problem, something that didn't involve my cousin's dowry. Though I knew little of his father, I knew his company was the most important thing to their family. It was a source of pride, of livelihood, and respect.

Linus would never abandon his family, even for love. I could respect that. And I would make sure he wouldn't have to give up anything for me.

The urge to solve this problem rose fiercely in my gut. The only way to control my future was to solve his family's money problems. I tapped my fingers against my numbed lips, thinking. Maybe I could pawn Linus' ring. I was sure it would be worth a substantial sum of money. Then I could use that money to make and sell dresses or...

It wasn't enough.

I wasn't enough.

"What a lovely locket."

I jerked upright and quickly unfolded myself from the floor, stifling a groan as my stiff joints popped. But it wasn't the innkeeper ready to demand payment. Instead, a man in a dark coat and a grey hat obscuring his eyes sat in a roughly hewn wooden chair a few feet away.

"Thank you." I stammered; sure he hadn't been there a moment ago. "It was my mother's."

I hoped the dark hid my tears and the fact I had been sobbing on the dirty floor of an inn.

The man wore a soft smile and his salt and pepper beard cut close to his skin. "May I see it?" he asked.

He had a pleasant, almost soothing voice. The stranger reached out a slightly wrinkled hand. He looked harmless. Nothing more than an old man. Even so, I hesitated, my fingers clasped around my single earthly possession.

"I only wish to look at it." His mouth smiled kindly beneath the shadows obscuring his eyes. "It reminds me a great deal of a similar trinket I gifted my wife many years ago."

Making sure I wrapped the chain around my fingers, I held the locket out. He leaned forward, keeping a respectable distance. A knot in my stomach loosened some. The soft light made the simple accessory look more elegant than usual; a silver face etched in a swirling pattern, inlaid with gold foil.

"It is lovely, Miss—what may I call you?"

"Hazel." I withdrew my hand. It would do no good to share my last name. He might be familiar with Veara Island, and I didn't want to deal with a person who knew the mortification I had endured at the ball.

"I bought a nearly identical locket for my wife when we were courting," he said, voice thoughtful and melodic with a peculiar accent. He motioned for me to sit across from him. "I quite impressed her with my skills at picking out jewelry."

"Us women are always partial to that talent." I managed a fragile smile and fastened the necklace back around my neck. Instead of tucking the locket away in my bodice, I allowed it to hang freely. Away from my aunt and uncle's home, the sight of it would offend no one.

"And might I assume the ring on that chain was chosen by a man with skills like myself?" The man smiled again. I wished I could see his eyes. Though his voice was kind and warm, I couldn't be sure if he mocked me.

"Yes." I winced.

"Usually, a girl as young as yourself would smile when saying something like that." The man made a *tsk* sound and folded his hands under his chin.

I could only force an insincere smile. Anxiety gnawed at my stomach. How could I find the money I needed to save Linus' business? Where would I sleep? Not a single soul on the island would take me in, not with my mother's past. Adelaide would try, but her father would sniff me out and punish her for it.

"Is the man who gave you that ring the reason you were crying?" he asked. "I do not mean to offend. I just can't, in good conscience, allow a young woman to be so distressed in my presence. Not if I can help."

"That's kind of you to offer, sir, but I'm fine," I said firmly, eyes trained on the fire instead of his half-hidden face.

"Forgive me, but it seems you require help, even if you don't want charity." The man leaned forward, the light briefly illuminating the rest of his face as the flames flickered.

He looked fairly normal, but his eyes were strange. They spoke of quicksilver and secrets. But then the light changed, and they were obscured once more.

"I don't..." I trailed off, my voice sticking in my throat. I was truly pathetic. A girl with no name, no home, no possessions, and no hope. Despair sank onto my shoulders like the anchors holding the ships to the craggy seafloor.

"Please, I mean you no harm. My name is Nicklaus Aldane. I believe we are alike. We both came to this place in search of something, am I correct?"

"Yes," I whispered. His eyes jogged something in my memory, foggy and distant, like something I remembered from an old story.

"Tell me, and I will help you in any way I can." His words carried the command of a general.

I did. Maybe it was simply the exhaustion, but my mind felt fuzzy, like I was floating. I felt a little more comfortable, a little less cold and aching. He wanted to help a young girl crying in the dark during a dangerous festival. Was that so hard to believe?

The words tumbled from my lips as if he had pulled them with a cord.

I told him everything. How Linus and I had met, and how I felt about finding someone who wanted to marry me. I told him about our secret engagement, of how I had hoped to be free of this island and the terrible past and future awaiting me here. And I told him about Linus' problems with money and his forced marriage to my cousin. When I was done, I felt strangely relieved, like I hadn't imagined it after all.

Nicklaus was quiet for a moment. Then he nodded, his dark velvet hat bobbing once. "You need help." He wasn't asking. "I am willing to offer it."

"Why?" Something warned me to pay close attention.

He grinned, white teeth glinting in the dim light. "I would like to believe I am a kind man. Besides, if my wife were here, she would wring my neck for not offering my help when I am more than capable of doing so."

"You love your wife?" I asked, my eyes narrowed.

He laughed once, a surprised, sharp sound as if I had asked the world's most childish question. When I didn't laugh with him, he sobered, running his fingers over his beard.

"Yes, of course."

"Why is she not here with you?"

I had never seen genuine love before, not in a marriage, only pain and heartbreak and abandonment.

"That, my dear, leads us to an important point. I want to help you, but I need something myself. If you will do something for me, I will ensure you have all the money you could ever want or need."

"But why? You don't even know me." I shook my head and leaned back in the hard chair. Growing up reviled by my small gossiping community had taught me an important lesson. No one offers help for free.

"I came to the island, as I suspect you know, for the festival. But as the cold has made it clear, I am too old to get to the Bazaar, much less search for what I need day after day."

"You want me to help you find the Bazaar?" I raised my eyebrows incredulously. "I have heard the stories, but I have to tell you I don't believe it exists."

The damp of my dress made my skin itch as I crossed my arms.

Nicklaus lifted his shoulders in a shrug. "It is real. Many people find the Bazaar each Alignment, but most never return. They are too willing and too eager to find the objects of their desire. So, you see, it is another reason I cannot go. The Bazaar knows what I am looking for and will use it against me."

"I don't understand."

I folded my arms tighter around me, my skin erupting into goosebumps despite the warmth of the fire. The way he spoke about the Bazaar... it was strange. Almost reverent. Something in me shied away from the thought of a land where anything could be bought or sold and youth was eternal. Where monsters waited to ravage mortals.

"Ah, yes, that is to be expected." He leaned forward so I could see the barest hint of his shimmering eyes. "You need not believe in something for it to be true though, Hazel."

My tongue stuck to the roof of my mouth. "Why do you want my help?"

Nicklaus reclined again, his face smooth and calm. "What have you to lose if you help me? I ask for nothing besides assistance."

I considered it for a moment. He wanted me to fetch something from the Bazaar. I could refuse. My stomach sank at the thought. I had nowhere to go, nothing to sell or barter. I was utterly alone and without options. Abandoned. Hopeless.

Desperate.

"Very well." I cleared my throat and straightened my soggy dress. "I'll help you if I can, but I need to know what you want from me, exactly. How can I be sure you will make good on your promise?"

"You are right to be wary, but I swear it is an honest deal. All I want is for you to enter the Bazaar on my behalf. There is something I desperately need for my wife. If I go, there is no guarantee I will find it. The Bazaar is a tricky place, it preys upon your deepest desires. If I do not return in time, my wife will die."

I hesitated. His voice was so earnest, so pleading. His lips trembled as if he were breaths away from breaking down. The chair creaked under his weight as he leaned forward, hands gripping the arms so tightly the tendons stood taut and white.

"I can't be without my wife, Hazel. Can you understand that?"

My heart caught when his voice cracked and broke mid-plea.

"I—" My mouth opened and shut a few times before I let out a long breath. "I understand, more than anything. This thing you want me to buy, how do I find it? How much does it cost?"

"No, if you think like that, you won't last a minute in the Bazaar." Nicklaus shook his head, but his voice dripped with near palpable relief. "Things cannot be bought and sold as you imagine. Everything you think you know is a lie in the Bazaar. The less you know, the easier it is to find what you are after."

"What do you mean?" I asked. A band of tension wrapped around my forehead as I tried to unravel his words.

"All you truly need to know is this: find the palace of the King of the Bazaar on the highest hill. It will be impossible to miss. There you will need to enter his vaults, where many ancient artifacts are hidden away. Within the vaults, you will locate a spring of water."

"What is so special about this water? Can't you be more specific about where it is?" I shook my head, trying to figure out if Nicklaus was crazy or not.

He laughed mirthlessly before he cast a look over his shoulder to the rickety old grandfather clock ticking steadily on in the corner. With each movement of the minute hand, his shoulders drew tighter together.

"I can't give away too much. The water has healing properties, enough to keep my wife healthy. We have been searching for cures for her ailment for years. I heard of all kinds of medicines in the Bazaar and I dared to hope. If I were not desperate, I would not have come."

My mouth felt dry and my palms grew clammy. "I can't promise you I will find this spring, or that I even believe your story—"

Nicklaus reached into his pitch-black overcoat and withdrew a drawstring purse. He set it in my lap and leaned back as if it should answer every question. I knit my brows together and hefted the bag, tugging the fastening loose. My mouth dropped open.

Gold coins, dozens of them. It was enough to buy a mansion equal to that of my aunt.

"This is too much," I stammered, wondering if the firelight played tricks on me. I shook my head, and yet the coins remained heavy and real. The sight set my heart racing with something exhilarating and terrifying. *Hope.*

"I have more money than I know what to do with, but I cannot buy what my wife needs." Niklaus dragged a hand down his face, his voice trembling. "That water exists in a place where the gods themselves once roamed. It can help her; I am sure of it. But I can't go."

Niklaus sounded so truly heartbroken I couldn't help but feel pity for him. He was an old man who had been hoodwinked by fairy tales of gods and magic. If this gave him some consolation or any measure of hope, how could I refuse?

"I want to help you, I do. But how can I know the Bazaar is real?" I closed the mouth of the bag, banishing the glittering gold from my eyes. There was no way I could take the money without being sure he knew my doubts completely.

"I swear to you it is, Hazel. I have been there, just once, when I was a younger man thirty years ago. It is an intoxicating place, so easy to get lost in." His voice went dreamy and sounded so very far away. "But I left, afraid I would roam the Bazaar forever. I did not get treasure or riches like everyone who enters wishes, but I gained something more valuable. Knowledge. And now that I need something from that place, and I have found you, I can use that knowledge."

"And what is that?" I tried to imagine Niklaus as a young man, roaming this island while the seven planets sat overhead in the night sky, just as they did now.

His voice dropped low and deep, the perfect tone for secrets. "If you know what you want, you will never find it."

I looked at him for a long moment, trying to peek beneath the shadow of his hat, but I couldn't see beyond the velvet brim. He did not seem to be lying or after something dishonest. But I knew better than to trust blindly.

"And if I do not find the water?" I asked, every muscle coiling in dread. The money in my lap could easily be snatched away, and with it, my future.

And Linus.

Nicklaus let out a slow breath and reached to take my hand in one of his. His palms were rough as if he had worked with them for most of his life. They were at odds with his fine clothes and, apparently, vast wealth.

"This money is yours to keep, regardless. But I knew the moment I saw you that you were an honest type of person. If you take the coins, I know you will hold up your end of the agreement. Am I wrong in this assumption of your character?"

I shook my head slowly. I was of low birth, without home or fortune or consequence. But I was not a liar. My integrity was all that I had.

"As I suspected. The moment I saw that locket, I knew you would help me. I felt as if the Fates had willed it," Nicklaus said, a smile clear in his voice. He released my hand and rubbed his palms together with nervous energy.

The clock released a hollow clunking sound and Nicklaus jumped to his feet, far sprier than a man of his age ought to have been. He pulled me towards the door of the inn. I stumbled after him, jamming the coin purse in my pocket.

"Where are we going?" I asked. He pushed the doors open and my breath left my body as freezing cold air wrapped around my throat. Nicklaus checked his pocket watch and then squinted up at the sky.

Seven points of light glowed brighter than the other stars. They hovered in a near-perfect line. The thickest part of the night was coming fast. Soon, the planets would align and the festival would truly begin.

"We must hurry, it is almost time."

"Time for what?"

My feet stung, still sore from my frozen flight across the island. But Nicklaus continued his fevered walk, pulling me behind him. The crowds grew dense, throngs of people from all across the empire curious to see if the tales were true. If a magical land full of treasure and secrets would appear.

The usually quiet town center was alive with activity, the main street packed with stalls and vendors and all manner of dancing revelers. Fires burned on pallets in the middle of the street. Ancient herbs, woven into crowns, rested on the dancers' heads.

I balked at the display of humanity and strange ancient customs. My aunt would have denounced everyone present as sinners, worshipers of the old gods. Part of me wanted to keep watching the odd display of old, backward religion.

I could see why everyone on the island locked themselves away during this time of year. It was, in a word, chaos. Beautiful, tempting chaos.

Niklaus did not seem interested in the festival itself. Instead, he tugged me forward, leading us past the thick of the commotion and towards the craggy rocks of the point, where the island's lone lighthouse reflected a long shaft of light onto the black waters.

We finally stopped, somewhere between the shelf of black rock and the dark pebbly shore. I strained to see in the dark and rested my hand against the cold surface of a large boulder. The shaft of light made another rotation, flickering across breaking waves.

"I don't see anything," I said slowly.

Strangely, a part of me had wanted to see something magical

tonight. Maybe it was Nicklaus's desperate plea to help save his wife. Maybe it was the cold and the feverish energy surrounding the town. Or maybe it was my desperation to be with Linus.

"I didn't expect we would." Nicklaus shut his pocket watch with a click. He tucked it into his waistcoat and turned to me, his face still mostly obscured by his hat.

I licked my lips, hope dying like an ember. "Are you certain I can keep the money? It's too much, especially if I can't help you."

Nicklaus shook his head and rested a gentle hand on my shoulder. "It is nothing, I promise you. All I want is for my wife to be healthy again, and the only way to be certain of it is the water from the palace. There will be far more than that measly bag once you return. I can promise you that. You will want for nothing the rest of your days and the same with your fiancé."

My heart lifted at the thought. The idea of a life with Linus, away from this freezing little island, was like the rush of fine wine through my veins. He wouldn't have to marry Veronica. He loved me. I just had to bring us together.

Nicklaus reached into his jacket again and pulled out a flask, a little larger than my palm. Setting it in my hand, he looked up at the moon and the seven planets peeking between the clouds and pushed me one step closer to the shore.

"Take this, use it to bottle the water. Whatever you do, you must not let it touch your skin or it will render the water powerless. And above all, you mustn't drink it."

"What kind of water is it? How will I know it's the right fountain?" I shivered when he prodded me forward again, his eyes cast towards the heavens.

The moon broke from behind the clouds and for a brief, impossible moment, I thought I felt a warm, humid wind and saw fuzzy orange lights in the distance. But when I shook my head, the moonlight faded, and with it the vision.

"We need to hurry. You will have only seven days to find the spring and return, or the festival will end and you will be trapped in the Bazaar until it comes back to the island in another thirty years."

"Trapped?" I asked, dubiously.

Nicklaus did not entertain my question. His nervousness was tangible. My doubt slipped again. A rush of cold uncertainty tickled at the back of my neck. I tried to bite back the thought and ran my fingers along the coin purse in my pocket. A kindly old man needed my help. I should take his requests seriously until I was sure the Bazaar was a fantasy.

"You need to walk directly towards the moon. At precisely 2 'o'clock the Bazaar will open until the moon sets. If you are not ready, you will miss your opportunity until tomorrow night. You only have a few moments."

"Towards the moon? But that is directly into the sea."

"It looks that way," he agreed, voice strained and eager. "Please, trust me. In only a few minutes, you will see that I am not a crazy old fool. And you must remember: do not touch or drink the water. And you must tell no one you meet what you seek. It could cost you your life. You must swear it to me, Hazel."

Niklaus stuck out his hand and tentatively I took it. His fingers gripped mine tightly as he shook it once with the same finality of a judge's gavel. A thrill of energy rushed up my arm, colder than even the water lapping the shore.

"I promise."

An invisible band wrapped around my throat, burning hotter than a fire. But the feeling faded so quickly, leaving only a numb ache, I must have imagined it.

Niklaus' shoulders sagged with relief. "You will know the spring when you see it. Remember, you have only seven days."

"I think I understand." My voice was small, unsure. But the coins in the pocket of my gown were real and grounded me. I could try this if it meant I could be with Linus.

I would do anything.

Nicklaus pointed me towards the moon, bravely baring its face through the thick layer of clouds that broke up over the ocean. Seven points of light blended into a perfect line, pointing to the craggy face of the moon.

A burst of energy rippled across the sea, like ice from a glacier had tumbled into the water. I heard a gasp and then a cheer roll across the crowds frolicking in the streets. I stumbled into the water, my toes stinging with cold.

The very ocean trembled. Music filled my ears. The scent of honey and spice tickled my nose. I took another few steps forward. The smells grew stronger, richer. I hesitated, wondering if the cold was finally going to claim my senses.

The water lapped at my worn-out boots, staining them. My ears rang and my vision blurred. All I could see were seven points of light shining on the ocean.

I looked over my shoulder and back at Nicklaus, who nodded encouragingly, his hand covering his heart. He looked different in the moon's light and the shining planets, glimmering like diamonds above. Knowing and powerful and a million other things I couldn't seem to focus on.

"Hazel!" he called, the wind making his voice far away and small. "There is one last thing you must remember."

I turned in the ocean up to my calves as the smell of exotic spices and sweet molasses coated my tongue. My head felt fuzzy, like I'd had too much champagne. But I'd not had a drop to drink all night.

"Do not sell what you cannot part with and do not buy that which price is too dear."

I couldn't ask him what the riddle meant. A gust of hot wind tore across the water. My eyes squinted shut, and I took a jerking step backward, expecting to fall into the shallow, salty sea.

But my hands collided with something dry and hard. Mist swirled as voices and music rolled in my ears. I tried to get to my feet but fell again, the world spinning around in a haze of silver, curling mist.

Shivers of hot and cold stole over my body, running across my limbs and up into my scalp. I coughed and curled onto my side, pinching my eyes shut. The nausea knotted in my middle slowly retreated, releasing its stony fingers one by one. I sucked in a breath and opened my eyes.

A menagerie of color and hues. Smoke and incense curled through the air, filling my nose with the scent of exotic wood and promises. I pushed off of the warm stone ground. Honey-colored blocks of limestone, hewn in neat rectangles, lined a narrow winding road. The sky was dark, except for bursts of silver starlight hanging in a canopy across the air like a tapestry.

The road curved like a serpent, breaking off into a thousand points. Lining the sides were stone and mud-brick buildings decorated in stunning drapes of fabric. Stone archways dotted the roads. The colors hurt my eyes, burning them as I tried to gain my shaky footing.

The silent black ocean was gone, replaced with a sprawling market. The air was thick and balmy, the frigid chill of winter gone and long forgotten as my skin warmed and colored once again.

I was not on Veara island anymore. There was no hint of the North Sea or the storm that had raged only hours before. What once was reality fled. In its place was a world of myth and legend that reeked of magic, secrets, and sin. And I realized the truth.

I had stumbled into the Bazaar.

FIVE

"Excuse me, how do I find the palace?" I tried to stop a man dressed in a strange type of tunic I had never seen before. It was long and flared out slightly at his hips. He hardly spared me a glance and pulled his sleeve away.

I released a frustrated growl. He was not the first person I had asked for directions.

Although it was night, the Bazaar was lit with brilliantly colored lamps and burning fires. People in vibrant gowns and foreign clothing danced and sang and celebrated. The streets were narrow, unless they opened into large squares packed with people and merchants with tables laden with many wares.

"Please, ma'am, can you tell me how to get to the palace?" I shouted to be heard, tapping on the arm of a woman with fiery red hair. She looked at me, but her eyes were far away, like she could not see past the brim of her goblet filled with deep purple wine. The color of a bruise.

"What kind of question is that?" she asked in a lilting accent.

I shook my head, not sure what to say. Then she laughed and turned back to the man she had been talking and drinking with, ignoring me completely.

No matter how many times I tried to ask for help, the result was no different.

A headache knotted at the back of my skull. I stumbled a few steps, sitting hard on the edge of a well. The colors hurt to look at. The buildings were tall and narrow, and the air shimmered as if it were alive with magic. Voices assaulted my ears. I dropped my head into my hands.

I did not know how long I'd been in the Bazaar. It felt like only a moment, and yet I had asked dozens of people for help to get to the palace Nicklaus had told me about. It seemed no one noticed me at all. The hundreds of people crowding the streets were too busy sipping wine and dancing.

I kneading my forehead as I tried to catch my breath. The sudden warmth of the air was jarring. The enticing smells of foods wafted through the air, reminding me how famished I was and how my throat burned with thirst.

"Why don't you join us?" The woman with red hair asked. I looked up through my fingers. Her eyes still had that same far-off look, but she extended a cup of wine. Sand felt like it poured down my throat. With trembling fingers, I took the goblet.

I took a sip, the liquid instantly flooding my veins with warmth. A strange sensation buzzed in my head. I shook it, trying to remember what I was doing sitting on the edge of a well. It seemed so odd to be sitting when a party was going on.

"Come on." The red-haired woman extended her hand and pulled me to my feet, which suddenly didn't hurt. "We are celebrating! It is the Alignment, after all."

She led us away from the bustling square and down one of the hundreds of streets that ran like the rivulets of a delta. My skin warmed, my lips no longer parched and cracked. I took another sip from the goblet and followed the woman further into the belly of the Bazaar, humming along to the music in the air.

We wound through the streets, brushing past others who threw their heads back and laughed and talked together. Aches and pains faded until I felt like I floated. I felt good. When had I ever felt so good?

The woman stopped at a stone doorway. Sheer curtains obscured what lay within a one-room building.

"What are we doing here?" I asked. My voice slurred, and I laughed, though I was sure she had said nothing particularly funny.

"You'll see," she chuckled, and pulled me through the curtains.

I blinked and coughed as the rich scent of incense stung my eyes. A pile of heaping pillows covered the floor, as vibrant as jewels. They looked so soft and inviting, I didn't hesitate when she told me to sit down.

I lay back, my bronze hair flung around me as I sank into the cushions. The walls were coated in rich tapestries. Sipping more of the wine, I skimmed the interesting weaves of fabric. They were covered in expert stitching. Tales of a hero or another danced across the draperies. I couldn't tell what hero or story. I didn't really care.

My head lolled to the side, my limbs heavy and languid. A dragon-like creature, woven of brilliant colors, danced along a massive tapestry. An orchard with heavy golden fruit. A fountain of bubbling water where people danced. The images shimmered and moved like they were animated somehow.

I giggled at the sight.

"What have you brought me this time, Aimar?" a man purred in a voice as rich as the surrounding smoke. I couldn't help but smile up at him as he wrapped his arm around the red-haired woman he had called Aimar.

"She just entered the Bazaar tonight, the poor thing. Said she was looking for the palace," Aimar pouted.

The man's face broke into a dazzling grin. His skin was like bronze, his hair long, hanging to his waist in a series of complex braids threaded with gold. He wore a deep purple robe, open at the waist to expose acres of smooth skin.

"And what treasure are you seeking in the Bazaar?" he asked, sinking into the pile of pillows. Aimar sat next to him, leaning on her elbows and watching me like a cat tracks a bird.

My brow furrowed, and my eyes wandered around the room aimlessly. "I don't recall," I hummed. "Isn't that funny?"

"Hilarious." Aimar rolled her eyes. The man *tsked* at her, tapping her lower lip with a long, elegant finger. She sighed and reclined further into the bed of pillows.

The man turned and grinned once again. I couldn't help but smile back and stole another sip from the glass in my fingers.

"You don't know why you're here?" he asked.

"No," I laughed, my brain growing more clouded. "How odd!"

The man's smile faded a little, and he and Aimar exchanged hungry looks. I thought for a moment that I had come to the Bazaar for a reason, but it kept flitting away anytime my mind tried to grasp it. It felt too hard to care.

"It doesn't matter, Darius. Look at her. She will pay whatever it is you ask." Aimar heaved a breath, looking bored. Darius's silky black hair ran across his shoulders as he pushed himself more upright. His dark eyes commanded my gaze.

"What is it that you want? I am a merchant, of sorts, with the skills necessary to give you whatever it is you crave," Darius spoke, his voice sending shivers across my skin.

Something rattled loose in my brain at his words. Something about prices and payments and warnings. But when I thought too hard a sharp pain pricked behind my eyes, so I stopped trying to fetch the memory.

What did it matter? What did anything matter?

"Can you get me more wine?" I asked, pouting when I tipped my head back but no more deep lavender liquid trickled into my mouth. Darius raised a sleek black brow and shared a look with Aimar.

"Maybe later," he said. "Now, surely there is something you might want, something you desired so desperately it drew you to the Bazaar."

"Nope." I snickered, my eyes slipping from his face. I didn't think the Bazaar had anything I wanted in particular. Except, there was something about a kind old man. Something he pleaded for.

I shook my head and giggled again. Darius sighed. He turned and crooked his finger to a curtain hanging from the ceiling, cutting the room in half.

A procession of women, their arms laden with trays of golden amulets and trinkets, corked bottles, and jars of powders, appeared. I clapped as they set the trays on a low table in the center of the pillows. Darius knelt and beckoned me closer. I scooted on my knees; my face bent towards the trays.

The women moved to lounge beside Aimar. They were all beautiful and different. Some looked like those from the Nederhølm coast: pale hair and ivory skin. Others looked like those from the western kingdoms. Bronze skin, black hair, and high cheekbones.

Nederhølm. Veara Island. The word rang in my mind. My home, the empire, and the freezing North Sea. *Home.*

Why did it matter? I wasn't sure it did...

"I can grant you anything you wish," Darius murmured, his lips pulling into a seductive smile.

His long fingers flourished over the presentation of goods. The offerings moved and changed like living things, shifting before me as if they couldn't decide on a form. He held his sleeve aside and plucked a jar from the table. The crystal stopper glimmered in the low light granted by the oil lamps dangling from the ceiling.

The women reached for platters of fruit I had not noticed before. There were pomegranates so bright red they seemed on fire. I watched, transfixed, as they broke them open and dipped their fingers in the fruit. Scarlet juice dripped from their mouths, gleaming like blood. They devoured golden apples and strange looking peaches next. My mouth watered.

"I can grant you bottled courage," Darius purred and opened the bottle, passing it under his nose. "I can give you brewed glory. Or, I can give you endless knowledge that would rival that of the wisest scribes."

I watched as he opened a box full of scrolls. The words on the thick parchment seemed to glow with power, promising me untold understanding, the kind that could end kingdoms. My fingers itched to unroll them and read.

"I don't think that is what I came here for," I said. The warmth filling my body from the wine turned hot and uncomfortable. I shifted on the pillows, a thousand hands crawled along my skin.

"But there is no doubt it is what you want." Darius grinned, his teeth baring like a panther's. My heart raced, as though it had been a stone in my chest until that moment. Blood moved through my veins again, and with it, a warning.

"There is something I need to find. Someone needs me to do something for them..." I trailed off, my thoughts sticking like a boot in the mud at low tide.

What was it? My shoulders ached and so did the soles of my feet, like I had walked a hundred miles. I twisted, looking around. Where was I?

"All you could ever need is right here," he insisted. "Take the potions I offer. There is only one thing I ask in return."

"What is that?" I rubbed at my forehead, splitting with a terrible ache.

Darius shrugged, his open robe slipping down a chiseled arm. My mouth watered again. "There is only one thing I trade in. You can have your pick of anything you see before you, for a piece of your soul."

"My soul?" I laughed at the ridiculous idea.

The women lounging in the room smiled lazily. Their lips gleamed in stained red; their eyes swimming with the same far-off look as Aimar. Then I noticed something strange about them, something I could not see before.

Their eyes were not just unfocused, they were completely white.

"It is the rarest thing of all to possess a part of someone's very being. But it will not hurt, I swear it. And what is a tiny portion of a soul for all the knowledge anyone could ever crave?" Darius insisted, his eyes narrowing, turning into darkened slits.

"You can't be serious." I laughed uneasily, pushing myself to my feet. They burned, and I grimaced.

What was once the hint of a headache changed to a blazing fire in my skull. My stomach seized, and I whimpered. Sweat broke out across my skin, sticking my hair to my neck. Had I been poisoned? It was like my body rejected the very air I breathed.

"I am always serious, my darling girl," Darius murmured, rising to his feet. The women followed suit, their listless looks scouring the body of their master. Darius was like a stalking lion and the women were his pride of hungry lionesses. I was a trapped animal, foolish and injured and frightened.

The tapestries on the wall shimmered, shifting and turning black and silver. They showed a starry night and a glittering palace on a hill. A woman ran across the sky, chased by a terrifying creature without shape.

"I don't want anything you have to sell. I'm not looking to buy," I whispered, taking a step back.

The oil lamps dimmed to almost nothing. Something was wrong. I had to leave.

"Then you should not have come," Darius hissed.

He took a step forward as I fell back another. I darted my gaze around the room, searching for a way out. The door was right there, with only gauzy curtains blocking the way. Darius reached for my wrist, seizing it in a painful grip.

"Let me go," I demanded.

I could feel my thoughts clearing; the effects of the wine and the Bazaar falling away like scales. Wrenching my arm downward, I broke his grip on my wrist and lunged for the door. One woman reached for my hair, tangled and damp with sweat. I let out a cry and went tumbling backward.

I clawed desperately, breaking skin. A woman hissed and covered bright red scratches on her cheek with a hand. Milky white eyes glared back at me. I screamed.

Darius raised his hands as if offering surrender. "This will go far easier if you simply pay me for what I am owed."

"I don't want what you're selling. I owe you nothing," I insisted, breathing ragged.

My back pressed against the wall. The curtains brushed my arm when a warm breeze pushed through the streets. Though people wandered the roads outside, none seemed to care about my scream of distress. I swallowed hard, a hazy plan cobbling together.

Darius let out a low, throaty laugh. "That is not true in the least."

He took another step forward, a knife, unlike anything I had ever seen before, weighing down his palm. It looked to be made of pure glass, impossibly clear and wickedly sharp. I felt intuitively that it would not kill me, but instead take something worth far more than blood.

Before he could pierce me with the knife, I reached up and yanked a brass chain holding a large oil lamp aloft. It went crashing down, spilling searing hot oil all over Darius and the other women. A few droplets stung my skin, and I bit back a cry. I flew from the room and burst into the street.

Darius' screams of agony and anger echoed off the faces of buildings.

I ran without thinking about where I should go. The streets went on forever, parting and shifting and changing as if there was no logic or planning at all. Every turn looked identical. Narrow roads lined with stalls and vendors and buildings parted for squares and fountains. Roads twisted among themselves like writhing snakes.

All I knew was I had to get away. I ran until my lungs were scorched and my legs gave out. I stumbled through a canal, the vivid blue water reaching up to my thighs. Finally, I stopped, collapsing against a wooden railing; The porch I leaned against attached to a tavern.

I dropped my head back against the sandstone wall, gasping in wracking coughs. I was in a waking nightmare.

Though my thoughts were clearer than they had been in Darius' souk, something important scampered around the edges of my mind. There was something that I desperately needed to do. Someone needed my help.

More laughter raked my ears, and I pulled my eyelids open. The tavern was one of the largest buildings I had seen yet, crafted of sandstone instead of the earthy mud brick and stucco. Three stories studded with windows, deep teal curtains swirling in the breeze.

It was in one of the busiest sections of the Bazaar I had yet seen. A huge, oblong square where more of the endless stalls and shops covered an open-air market. Arches and columns supported the ceiling of stars. Canals tangled through bridges.

I took a shuddering breath. I couldn't just stay there. But as I got to my feet, something shimmering a purply silver caught my eye. Darius' robe. A gasp stuck in my throat and I pressed my spine flush against the cold stone wall.

The bright red hair of Aimar appeared next to him through a thick crowd of revelers. A long canal of beautiful water decorated with vibrant pink lilies stretched between us, cutting the street in half. Long reed boats glided along, obscuring the pair.

I ducked inside the heavy wooden door of the tavern. The casement of a window scratched my arm, and I crouched lower, parting the curtains with my fingers. Darius and Aimar spoke to a merchant lounging on a bright carpet, a twisting brass pipe smoking in his hands. He shook his head and Darius' shoulders tensed. Darius turned in the tavern's direction and I slapped my hand over my mouth to stifle a scream.

His face rippled with bright red welts, one eye swollen shut. He looked fearsome, bloodthirsty. For a moment he looked right at me, but then he barked something at Aimar and they moved on, pushing through the crowds.

I studied the streets for a few more minutes until I was sure they were not coming back. The smell of food wafted from within the tavern's kitchens, making my stomach growl. But I couldn't think of food right now. I had to remember what I was doing in such a strange place.

"What can I get you?" An airy voice, as mesmerizing as the sounds of singing waves, startled me from my crouched position. I jumped, bumping into a table with my hip. I winced and pushed my hair out of my face to focus on the woman looking down at me.

"Nothing," I stammered.

She had to be at least two feet taller than I was, with black hair cut close to her scalp. Her skin was a beautiful, deep russet color and adorned with golden bracelets, necklaces, and armbands. But it was her eyes that stole my voice. They were a vibrant, liquid gold as if she had trapped the sun in her irises. Somehow, I knew she was not human.

"We are busy tonight," she said, her eyes narrowing to study me. "Would you like food? Something to drink?"

"I-I don't know."

Her brows pulled together, studying me like an insect pinned to a board. I tried to step away from her probing gaze. It burned like a hot poker trailing my skin. What was she trying to see?

The door slammed open, rattling against the back wall. I yelped and ducked down again, throwing my arms over my head. Darius was here to finish the job, to take what he thought he deserved.

"Are you alright?" the tall woman with the golden eyes asked. I looked up as a group of men, all dressed in clothes from distant lands, stumbled into the tavern and sat by a low bar offering drinks and food I had never heard of.

I shook my head, my chest so tight I couldn't take another breath.

The woman with gold eyes hesitated for a moment before she put a hand on my shoulder. She looked worried. Almost kind.

"What is it?" she asked.

"I don't..." I stammered, my voice catching in my throat.

In a far corner, there sat another man with his back to me, dressed in the darkest black I had ever seen. It was like the shadows clung to his heavy cloak. Something about him brushed at the edge of my memory. I couldn't quite recall, but something was familiar about that impossibly black cloak...

My voice came out strained and small. "I'm trying to find something."

The woman clucked her tongue against the roof of her mouth and reached out her hand. Hesitating, I let her pull me to my feet. She crossed her arms, head cocked to the side as she studied me again, golden eyes boring straight through. Finally, she sighed and turned around, beckoning me with one hand.

"Come with me, you look like you need someplace to rest."

I stood there for a stunned moment; my feet rooted to the spot. The crowd grew thicker as more people piled into the tavern, ordering and shouting for food and drinks. The man in black disappeared, a figment of my imagination, a result of that strange wine.

The woman stopped and half turned, flaring her eyes and setting a hand on her hip. "Well?"

I followed her up a set of stairs and to the top floor. Rooms lined a web of narrow halls. Some sat open with people sleeping on rugs or bedrolls. Others were shut tight, with signs in various languages telling others to keep out.

I wrapped my arms around myself. My dress was still wet from my tromp through the canal. It was incredibly dirty from my travel through the Bazaar and the freezing rainstorm. I stopped as the woman took out a large brass key and pushed open the door to a room at the end of a hall.

Rainstorm.

I remembered something.

I had been running across a darkened island, my skin so cold it was as if it would shatter. An inn, different in a thousand ways from this one. Someone who wanted something from me... what was it again?

"You can stay here. You should sleep and eat something, or you won't last much longer," the woman said, stepping aside and ushering me into the room.

It was small but quiet and comfortable. A pair of shutters stood open, showing the golden lights of the Bazaar and the silver studs of stars stretching across the black sky.

I hesitated, only partway in the room. "I don't have to pay with my soul, do I?"

I would not make that mistake again.

"It is free of charge." The woman shook her head. "You look like you need help. My name is Saskia. I own the tavern."

I couldn't trust another person in the Bazaar again. "I won't be trapped into paying with something I am not willing to part with."

"I require traditional payment. Gold, silver, bronze, maybe jewels, but nothing like the other patrons here. Am I not able to give you a simple room without expecting something in return?"

The way she said it made me feel like I had been too harsh and maybe even a little rude. Her golden eyes flashed with deep emotion, one that spoke of years of pain.

"Oh, well, this is—that is kind." I tightened my arms around myself again, conscious of my disheveled appearance.

Mud and dust streaked my dress and skin. I was certain I smelled terribly, and my hair knotted around the nape of my neck. Saskia leaned against the doorjamb, golden eyes sweeping the room and then me.

"You're rather conscious, for a human."

"I don't know what you mean," I said, grimacing.

Saskia waved her hand dismissively and handed me the brass key. "Never mind. Things will make more sense once you sleep for a while. The door locks from the inside once you have the key. No one will be able to come in. Once you wake, come downstairs and find me."

"Thank you," I stammered, wanting to ask a thousand questions.

But Saskia had already walked away, her amber-colored dress trailing after her. The fabric shimmered as she descended the stairs without a backward glance.

I shut the door firmly and locked it, walking backward until my legs bumped into a bed. A beautiful blue carpet woven of the finest wool covered the floor. The bed looked immeasurably comfortable, the mattress soft and inviting. I sank into it, my muscles groaning in protest.

It felt like I had not slept in a week. My eyes sagged, heavy and scratching. I dropped onto my side and sank further into the bed. The commotion outside faded to a whisper and my eyelids slid shut. Something slipped across my chest and landed on my arm.

Groaning, I peeked at it through my lashes. A locket on a chain. A ruby ring lay next to it, resting against the skin of my inner arm.

I lost the battle against sleep, images of the ring and a sandy-haired boy flitted through my mind as I drifted off into oblivion.

SIX

Sleep did not release me easily. After a series of strange dreams and whispered memories, I sat up slowly, every part of me sore and raw. I passed the heel of my hand over my eyes before swinging my legs down and testing my weight on my feet. Wincing, I pushed myself up and struggled to the window.

The sky was still inky dark. The same curtain of stars glimmered bright and beautiful over the Bazaar. I thought I had imagined it all, like a fever dream as the result of near hypothermia from my time in the cold. But everything remained as beautiful and odd as before.

My stomach turned, growling from ravenous hunger.

I could not tell how long I had been in the Bazaar, and the perpetual blanket of night wasn't helping. But based on how long I'd slept and the hunger I felt, it had to have been many hours, perhaps even a day.

The thought sent my heart fluttering and my stomach-turning. I had to find out how much time had passed and what day of the Alignment it was. And then I remembered.

The island. The cold. A kind old man. Linus. The images flashed in bursts. My memory had returned.

I remembered Nicklaus, his plea for me to find the spring water in the palace of the King of the Bazaar. I remembered Linus, his blue eyes pained as they threw me from my aunt and uncle's home. It felt like a lifetime ago.

Turning from the window, I squeezed my fists. I had to get moving. I paced towards the door, but something caught my eye and turned my stomach to lead. Something that had not been there when I'd fallen asleep. A package wrapped in a silver ribbon on a chair in the corner of the room.

I tested the door handle, but it remained locked. The window was far too high off the ground for someone to climb. I chewed on my thumbnail, considering the gift. Chest tight, I picked up the package carefully, worried it might burn me with some type of poison.

The paper reflected like the night sky. I carefully tugged on the ribbon and the package unfurled gracefully, a tumble of lace and silk following afterward. A beautiful gown sprawled across my lap.

The bodice was tight fitted, dark blue linen overlaid with black lace. The capped sleeves gathered tufts of rich, royal blue. It would be easy to walk in the loose, simple skirt. A beautiful morning gown like the ladies on the island wore in summer. I flinched. Was this some type of joke? A mockery of my name and status?

A folded piece of parchment winked with pearlescent paper, and fluttered from the package. I set the dress on the bed and plucked the note from the ground. Breaking a pitch-black wax seal with my nail, I unfolded it. Beautiful, curling script stared back at me.

I have heard much about you in the short time you have been in my Bazaar. Take this gift as a token of goodwill. I look forward to meeting you.

-Zaire

Zaire? I bit down on my lower lip, passing it between my teeth. Perhaps Darius had found me and now taunted me. Threatened me. Niklaus' warnings surfaced. Nothing in the Bazaar is as it seems.

My fingers trailed the satin. It was just a dress, wasn't it? Besides, the gown I had worn to the ball was torn and dirty and completely ruined. It was nice to have something I hadn't made myself.

Though the note and the mysterious sender made my skin crawl, I undressed and cleaned myself as quickly as I could with a basin of water before changing. I locked the purse of coins from Niklaus in the trunk by the bed. I had a feeling gold would do me no good in this place.

The dress fit perfectly. Zaire, whoever he was, knew my measurements down to the exact number. I tried not to let the thought make me nauseous and focused on cleaning and brushing out my tangled hair.

It shone in the warm light that always seemed to fill the Bazaar. My hair fell in loose waves down to my waist and I pulled half of it back from my face, ignoring the widow's peak that became more prominent.

Once my appearance was more presentable, I took a deep breath and unlocked the door. I half expected to see someone waiting for me, ready to collect payment for the dress. But the hall was empty and quiet.

I shut the door and tucked the key in my pocket, wrapping the note around it. The key clinked against the metal flask against my hip, reminding me I was here for one purpose: the water in the palace. I could not worry about dresses and strange notes and men wishing to buy my soul. I was running out of time.

The tavern was quiet, nearly empty, when my feet hit the last step of the staircase. Dozens of tables and chairs flanked the low bar. A stone fireplace sat across from it, though the hearth burned only coals. A few patrons sprawled on the tables, face down with their hands still clasping goblets or tankards. I winced away from the familiar bruise-purple wine on a nearby table.

"You're awake," Saskia, the tavern owner, said. "I was wondering if I should fetch you."

"How long have I been asleep?" I asked, fingers fluttering nervously over the railing.

Saskia sighed in a way that reminded me a little of Adelaide and pointed at a chair by the bar. I moved sluggishly, my limbs still tired and sore. I sat on the stool and Saskia slid a plate of bread and some type of porridge to me. Picking at the food carefully, my stomach turned at the memory of what the wine had done to my mind.

"You've been upstairs quite a few hours, maybe nine," she said, lifting one shoulder before returning to scrubbing glasses behind the rough wooden bar.

My mouth went dry, and I wheezed around a mouthful of bread. Saskia slid a glass of water over. Nine hours had slipped by just since I had been in the tavern. My stomach soured when I tried to recall how long I had wandered before that.

"How many nights of the Alignment are left?" I asked, my hand tightening around the glass so hard I thought I might shatter it.

Saskia's eyes narrowed again, making me feel as if I were doing something wrong. "There are six nights left now."

"Thank the Fates," I whispered. I'd lost an entire day, but there were still six nights left.

I dropped my forehead into one hand, the other tracing the ruby ring forlornly. I wished Linus were there to tell me it would all be all right. But he was probably with Veronica, planning for their wedding. The thought turned to dust on my tongue and I dropped the ring.

"How do I get to the palace from here?" I pushed the plate of food aside after only a few bites. I was far too anxious to eat.

Saskia raised a sculpted black brow and leaned her forearms on the counter. Her liquid gold eyes were almost frightening when combined with her astounding height.

"What is it you are doing in the Bazaar, exactly?"

"I need to get something from the palace." I choked, unable to share more. My fingers wandered to my throat, trying to ease the sudden knot. I breathed in sharply, remembering the promise I'd made to Niklaus. How I'd sworn not to reveal what I was looking for.

An enchantment? Sharp knives and handshakes danced across my mind. I swallowed hard. I should not give promises so freely in the Bazaar.

"A man sent me here to find medicine for someone he loves." I tested the words slowly as they slipped past my lips. I did not choke again. There. Something close to the truth.

"Do you see up there on the hill? That is the palace." Saskia breathed out slowly through her nose before she turned to the window behind the bar and pushed the shutters open.

I followed the line of her finger to the highest point in the Bazaar. It was impossible to miss. The palace was a behemoth, giant and imposing and glittering like the facets of a jewel. Even from far away, perched at the precipice of an imposing hill lined with lanterns, I could tell it was unlike anything I'd seen before.

The governor's mansion on Veara Island was impressive. I'd never seen Nederhølm Keep, only watercolors and sketches. The palace of the King of the Bazaar eclipsed them all.

It was much like the Bazaar itself, cobbled together from the finest architectures of every land imaginable. It was like a piece of history. Grand ionic columns supported a marble portico. Large blocks of limestone made up the sturdy base. Ornate roofs, made of curling gold, topped off the many towers and wings. It was a strange mix between an ancient temple and a castle.

My eyes traced a path up the hill and to the palace.

It could take hours to get there. But the winding roads of the Bazaar were confusing and erratic. I thought a week would be more than enough to find a simple spring. Now I knew what Nicklaus meant about being too old to wander the Bazaar.

"Can you tell me how to get there?" I asked.

Saskia looked at me with pity and crossed her long arms. "You're not like any human I have met before. You say you are in the Bazaar for someone else?"

"What do you mean?" I barely broke my eyes away from the palace shining on the hilltop. I felt an itch to run to it, to find the fountain and get as far away from this strange world as I could.

"You know where you are, don't you?"

"The Bazaar. When I entered, it was off the coast of Veara island." I felt my patience slipping.

"That is not what I mean. Anyone who comes to the Bazaar is searching for something for themselves. Usually, they find it, or some semblance of it, before they get very far. By the time travelers reach my tavern, they are usually missing at least half of their soul. You are the only one I have met that is still whole."

I cringed at the memory of Darius and his wickedly sharp knife and rubbed at my nearly bare arms.

"Well then, I am not most people here." I hesitated. "Please, can you tell me how to reach the palace? I need to get what I came for and return home before the Alignment is over."

Saskia took in a slow breath and came to sit beside me, still towering in her height despite being seated. "I would not go to the palace if I were you."

"Why not?" I blinked at the tall woman.

Saskia clenched her jaw. "The King of the Bazaar lives there. He is not someone to be trifled with. I do not enjoy seeing mortals sell themselves off piece by piece, human. You should leave while you can."

"As much as I might want to, it's not possible." I shook my head once. "I made a promise, and I intended to keep it. I *have* to keep it."

Saskia's mouth twisted, her eyes darkening with something like sadness. "If you insist on going, you can try staying high up or looking over the roofs of buildings to find your bearings. There are no maps of the Bazaar."

My pulse thrilled, half hope, half dread.

"How does anyone find their way?" I leaned heavily on the countertop, another headache threatening to overtake me.

"Most don't, many do not care. Once you find what you desire, it is easy to lose focus."

"What is this place? Who are all the people here? Will they leave by the end of the Alignment?"

Saskia laughed, amusement softening her fierce features. "I cannot answer all of your questions. But I know this: the Bazaar collects people and things that have nowhere else to go. Forgotten things. The Bazaar shifts and changes based on your thoughts and desires. It wants to give you exactly what you yearn for so that you stay forever."

"You make it sound like the Bazaar is alive." I shifted uneasily. An unbearable tingle stole across my arms and I scratched at them.

Saskia's smile faded until she was at once very serious. "It is."

A cool breeze, the first I'd felt since arriving, washed over me. I shuddered and wound my fingers through the fabric of my skirt, wishing I had my old wrap to pull around me. Saskia's eyes fell to the dress, and she arched her brow.

"Did you leave this in my room while I was sleeping?" I cleared my throat, heat stealing over my cheeks.

"No. As I said, the door locks from the inside once you hold the key. It will open only to you."

"There was a note from someone named Zaire."

Saskia's face paled. She looked towards the palace once before she slammed the shutters closed and picked up another set of glasses to wipe down. Her movements were sharp and deliberate. My stomach spooled into a tight knot.

"Should I be afraid?" I asked.

"I am sure it is nothing," Saskia said, but her eyes looked troubled. "You say you need to return to your island before the festival ends. If you do not hurry, the Bazaar will move on in search of more people and you will be stuck here. I am sorry I can't be of more help but you must begin your search if you want to leave in time."

"How can I find my way back here?" I asked, suddenly terrified to leave the only place I had felt remotely safe.

"The tavern is at a crossroads of sorts. Most people stumble across it a few times a day. For those who are lost it is even easier to find."

Another riddle.

I fought the urge to sigh. She had been kind to me, after all. Fed me. Given me a room without charging money or something darker. I stood and looked towards the door and the quiet Bazaar. Though daybreak had never come, some part of me felt that on Veara island a blood-red sunrise had already passed.

"Thank you," I breathed.

I wanted to ask why she helped me, who Zaire was, but I hesitated. Niklaus' warnings rang like a bell in my head. I couldn't trust anyone in the Bazaar. It turns things around, tricks you. I couldn't blindly trust Saskia, no matter how badly I wanted to.

Her gold eyes darkened again, as if looking into the face of a departed friend. "Be careful out there, little mortal. Take nothing the merchant's offer."

"I won't."

Saskia smiled a little before returning to her work. I headed for the door, purpose pushing through my veins like fire. But as I crossed the dining hall, a wisp of darkness caught my eye.

A familiar figure dressed in inky black.

He slumped against the wall, his head lolling to the side as if asleep. It was the man I had sensed watching me when I'd first stumbled into the tavern. The man, the *thing*, that had stalked me on the island. He didn't move or even flinch.

He must have been waiting for me all night. A million explanations darted across my thoughts. But only one mattered. He wanted something from me, and if he was from the Bazaar, it could only mean something terrible.

I stumbled back a step and knocked into a barrel. It banged against the wall, but the sleeping man didn't move. My heart thudded as I scrabbled for the door handle. Leave. I had to leave before he woke up.

My breath came in shallow, rattling gasps. I opened the door and fled into the Bazaar once more.

SEVEN

I ran hard, glancing behind me every few steps. But no one followed. After a while, the muggy air became difficult to breathe; the temperature balmy and humid. Soon, uncomfortable sweat stuck to my skin. I slowed, gasping, and studied my surroundings, memorizing and trying to plot a path in my mind.

The tavern stood behind me, small enough it looked like a child's toy. The hill with the palace was the highest point of the Bazaar, framed in by imposing black granite mountains that absorbed the light. But stretches of buildings and the colorful cloths that draped between the roofs hid it from view more often than not.

I slogged through the empty streets until a break between two low-slung buildings showed glimmering marble. With the turrets of the palace in my sight, I picked up the pace.

My heart lodged somewhere in my throat as I walked. It was eerily quiet, so different from the raucous party from last night. Though I was sure it was perhaps midday back home, no one in the Bazaar was up. Time felt warped and liquid with the permanent star-filled sky. Without the sun as a guide, I couldn't be sure how long I walked.

Crumbling columns faded to modern-looking buildings made from sturdy grey stone. Empty stalls stood in the warm breeze; their wares hidden away. The canals that ran between the streets glimmered like mercury. Pink lilies bobbed on the surface, enticing and bright. But slick green hands stroked the petals, as if teasing me to come closer. I winced and kept going.

The buildings faded. The merchant's stalls grew thinner and the street rougher and narrower until dark honey-colored walls rose in a sort of canyon.

I'd reached a dead end. Grumbling, I turned around, only to hear stone grind together. I whirled as dust and small stones skittered across my boots. The wall split apart, offering two paths that had not been there a moment ago.

Saskia's warning that the Bazaar was alive flitted through my mind.

I gulped and considered the identical paths. They were tunnels, really, with mere pinpricks of light signifying they had an opening. But part of me wondered if the Bazaar would simply change again, sealing me inside a dark tomb.

Saskia said the Bazaar collected things. People. Did it want to collect me?

I turned around again, determined to go back the way I'd come. My nose collided with another dead end. The alley I'd just walked through had completely disappeared. I rubbed my aching nose with one hand before turning back to the forked tunnel.

A frustrated sound tumbled from my lips. Now *three* identical tunnels taunted me with their open mouths.

"Wonderful," I mumbled.

Wind whistled through the tunnels. I had no idea which to take. Did it matter? I studied the channels. A humid wind brushed my face, smelling of decay and secrets.

I gripped the canister in my pocket, reminding myself what I was there for, and took the tunnel on the left. My breath echoed off the walls, amplifying and resounding. Like I wasn't alone.

My feet slipped on small pebbles and hidden crevices as I pushed forward, my breathing shallow and raspy. It did not take long before I noticed that the end of the tunnel was not getting any closer. The now-familiar sound of grinding stone echoed, and I caught my breath, slowly looking over my shoulder.

Behind me, there was only darkness. Only one way out.

I wanted to kick the wall, to curse the Bazaar for playing tricks on me, when I heard something strange. Heavy, labored breathing echoed from somewhere behind in the near-perfect darkness.

Cold sweat slicked my palms. Dragging feet, large and cumbersome, accompanied the rattling gasps. I stopped breathing; tried to remain as silent as possible. *Where was the sound coming from?* The tunnel echoed too much to tell.

The breathing grew louder, the footsteps picking up their pace. My thoughts went blank with blind panic. Another rattling breath, deep and hungry. I ran towards the light at the end of the tunnel, some primal instinct urging me to flee as fast as I could.

A roar thundered behind me. The roar of a hidden monster. Memories of the tapestry from Darius's den stung my eyes. The shimmering palace on the hill, a woman chased across a black sky by a terrible beast without form. Hot breath fanned against my neck and shoulders.

I screamed.

The Bazaar would have laughed at me if it could. The tunnel shortened, the seemingly unreachable exit materializing only a few paces ahead. My legs burned and the heavy bottle in my pocket clanged against my hipbone, bruising it. Just when I felt the brush of something sharp on the back of my neck, I burst into the orange lamplight.

The tunnel slid shut. A terrible boom sounded as something heavy collided with the wall. Dust and stones tumbled from the sealed passage. I fell, scrambling on my hands until my back hit a low wall. Another cacophonous boom. A wail of anger and hunger. I covered my ears, tucking my legs close to my body.

After what felt like an eternity, the pounding of gargantuan fists faded and the tunnel was just a smooth wall. I coughed and fanned the settling dust away, breathing hard. I felt my pocket again. The silver canister rested silent and useless against my leg. Why hadn't Niklaus warned me? Why hadn't he given me a weapon?

More wracking coughs choked my lungs. I took in a gasp of air and blinked away the last of the grime, trying to find my bearings. My wits. The streets were still empty, save for the colorful rugs, lamps, and drapes of sailing fabric.

A ladder sat against the wall of some sort of bakery. The words on the sign were in a language I did not know, and from within the walls, I smelled something heavenly and tempting. But my nerves were too rattled to be seduced by the strange goods the Bazaar tried to lure with. It had just tried to kill me not a second ago.

I pushed my hair from my face and climbed up a few rungs, hands shaking, until my head cleared the roof.

The streets in this part of the Bazaar were not so tangled with the canals. Instead, a sort of small port sat in the center of the largest square. Reed boats were tied off, bobbing gently in the starlight. Stalls lined the high walls surrounding the rectangular retention area.

Beyond sat the hill with the palace. I squinted hard, making out small, dark figures moving through the distant halls. It seemed marginally closer than it had been when I first set out, however long ago that had been. I gritted my teeth. *I can do this.* Grabbing my skirts in one hand, I made my way back down the ladder.

Following the image in my head, I squeezed around a few buildings until I reached the larger square with the boats. Hiking my skirts up, I jumped into an empty reed boat in the makeshift wharf. Hopefully, they were for everyone to use and I wasn't stealing. I shuddered to think what punishments they set for thieves.

With a long wooden oar, I pushed off through the shallow channel, jaw tight. If the Bazaar wanted to play games, I would have to play better. Linus' ring rested against my breastbone and I thought of him. Nicklaus relied on me, too. I had to be better than some petty, vindictive market.

The oar scraped the bottom of the canal, and I pushed, sending the boat forward. It glided through forests of lily pads, fields of hanging vines, and flocks of odd-looking birds. The silence of the Bazaar chafed my nerves. But then I heard a screeching voice as I passed beneath a massive fig tree. I hesitated, scanning the branches and swirling roots. Another scratchy sound. A laugh?

Birds, the same ugly ones I'd noticed on the wharf, dotted the looming fig tree. They were white, with fat little bodies and long black necks, ending in a curved hook beak. They watched me with beady, unblinking eyes.

"Hazel," one squawked. "Poor Hazel. Chased by the shadows. Lost in the market."

My blood ran cold. I oared harder, sending the boat flying across the water, ignoring the burn in my shoulders. I rounded a bend and stifled a scream when another flock of birds greeted me, perched on a low bridge above my head.

The birds watched, heads twitching. I felt lightheaded, my very blood turning cold.

One squawked, "Chased by shadows. Chased by gods. Poor Hazel, she'll never find what she seeks."

"Stop it!" I swung the oar. The bird made a laughing sound before it fluttered off into the sky with its foul brethren.

My fingers shook as I lowered the oar back into the water. The boat shuddered, my knees weak and trembling. But I tried to forget what the birds had said, and the monster in the tunnel, and paddled forward once more.

The channels and waterways crisscrossing the Bazaar looked relatively logical from up high. Now, navigating the smooth water, I was sure of it. They were mostly straight, moving in patterned lines and angles.

Anticipation lightened my chest when the water gained a current, driving me forward. A low bridge loomed up ahead, and I was sure once I passed underneath, the palace would sprawl out before me and my journey would almost be over.

I ducked down, my hair brushing the crest of the bridge. Then the stars reappeared, winking down at me like they were celebrating my victory as well. I wanted to sob in relief.

The boat scraped the bottom of a canal, ending in a circle with a beautiful fountain in the middle. Taking a deep breath to calm my fluttering stomach, I stepped onto dry ground.

"Back so soon?"

"Saskia? How—?"

I whirled from the glimmering fountain and blue waters. The tavern and its sandstone stared back at me. The circular canal led to a series of steps and straight to another set of large doors at the back of the building. My mouth dangled, and I whipped my head towards the hill. The palace seemed to laugh at me, looking haughty and impossibly far away.

"You've only been gone for a quarter of an hour," Saskia said, pulling chairs from off of the tables outside. "Did you forget something in your room?"

A quarter of an hour? I had been gone far longer than that! My stomach churned.

My voice stuck in my throat. "How is this possible? I was so close to the palace! I thought I was almost there."

"The Bazaar will not give up its secrets easily, even for someone like you."

"Someone like me?" I wanted to sit down and give up, to scream and rage. But neither would bring me closer to Linus.

Saskia pursed her lips and glanced at the palace like it was a cancerous growth. She turned back to the tavern and beckoned me to follow. I fought back the urge to sob. Feet weighing me down like an anchor, I followed her.

"If you insist on wandering blindly, at least take some food and water. Time moves differently here, especially when you are trying to find something in particular. You don't want to faint from hunger."

"Why is it so difficult to get to the palace?" I sat at the bar. "It feels like I've been walking for hours, but the palace is always the same distance away, no matter where I am."

"I cannot say." Saskia handed me a wrapped bundle of food. "It has been many centuries since anyone entered the Bazaar looking for something not for themselves, but for another person. It is not usually how things work here."

"Centuries?" I rubbed at my forehead, Mother's locket burning against my skin.

"Yes, as long as I can remember." Saskia smirked while I gaped at her, open-mouthed. "You need not look so surprised, Hazel. I remember little of my life before I came to the Bazaar several centuries ago, but I am fairly certain I am not human."

"What are you then?" I blinked.

"I am a siren," Saskia sighed, "though my powers are not of much use in a place such as the Bazaar."

So that is what she meant by her cryptic words yesterday on my first terrible night in the Bazaar. If she was not human, then perhaps more of the myths and legends were true. The good and the bad.

"But why did you come here?" I asked.

I hoped she didn't see the blood drain from my face. I had heard tales of sirens luring fishermen and sailors to their deaths below the waves. Of their cruelty and allure and thirst for blood. But Saskia, though beautiful and otherworldly, did not have any such effect on me.

She smiled, a little sadly. "As I told you before, the Bazaar collects forgotten things. It is the only place for creatures like me."

I traced my fingers forlornly along the bar. Saskia held another bundle of food to her chest and stepped around me. A slumped figure leaned against the farthest stool, eyes blankly staring into a tankard. The siren handed the young man the food. He looked up at her, but did not seem to register her. Not really.

"Take this, Matthias. Eat and I will take you back to the gates when you are stronger." Saskia crossed her arms, waiting for the man to pick apart the bread. Matthias looked at the food and back up at the tall siren.

"The gates?" He blinked slowly; eyes almost milky.

My stomach turned. He was mortal and clearly missing a large part of his soul. How could he have lost so much so quickly? The second night had not yet come and already he looked like the walking dead.

Saskia sighed, but her eyes remained kind. "You need to return to the island, remember? You asked me for help not an hour ago."

"I did?" Matthias picked up a piece of bread like it was coal. "Do you have something to sell? Perhaps a garment that could give me strength, or a talisman to help me gain favor in my father's court?"

I winced. Would Saskia slice him with those glass knives? Steal a part of his soul to feast on and set him loose until he was nothing but an empty husk of a man?

"No." The siren's face hardened. "And you've just lost your chance to eat. You're coming with me to the gates."

Matthias sputtered as the much taller woman pulled him to his feet by the cloak.

"You're taking him back?" I gaped.

Saskia's mouth flattened into a thin line. "I do my best to save any human that comes into my tavern. Some are a little averse to the idea at first. But he will feel better once he is back in the mortal lands."

"But why? You're a siren. A merchant here." I shook my head; sure she hid something.

Matthias' face went slack again, forgetting why he struggled.

Saskia passed a hand over her face and adjusted her grip on the limp man. "I know what it is to be hunted, Hazel. I could not save my sisters from the monsters that wished to end our kind all those years ago. But I can save others from a similar fate."

I looked down, eyes burning. "I have a sister."

"And you must be here for her in some regard."

I nodded, realizing she was right. I was here for Adelaide as much as Linus and Niklaus. To bridge the gap between our worlds. To have the right to be by her side. To spare her any more shame or pain.

She nodded, like we were sisters in a similar cause. "So you understand why I must help mortals. Why I wish to help you."

"I do." I studied my hands, my nails crusted with dust. "You're very kind."

Saskia's tired face brightened for a moment.

I opened my mouth to say something else, but bitter dread settled in my stomach. My skin pricked with awareness. A familiar flash of darkness curled in the corner of the tavern. I gripped the lip of the table, breath whooshing from my lungs.

The man dressed in black. This time, he was awake, and I was certain he watched me. His dark eyes flared, and my stomach dropped. He stood abruptly.

Stony fear seeped through my bones. I jumped to my feet, my fingers tightening around the bundle of food. The tavern wasn't safe anymore. Perhaps it never was.

"I need to get moving," I said curtly, flashes of Darius and his greedy eyes in my mind. "Thank you for your help and the food, but I need to reach the palace."

"Good luck," Saskia called, her brow creased with obvious confusion as she grabbed Matthias' hood again.

I turned swiftly, racing out of the tavern and towards the circular canal. The man in black hovered by the doorway for a moment, his heavy gaze weighing on my shoulders.

He was after me. After what Nicklaus had sent me to find. I was sure of it, as sure as the fear coursing through my blood. I ducked around a corner, my eyes fixed on the palace, and ran.

The Bazaar was coming alive. People tended to their shops and began searching for their next purchase. Voices and music buzzed through the air again, filling me with a sense of trepidation. Time was passing me by like an insect in amber.

I glanced over my shoulder, terrified to see a dark figure close behind. But there was no one. The empty alley was quiet and lonely. That was almost worse. I knew he was following me, even if I couldn't see him.

Swallowing hard, I clutched my ring and locket. *Linus, think of Linus. He needs you*, I repeated to myself.

I took a deep breath and focused once more on the palace.

Night Two

EIGHT

The crowds were dense on the second night of the Alignment. Shoulders and faces and hands blurred at every step, and yet I had never been more alone. No one would answer how to get to the palace. Most people did not seem to care at all. They could not see past their cups and the merchant's wares.

The streets slithered beneath my feet, shifting and changing stones. I stumbled a little, catching myself against one of the mud-brick walls. I had entered an entirely new section of the Bazaar. It looked like the paintings of the western kingdoms I had seen in books brought by the sailors in the port.

There were towers topped with domed roofs and coated in flaking gold leaf. Beautiful wool rugs and heavy canvas tents lined the narrow, dusty streets. Smoking pipes released a heady, sweet fume into the air. Ceramic lamps made of mosaic glass scattered shards of colored light.

Stranger than the ever-changing scenery was the people. Many creatures bounded around, some small and unassuming. Others were large and terrifying. I knew in some part of my mind that if Saskia was not human and the Bazaar collected strange beings, that creatures of myth and legend might roam the streets.

But thought and truth are different.

Most beings were fairly humanoid. But as I pushed past crowds of robed people, strange features came into focus. The first thing I noticed was the heads. A peculiar species walked with a human gait and had normal arms and legs, but their heads were that of all sorts of animals. Falcons, lynxes, wolves, and lions.

I ducked my head, trying to keep from staring.

Dodging around a merchant selling strange watches, my worn boot caught on a long smoking pipe. I tumbled, bumping into the back of a man dressed in flowing burgundy robes. As he turned to glower at me, beady, black eyes stared from the face of a massive eagle. I gasped and fell back, my shoulder colliding with a wall. He spoke in a clacking language, shrieking and snapping at me.

My tongue froze to the roof of my mouth and I stared at him and his strange face, my eyes wide. He muttered something else in his squawking tongue before he turned back to selecting wares from a hungry-looking merchant.

I slid along the wall, my hands seeking the smooth stone. Stranger things emerged as I pushed further into the Bazaar. Statues that seemed to move, watching me and changing podiums. Shadows that breathed on my neck and tugged on my hair before giggling and swirling away. More birds watched from the rooftops and spoke with the voices of humans and whispered terrible things.

I must have trekked over three miles through those winding roads, climbing rooftops and scaling rickety ladders to gather my bearings. Sometimes, the palace was tantalizingly nearby. So close, I could see lanterns glowing in windows. Other times it was further than ever before, so distant it was nothing but a smudge on the horizon of endless, tumbling buildings.

Sweat slipped down my spine. I kept hiking, pushing my tangled bronze hair back. Hours tumbled by. The tavern appeared in my path once more. And then again. And then a fourth time. My legs ached and my feet stung. Still, I gritted my teeth and continued fighting my way through the crowds, through the smells and sounds of debauchery, and kept my eyes on the castle.

But hours later, fatigued and streaked with dust, I crossed a canal into a familiar open square. Tears pricked at my eyes. Saskia's tavern. My necklace burned against my skin, a scorching reminder of everything I had to lose. But it was impossible. The Bazaar would not let me go.

I collapsed at a table outside, too embarrassed to go in and see Saskia so soon. She would be kind, I was sure. Offer to lead me back to the gates before I could get lost or hurt. But what of Linus? What about my sister or Niklaus? I had no other options. She would not understand.

My throat stung as I tried once more to fight back the tears of frustration slipping down my cheeks. All I could think was that Linus was with Veronica, cozy by a fire. Holding hands and celebrating. And I was lost and miserable.

"You're looking for a guide," a deep male voice spoke next to my ear.

I jumped, my elbow colliding with the edge of the table. A garbled sound slid past my lips as I jolted, teetering on my chair. The man, the one who had been following me and torturing me for days, leaned against the wall of the tavern beside me, his eyes a startling warm brown. Like mine.

"You are rather lost, aren't you?" he said, his expression languid and faintly amused.

"You've been watching me, following me on the island," I gasped. "What do you want? I won't sell anything."

I nearly fell out of my chair, scuttling back as far as I could. My shoulder blades brushed the rail of the porch, keeping me pinned in place. It was so loud outside, with all the people laughing and drinking. Saskia wouldn't hear me if I screamed.

"Relax, darling." He pulled his hood from his head. A tumble of ink-black hair fell in soft waves around his face. "I'm not looking to buy. I am only offering my help."

He advanced a step, dust clinging to his dark leather boots. I jerked away like he might seize me by the throat.

"Stay back!" I warned, looking around for any weapon. My hair fell in front of my eyes as I stood. I considered grabbing a chair and breaking it over his head. The thought was ridiculous. I was so weak with hunger and exhaustion; I doubted I could lift it at all.

"I will not hurt you," he said in an accent that was impossible to place. It was melodious and smooth. The voice of a predator lulling its prey.

"Why have you been following me? You were at the ports and then at my aunt's house." I demanded. My legs quaked, and I hoped my skirts hid that fact.

The man crossed his arms. He wore curious dark black robes and black breeches. A scabbard with a curved blade slung around his hips. His face remained smooth except for the hint of a sarcastic smile teasing at the corner of his mouth.

"I've been watching you try, and fail, to navigate the maze." His dark hair fell to his sharp jaw, covered in stubble, and he pushed it back with one hand.

"The maze? It's a Bazaar." I tried to back up, pressing the railing so hard into my spine it bit through the bodice of my dress.

"They are one and the same." He lifted a shoulder, and black smoke curled off his clothes. "The Bazaar is a maze meant to confuse and distract you. So far, it seems to have done a marvelous job of both."

A huff slipped between my teeth, my annoyance briefly overriding my fear. "Tell me why you've been following me. How did you get to the island before the Alignment?"

He stepped closer, and I caught the scent of leather and spices. Only a foot separated us. I kept my chin up, forcing the trembling in my lip to stop. The man looked human, except his eyes weren't glassy and white. The only other people I'd met that were unaffected by the Bazaar's spell were ones like Darius and other merchants. Not to be trusted.

He leaned closer, inspecting me like an expensive necklace. "I work for some powerful people in the Bazaar. They provide me with access to the outside world on rare occasions. And I am only following you to understand what makes you different."

"That's not good enough," I stuttered, my tongue growing clumsy with panic.

"I am offering my services, darling." He lowered his eyes, studying my dress. One eyebrow quirked, and I felt the rush of blood to my cheeks. "My benefactor wishes me to help you."

I narrowed my eyes, sensing deceit layered under his innocent tone. He smiled, and I felt a hot ring of embarrassment crawl up my chest. That smile looked far too familiar. It was, in a word, *devastating*. Like those of sailors eyeing Veronica in her flashy, revealing gowns from their ships. It was a knowing smile, like he was playing with me.

Damn him and his benefactor.

I shoved past, relieved when he did not reach out to grab me. "Stay away."

"I am not lying," he laughed, a low rumbling echoing in his chest. "I have been watching you try to find your way in the Bazaar and want to offer my help."

I hesitated, hating that his words affected me. Slowly, I turned back to where he languidly leaned against the porch railing. "Why?"

He mimicked my position, crossing his arms over the broad expanse of his chest. "I was curious to see if you could find your way on your own, given your unique *condition*. I am sure you could, given enough time. But time is a commodity that cannot be bought and sold here—and you are running out of it." He licked his lips, and my eyes followed the movement. "But I am willing to help you, free of charge. It would please my benefactor greatly."

I narrowed my eyes, waiting for him to lunge at me. "Who is your benefactor, and how could you help me?"

He was silent, his face drawn. I waited a few seconds. Quiet stretched between us. I shook my head and made a move to leave the square, intent on leaving this man and his intense gaze.

His smooth voice carried like a caress. "I have been here a long time. I am one of the few that knows exactly how to get to the palace."

Ice filled my stomach, and I tightened my fingers into a fist. I'd never mentioned the palace. I glanced around at the other people in the square. No one else seemed to notice the man. It was like the shadows clung to him. Like he was a part of them.

The words of the terrifying birds haunted me. *Followed by shadows.*

My fingers curled tighter. "How do you know that?"

He shrugged, pushing a wave of hair from his eyes. "Perhaps I know more than others."

"Or you've been eavesdropping since the island."

He snorted again. But it was the only likely explanation. I could not trust this man. He'd been sent to follow me by someone else. A benefactor who sent me dresses in a locked room. I shuddered.

"Are you accepting my offer?" he asked.

"No." I backed away, eyes darting as I pushed through the crowds. "I don't want your help."

The smell of spices and the hum of the dazed crowd washed over me. I gripped my locket. My ring. I would get to the palace and flee the Bazaar with no one's help but my own if it was the last thing I did.

"You will," he called.

I didn't turn around.

I left the large square housing the tavern and retreated into a narrow, forgotten-looking alley. It stretched on for a long time. Desolate. For the past day and a half, I'd taken the most obvious routes, as anyone would. Perhaps I needed to change my tactic. Nicklaus had said I wouldn't get far thinking along the lines of simplicity.

My skin felt clammy as I mulled over the shadow man's words.

That arrogant man had tried to manipulate me into following him. I wouldn't fall into his trap. Shaking my head, I blew out a shaky breath. The Bazaar was only a place. There was a way to the palace. I just hadn't found it yet. And I certainly didn't need help from a man who had been watching me with honey-brown eyes.

The alley grew more and more narrow as I walked. After a while, the grey stone walls brushed both of my shoulders. I swallowed, reaching for the flask of water Saskia had given me. My fingers curled around Nicklaus' canister. I'd forgotten the water at the table outside the tavern, along with the food. I shut my eyes, my lips dry and cracking like I was in the middle of an arid desert.

By the Fates, was I cursed to wander this place forever? I snapped my eyes open and kicked at the dusty road. A choking scream ripped through my teeth as I planted my fist against the wall.

I hated the Bazaar.

Shutting my eyes again, I leaned my forehead against the cool stone. One deep breath. Another. I couldn't lose my temper or give in to despair. There were still six nights left. I could figure everything out before the end of the Alignment. I gripped my locket and ring in my fist and pushed off the wall.

Forging on; I clomped through puddles of tepid, filthy water. It was almost as if the Bazaar mocked me. The road grew more uneven. Ivy choked each crumbling brick. The air turned stale. Even the typical orange glow of lanterns faded to a dingy grey coldness.

Maybe the unassuming alleyway wasn't the right choice after all.

My brash confidence faded to a dim ember before puffing out completely. I looked over my shoulder and saw nothing but low-hanging mist and the endless yawn of the alley behind me. A sick sense of familiarity washed over my skin.

I was once again alone in a tight, darkened tunnel. A warm breeze tickled my neck, like the breath of an invisible beast. I gulped down air as sweat stuck to my skin. Each muscle between my ribs tightened. Linus' ring singed against my skin and I clutched it, forcing one foot in front of the other.

Mist curled and gathered around my skirts, tugging and clinging and wrapping around me like a ghostly cat. The walls of the alley closed in, pushing my shoulders rather than merely brushing them. I turned sideways, scuttling like the sand crabs back home, and reached out blindly in the thick mist.

Fog swirled. Reaching grey fingers seeped into the fibers of my skirt and pushed into my eyes and down my throat. A terrible thought niggled at the back of my mind. Hissed and whispered that I would fail. What if I fell from the Bazaar as easily as I had slipped into its sultry, terrifying streets? What would become of Nicklaus and his wife? Of me?

I burst out of the thick, coiling mist and staggered into a vast open space. I blinked against the starlight twinkling down once more, a strangely familiar blanket overhead. Seven points of pulsing light blazed in the blackness, watching as I turned in a circle, taking in my surroundings.

The alley opened onto a strange circular plateau. I craned my neck back. A sheer cliff face hung overhead like heavy fruit on a wilting limb. Ringing in one side of the clearing was a semi-circle of rock, like some sort of arena. A dead tree, parched and tilting, moped a few feet away. Empty doorways looked like eyes in the dark brown rock.

How strange.

I blinked, rubbing at the remnants of mist still clinging to my eyes. That's when I noticed something was amiss.

The circular arena was just that. A colosseum of crumbling stone, rising high in a ring. The cliff face soared above like a spectator's gallery. My pulse thundered against my throat. The palace loomed overhead, perched near the edge. I cursed, kicking at the sheer rise with my boot, a sob of resentment lodged in my chest.

I was so close, but so impossibly far away. The Bazaar had won again.

Stone slid across stone. Grinding and groaning. A terrible sound that sent my heart skittering somewhere in my throat. The alley I had come through slipped shut like a trapdoor, sealing me in the arena.

I ran for the tunnel, beating my fists against the immovable stone. The door didn't open. With a cry of frustration, I stepped back. My feet tangled on something and I went down hard, my breath knocked from my lungs.

Ropes and chains, half shrouded in lingering fog, tangled around my ankles and shabby boots. I shuffled backward, kicking wildly to free myself. My back hit the wilting tree. My heart thundered, my skin turned to ice, and I struggled to breathe.

I screamed into the empty air. Screamed until my throat tore and tears streamed down my cheeks. I was useless. A failure. Only two nights into the Bazaar and I had been trapped, tricked, mocked, and abused. I threw my head back against the flaking trunk of the tree. And again, just because it felt good to control something that happened to me.

After a while, when my throat burned, my tears ran dry, and my skull ached, I collapsed onto my side. I dug my fingers into the ashy soil, hardly caring that my new dress was dirty or that my tangled hair matted to my cheek.

For a terrible, selfish moment, I wanted to give up. Just lie there in the dark and let the Bazaar consume me like it had done to so many before. For the first time in days, days that felt longer than an eternity, I thought of those who relied on me and felt hollow. Hopeless.

They would be better off without me.

Low voices sounded from the openings in the stone colosseum. I flipped onto my belly, hiding as best as I could behind the dead tree. I measured my hiccuping breath, fear burning away my self pity.

A group emerged from within the tunnels as if they had been waiting. Sparks flew. Torches sailed into a darkened brazier. Fire erupted a dozen feet away, illuminating a group of sinister-looking people. Their eyes landed right on me.

"What do we have here?" a woman mused.

She stalked forward, dressed in hide armor and tattered leather. Her face was smeared in blue paint. War paint.

I scrambled to my feet, wiping my scraped palms on my dress. Blood glared back at me from the once beautiful gown. The fire in the brazier crackled and popped, sending a flurry of sparks into the air.

"Who are you?" I demanded, keeping my trembling chin in the air. *Think*, I demanded. But there were no more tunnels. No more options. They'd trapped me like an animal. Maybe it would be better to give up.

The woman stopped in front of me, resting her weight on a crude-looking club carved from an unnaturally huge femur bone. My throat was as dry as the dust beneath my feet.

"Interesting," a male voice called from the other side of the brazier, obscured in shadow. "It doesn't look like she's under the influence of the lotus wine or the merchants."

"What does that matter, Seti?" The woman sighed, looking bored. She hefted the club. The blue paint wound in spirals around her bicep and bare shoulder. Her hair was dirty and matted and her teeth glinted hungrily in the firelight.

"It doesn't." The man purred, his words tangling in a bizarre drawl. "A new plaything is always welcome in our arena."

Two men came into the light. But I couldn't call them men.

One was like those creatures I had seen earlier, half-man with the head of a falcon. Its... *his* eyes were sharp and unyielding. His chest was bare, a white tunic wrapped around his waist. A sharp, curved saber hung at his hip.

The other was more like an ogre, with tusks protruding from his lower lip, making his prominent forehead even more brutish. They reminded me of the gladiators of time gone by. Beaten and starved into killing machines with an unquenchable thirst for carnage. For blood.

"Stay away from me."

My voice cracked.

They laughed.

The trio didn't listen, instead; they pressed forward, leisurely walking, pushing me back. I held my hands out defensively, skin tingling. The woman lunged forward, and I tripped, careening sideways. My forearm collided with something hard.

Empty sockets. Bleached bone. The slackened jaw of a skull grinned back at me.

They laughed as I shrieked and rolled away, clambering to my feet. The dead tree loomed behind, pinning me in place. I dove for a dead branch lying next to another partial skeleton, a broken ax head lodged in the sternum.

"This won't even be fun, Nimuae," Seti cawed, the words strange coming from a beak. "She'll die so easily."

"Who cares? It's been ages since we've had any fun," the woman, Nimuae, said, her lip curling fiercely.

I brandished the dead branch, pointing the dry bark at them. The ogre-man grunted, somewhere between a hoot and a snarl, reaching for me. I shuddered at the spittle clinging to his lower lip and tusks. One hand wrapped around my throat and shook, dislodging the dry branch from my hand.

He cackled and let me go. I swayed; my bodice was so tight around my ribs that my lips went numb. By the Fates, I was going to die. Linus would marry Veronica. Nicklaus' wife would die. Everything was over.

"What do you want with me?" I asked. My voice trembled, almost hysterical. At that moment, I truly wanted to give up. End the fear and torment.

"Such odious questions," Nimuae grunted impatiently. "You

entered our arena, girl. Remember that when you're begging for death at the end of my sword."

"Bring her to the center," Seti barked to the ogre.

He grunted, seizing my arm so hard the tendons screamed in protest. I screeched and kicked at his legs and side as he dragged me across the dirt and stones. He could have been smirking or smacking his lips, imagining the way my flesh would taste, for all I knew.

He threw me down roughly, and I rolled twice until I collided with the burning hot brazier. My back arched away from the heated metal. I coughed and wiped at the dust caked on my cheek.

The ogre feigned a lunge, and I crouched defensively, my hands covering my head. He snickered, and the woman shot him a withering glare. Nimuae went to a rack of weapons and threw a rusty, blunt dagger in the dirt at my feet.

"We haven't had visitors to our arena in years," Nimuae murmured thoughtfully, tracing her finger along the edge of a huge broadsword. "As you can see from the bones littering this place, few are true challengers. I'm sure you won't be an exception. But what can you do? Entertainment is entertainment, and Ragnor is simply *starving*."

Her lips curled wickedly, eyes flicking towards the leering ogre. Nausea flooded my stomach, boiling through my limbs. Seti and Ragnor stood back as Nimuae hefted the sword. I imagined myself impaled on the corroded, jagged blade, like so many others had probably been before me.

"Pick it up," she snarled. "You want a fair fight, don't you?"

"I don't want to fight, please. I'm just trying to reach the palace. I didn't mean to trespass," I begged. It couldn't end like this; me cowering in the dirt beneath some bored gladiators.

Ragnor snorted again as Seti chuckled. His eyes darted around, taking in the arena and my pitiful state with a head swivel. It was a grotesque gladiator duel, and I was the bait to be toyed with.

"*Pick. It. Up. Now.*" She punctuated each word by slamming the tip of her sword into the dirt. "Or you'll be losing that pretty little head sooner than you thought."

My fingers shook, closing around the hilt of the pathetic dagger. I wanted to keep begging, but I knew that glint in Nimuae's eyes. Cruel, like Veronica and my aunt. No mercy would be given. Why waste my breath?

The men stood away, watching with bright anticipation in their eyes. Seti's beak clacked mindlessly as if imaging tearing my limbs apart. Nimuae lunged, experimentally stabbing the enormous blade. I dodged easily, but I was sure she was simply lulling me into a false sense of security.

The sailors at the port on Veara Island would do similar things when they boxed, placing bets on one another. A fake punch, a lazy dodge. Soon, one would become complacent and cocky and then they would be on their back in the dust.

The sword jabbed again, and I stumbled back, slapping it away with my palm. I hissed and clutched my hand to my chest.

The blade, though rusty and unwieldy, still stung my palm. Nimuae laughed, her eyes narrowing, probably analyzing the best way to disembowel me. She slashed, both hands bringing the sword down in a powerful arc. I yelped, lifting my hand as I fell to my knees. The dagger clanging uselessly against her hilt, sending pangs of vibrations through my wrist bones.

My dress clung to the sweat on my back and legs. Nimuae lunged again, slashing the lace and cleaving the skirt in two, nicking my thigh. I cried out, slapping my hand over the welling blood, the slit in the dress baring one leg to my mid-thigh. I pulled my hand back, the imprint of lace and blood sparking an idea.

The dress.

"Stop!" I yelled, holding the dagger out like it was a spear. "Or do you want to explain to Zaire why his special guest is dead and bloody in *your* arena?"

Victory.

Nimuae faltered. Her surprise sent her off balance, and the sword tugged her to the left. She cursed and dropped it, pulling a dagger from the belt at her waist.

She pointed it at me, painted face guarded. "If you're so special to him, why are you wandering the Bazaar like any lotus-hungry human?"

I narrowed my eyes at the words but swallowed back questions.

"I've been trying to get to the palace. He sent me a special invitation, along with this dress, as a gift."

"She's lying," Seti spat. "We should kill her and have it over with. I'm already bored."

Nimuae hesitated, and I kept my face impassive, haughty. I had said something right. Saskia's reaction to me asking about Zaire and the note wasn't just my imagination.

The note!

I plucked it from my pocket, thrusting it forward like Nimuae would a rusty weapon. "Does this convince you?"

Nimuae and Seti's eyes fell on the broken wax seal hanging from the paper. I doubted they could read, but the symbol in the black wax seemed to send a ripple of unease through them. Double crescents framed by some type of fruit embossed in black wax. It seemed unremarkable to me, but Nimuae's face paled.

"Maybe she's telling the truth," she muttered to Seti.

His sharp eyes analyzed the note, squinting and jerking side to side. His beak clicked in frustration and a shudder of repulsion tore through my stomach.

"It could easily be a forgery. Besides, hasn't Ragnor waited for his breakfast long enough?"

Seti threw the note back at me. My triumph faded like a dying star, collapsing in on itself spectacularly.

"Fine," I said, but my voice broke. "Zaire will make you regret it."

"Oh, somehow I'm sure he won't," Seti laughed.

He stepped forward, razor-sharp beak glinting red in the firelight. My muscles went rigid as I imagined how painful it would be to be torn apart and pierced through by a bird-headed man.

I closed my eyes, my dagger outstretched, waiting for the first burning cut.

A cry, the piercing screech of a falcon, rang off the circular walls of the arena. I gasped and dropped to my knees, expecting the warm trickle of blood to come at any second. But the same screech sounded again. Then a sickening crack. A thud. I felt nothing.

"Seti!" Nimuae wailed.

I wrenched my eyelids open to see a blur of black streak across the arena. A silver sword extended from a mass of swirling shadows, perched against Nimuae's neck. She held up her hands, her dagger falling to the dust with a muted thud.

"Wait!" she choked out, laughing uneasily. "We were just having fun. She trespassed on our territory. We did nothing wrong."

"As far as you're concerned," the man in black pressed the blade a little harder into her neck, "this arena, this entire Bazaar, belongs to Zaire. Is that clear?"

She nodded desperately, trying to keep the perfectly sharpened blade from piercing her skin. Seti made a sound between a groan and a caw. His arm was bent at a strange angle, and his beak looked cracked.

I couldn't muster up any pity, even as I got to my feet, my legs numb and trembling.

"What are you doing here?" I asked. I wished I sounded angry, or at least defensive. But annoyingly, I sounded grateful. Somehow, that was worse. I didn't want to be indebted to anyone, especially not in this Bazaar.

"I said you'd need my help, didn't I?" The man drenched in shadows slowly lowered his sword, putting it back into the scabbard beneath his long coat. His hood was up, obscuring half his face.

My jaw tightened. He'd been following me, expecting me to fail. *Again.* My gratitude faded as quickly as it had come.

"I was doing just fine," I quipped, wrapping my fingers around my necklace. A bald-faced lie.

He snorted before he turned back to Nimuae. "I think you'd better get to the palace to beg Zaire for forgiveness. You're late on your tax."

"Of course," Nimuae stuttered, casting a hateful look at me before she stepped backward, her eyes lowered from the mysterious man. She helped Seti up, who was busy cradling and whining over his arm, and then the trio of gladiators disappeared into the shadows of the tunnels.

"How did you find me?" I asked, dropping the dagger as if it burned. My shoulders ached and my hands stung from scraping on the ground. Bruises bloomed on my arm and neck where Ragnor had grabbed me, the skin hot and tender.

The man shrugged as if it was obvious. "I told you I know how to navigate the maze. Do you believe me now?"

"I don't understand." I shook my head. "Why are you doing this? Why did your benefactor tell you to follow me?"

One hand reached up and slid off his hood. He was quiet, as if pondering something.

I studied his face, searching for some sort of sign. His brown eyes were almost black in the dark. His face was chiseled, like he was the product of a fine family. I tried to guess where he could be from and why he could strike fear into Nimuae.

"Are you," I hesitated, stomach twisting, "are you Zaire?"

His eyebrows shot up and he let out a barking laugh. Shoulders shaking, he bent over, clasping one knee before he wiped under his eyes. He straightened, blinking up at the sky and chuckling.

I scowled at him.

"No, I am certainly not Zaire." He laughed again. "I'm Cassian."

I rubbed at the heat in my cheeks. "And who are *you*, Cassian? Why can you tell those... people what to do, and why do they listen?"

He sobered a little, squinting up at the palace. "It doesn't matter who I am. I know the Bazaar better than just about anyone here and can get you where you need to go."

"But why have you been watching me?" The feeling of his dark eyes, clear and looking right at me, sent a strange prickle over my skin. "Can't you answer that without being cryptic?" I laced my words with venom.

"I've been sent by someone."

"By who?" I crossed my arms, the bare skin pebbling into goosebumps.

He brushed his short stubble with one hand. "I can't tell you everything yet, but I promise I will answer your questions in due time *and* help you navigate the Bazaar. Under one condition."

"I knew there was something," I muttered, staggering against the wilting tree as my strength left my limbs. "And what would that be? A third of my soul? A blood-oath?"

"No," he chuckled, brown eyes flaring with something I couldn't name. "Nothing like that. All you need to do is agree to meet someone. Once you do, I'll take you wherever it is you wish to go."

"Who do I need to meet?" I dug my fingers into the flesh of my upper arms.

Part of me screamed not to trust Cassian and to avoid his benefactor at all costs. But mist crawled towards us again, and it was dark and frightening in this den of death and blood-sport. I wanted to escape, and I clearly couldn't get to the palace on my own. My heart dropped at the thought. What would my aunt think of me accepting help from a strange man who had followed me? What would Linus think?

"I'm not Zaire," Cassian said. "But he did send me to find you."

NINE

Cassian walked ahead, blazing a path through the Bazaar with no sign of hesitation. When the tunnels rearranged themselves, he didn't think twice about picking a path. It was almost like the streets unwound from their confusing tangle before him, parting like a curtain.

"How are you doing that?" I griped.

Cassian offered me his hand to help me over a rickety wooden bridge. Below, a deep blue canal hissed like it was boiling. I ignored my pride and accepted his help to cross the creaking bridge, not eager to be scorched by that dark water.

He held onto my hand a moment longer before I snatched it back. His hands were smooth and lightly calloused. I didn't mind the feeling.

"Doing what?" Cassian didn't even look over his shoulder.

I breathed out between my teeth, crossing my arms as he continued as if we were taking a leisurely evening stroll. "You seem to know exactly where you're going. How can anyone find their way in this place?"

"Few people are looking for *somewhere* in particular when they come to the Bazaar," Cassian mused, waiting a few moments for me to catch up. "Just *something*. There's a difference."

He slowed his step as if sensing my exhaustion. Soon we were walking side by side.

"You didn't answer my question," I pointed out.

Cassian smiled, a crease appearing on his cheek. "I've been here a long time. I know these streets, no matter how many times they change. It's my home."

"How can anyone call this place home?" I muttered, glaring at the shopkeeper's dangling talismans and other oddities. Their stalls lined the sides of the narrow streets. It was a sinful place. One where people gave into their base desires and got lost along the way.

I shut my eyes, remembering the despair in the gladiator's pit. Screaming against the Fates, the gods. Anything that would listen. I dragged my eyes open, my spirits sinking ever lower.

Cassian's brown eyes reflected the glittering lamplight when he looked at me. "Few do," he admitted. "But it's home to me. To these merchants."

I set my jaw. "And Zaire."

His smile weakened a little and his eyes softened. "Yes, him too."

"What does he want? Why did he send you to watch me before I even came to the Bazaar?" I shook my head, pushing my tangled bronze curls away from my face. I wished I had something to tie it back with, even if it would make my widow's peak stand out.

"He noticed you as the Bazaar was anchoring to the mortal world. He sensed your f—" Cassian choked on the words like he couldn't speak freely without being strangled. The cords of his neck strained for a moment, his face turning a little red.

It was almost like the effect of Niklaus' vow on my words. My blood heated at the thought and I narrowed my eyes. What oath had he made to Zaire? Why was he sworn to secrecy? Distrust wound through my veins.

"I'm sure you've noticed you're not like the other humans here," he finally spoke again, his voice still strained. He pointed to the people around us.

Some lounged on carpets, smoking pipes, and laughing. Others sipped from the same goblets I had when I first came to the Bazaar. Merchants flashed them dazzling grins and coaxed them into buying trinkets and vials of mysterious liquid. Flashes of glassy knives appeared, slicing without leaving a mark. I shuddered at the sight and clasped my arms around my middle.

"But what does that matter? I'm running out of time to get what I came for," I said.

"You'll never find it if you don't have Zaire's blessing." Cassian paused, pushing me gently in front of him to pass through a particularly narrow tunnel. His hands lingered on the bruises dotting my wrists. "He controls everything here. The Bazaar isn't letting you find your way because he hasn't told it to."

My skin prickled under his touch, even though he let go almost immediately. I rubbed my shoulders. Hard.

"Why does everyone talk like that? Like the Bazaar can think and feel."

My foot caught on a rock, and I nearly landed on my face. I wanted to scream again, blame him for my frustrations. But Cassian's hands shot out, lighting quick, and wrapped around my waist. A warm breeze and Cassian's firm hand on my back crawled under my skin. I pushed him away.

"This is a strange place. It's older than the gods themselves. Very few can find their way here, much less understand every secret it holds." Cassian released me, but the thrill of energy on my skin from where he had touched did not.

I didn't respond. His answers were only giving me more questions, anyway. Besides, fatigue had crept in from every side. Sweat and dust and scratches marked my skin. I wanted to lie down and sleep, but the second night of the Bazaar was almost done.

The crowds thinned out and the sides of the tunnels dropped away until I could once again see the shimmering stars. They differed from the ones I knew on Veara. These were brighter, their light stronger and more luminous. As if they were the eyes of the gods, watching from their new home.

The smooth ground grew soft beneath my boots. I glanced down. Tufts of luxuriously soft grass sprouted, waving in the wind. A wide, grassy plateau spread before us like the Bazaar had opened a door to another world. A grove emerged from the whipping grass. We left the snarled web of streets behind.

The shelf of grass and bright white boulders stretched on for a few dozen yards before dropping off steeply into nothingness. The palace glittered on the opposite side of the chasm. I let out a groan. It had been ludicrous to hope I would meet Zaire in the one place I desperately needed to go.

Cassian smiled apologetically. "He won't let you into his home until he's spoken to you."

"Of course not," I grumbled.

I rubbed the bruises on my neck and wrists, working out the tired muscles. Cassian's eyes followed the movement and his eyes darkened. He pressed his mouth into a hard line, brown eyes turning black.

"What?" I snipped.

"Come here." He held out one hand.

I glared at him, ready to throw a punch. "Why?"

He sighed and grabbed my hand anyway, hauling me forward. "These bruises and cuts, I don't like them."

"Yeah, well," I screwed my mouth to the side, trying to make sense of my hammering pulse, "maybe you should have interrupted those gladiators sooner."

"Maybe I should have *killed* those gladiators," he snarled, his usually carefree voice dropping completely.

I tilted my head, unsure how to take that declaration. Without another word, Cassian reached into his coat and withdrew an intricate glass vial. Holding my hands in one of his, he ripped the stopper out with his teeth and, without warning, dumped the contents on his free palm.

He reached out, smoothing the oddly thick liquid over my wrists.

"What are you doing?" I shrieked, trying to bat his hands away.

Cassian grunted and held me still, towering over me as he grimaced and smoothed more of the elixir onto my neck and the cut on my thigh. I sucked in a breath as his fingers danced over my skin, indignant and breathless.

"There." He dropped the vial carelessly on the grass. "You should be fully healed within the hour." With that, he motioned for me to keep walking. I stared at his receding back, broad and stiff. My skin tingled, and I glanced down just as the blooming bruises faded.

I opened my mouth, but couldn't find any words. I jogged after Cassian, my head swimming. Why had he not asked for payment?

We entered a grove of trees. The air grew sweet and the sound of a rushing stream filled my ears. Cassian stayed silent as we walked. Leaves rustled around gnarled trunks. A branch cracked and something leapt from behind a twisting tree.

I jumped, clutching onto Cassian's arm like I could use him as a shield. Another rustle and then a man with shaggy legs skipped around the grove. Cassian's eyes showed a flicker of surprise and he glanced down at my hand.

"What *was* that?" I hissed.

The creature didn't look at me. His unkempt goat's legs twitched as he grinned, and twisting horns hooked over his ears. A woman with green skin and long brown hair, dressed in gossamer robes, plucked an apple from a low-hanging bough and offered it to the goat-man.

"I wouldn't look at them, darling," Cassian said distastefully, his eyes still glued to my hand. "Or they may think you're flirting with them. Horrible ego's you know."

The satyr winked as I blushed. Cassian smirked, looking once more at where my hand held onto his well-muscled arm like a tourniquet.

"They aren't the only ones," I snipped and snatched my hand away. Cassian threw back his head and laughed. I grit my teeth.

The small grove ended in an unnaturally straight line. We stopped at the edge of a clearing. Cassian leaned one shoulder against a warped tree trunk.

"Zaire's over there." He jerked his chin towards a beautiful pond at the edge of the plateau where a dark figure gazed into the still water.

I hesitated. The bright meadow and cheery forest felt like a trap. Fake sunlight and strangely gleaming fruit. I'd almost prefer the harsh black rock and fierce winds of the North Sea. This facade of calm and warmth wasn't real.

"I'll be waiting right here." Cassian smiled encouragingly, his usual amusement absent from his face. "Don't give up yet, Hazel. Despair doesn't suit you."

I don't know why it worked, but the knot in my stomach slowly unraveled. I tore my eyes from the man dressed in shadows and his soft, tentative smile.

Another man sat on a rim of rocks at the edge of the bright blue pond. The little stream winding through the trees fed into it until the water tumbled over the edge of the chasm and fell into oblivion.

The reflection of dark hair and a blue velvet doublet gleamed over the water. He leaned back, piercing an apple in his hand with an intricate blade. At my approach, the man looked up, long lashes framing the most startling pair of eyes I'd ever seen.

"Hazel," he said, voice as smooth as honey and as dangerous as waves crashing against sharp rocks. "I've been so eager to meet you. Come, sit beside me."

"You know my name?" I asked, dumbly, and sat on the rim of smooth white limestone.

Zaire raised a dark eyebrow and turned to face me more fully. I couldn't tear my eyes away. He was beautiful.

His skin was smooth and radiant, the color of a polished bronze statue. Even though he was seated, I could tell he was tall. His arms and legs were lithe, like a panther. He wore a dark blue doublet embroidered in swirling patterns of silver and gold. But it was his eyes that truly arrested my attention. They were pure silver, exactly like melted coins, and shined just like the stars above.

"Of course," he purred, his voice winding around me like a spell. "This is my Bazaar, after all. I know all who come here."

I swallowed hard, casting a glance at Cassian. He flicked his gaze between Zaire and my face as he wiped a dagger with a cloth. My stomach felt hollow and cold. Maybe I had made a mistake in allowing Cassian to bring me here.

I jerked my eyes from my surly guide and inspected Zaire. "Why did you send Cassian after me? Why were you watching me back on Veara Island?"

Zaire grinned, bright white teeth glinting back at me. I fought the urge to shudder. He was handsome, there was no denying that. But he was also terrible, like the statues of the old gods at the abandoned temples across the kingdom. His eyes, silver and sharp, were filled with unmistakable power.

As he smiled, I noticed a flaw in his otherwise deliriously perfect face. Across his forehead, cutting through one eyebrow and down his left cheek, was a hideous scar. I did not know how I hadn't seen it before. It was so jagged and obvious now. He caught me looking, but if it offended him, he didn't let it show.

"I've noticed you practically from the moment the Bazaar connected to the mortal lands on the eve of the Alignment. You're unlike any human I've met in the past thousand years."

My breath snagged. A *thousand* years. How could that be? He looked no older than... well, I couldn't tell. He was young, but his face showed ages of experience and secrets.

I shook my head. "What is so special about me?"

"The fact that you have spent a little over a day without succumbing to the pleasures my Bazaar has to offer should answer that question. Not a single human has ever entered and retained their consciousness for more than a few minutes."

I tried not to blush at the way he said *pleasures* like it was a delicious secret. I shrugged, winding my hands together. My heart raced under his scrutiny. He sat perfectly still, watching me. Waiting.

The satyrs and green-skinned women laughed and danced through the branches of trees. I noticed other humans in the grove then, their eyes blank and far away. The satyrs dangled fruit before them tantalizingly and they accepted, biting into the flesh as if it were the sweetest thing they'd ever tasted. Bile rose in my throat.

"What kind of family do you come from?" he asked.

I started, feeling as if a warm hand settled around my shoulders, lulling me to speak. "Not a special one." The words tripped from my tongue and I tightened my jaw, fighting for control. "My mother died when I was young. I never knew my father."

"How tragic," he whispered, but his eyes were sharp and searching. "Perhaps that is why you found your way here. This place is for those that are lost and ignored. This world differs from the one you came from. You are not forgotten here."

It sounded like he was trying to solve a puzzle, not truly speaking to me.

"How can this place exist? Who are you?"

His silver tongue weaved a spell that made my eyelids heavy and my lips loose. A strange, alien part of me wanted to preen at his intense perusal of me. Wanted to mewl with appreciation and lean my cheek into his hand.

"Even I cannot answer those questions." One of his hands traced the blood on my bare thigh from my tousle in the arena. His lower lip jutted out as he examined his ruined gift. He snapped his fingers and one of the green-skinned women sashayed over to him as if she could not wait to be nearby.

"Fetch my special guest something more comfortable to wear."

The woman nodded and twirled away, her eyes spearing me with something very much like jealousy. My fingers tightened in my lap as Zaire leaned forward, his breath sweet and cool against my cheeks. His hand still burned against my exposed skin, the slit Nimuae had cut in my dress displaying far too much.

"Tell me something, Hazel," Zaire murmured, his mouth turning my name into something like a prayer. "What is it that you desire?"

A pair of women a few feet away sighed and turned towards him as if he had said something wonderfully scandalous. A human man sitting against a tree looked at Zaire too, his mouth pulling into a dreamy smile.

They all answered in a blur of words and wishes, desires and secrets that were deep and passionate and lurid. I blushed, red creeping and licking up my neck as they confessed to Zaire exactly what they most wanted, no matter how personal or desperate.

Cassian, still lazily leaning against the tree, lifted his brows like he was bored. But he watched me just the same, seeing how I would answer. A wave of... something washed over me, tugging on my tongue, begging for it to reveal what I most wanted. What I most hated. What I feared and loved and longed for.

"I... I just want to get what I came for and return home," I choked out. The buzzing, tugging sensation crawled along my skin, pushed against my tongue. It felt like fingers thumbing through my thoughts, searching. Reading me.

Zaire's eyes bored into mine, and I felt as if he were trying to pull something from deep within. His silver eyes coaxed and prodded. He leaned closer, his full lips almost brushing my ear as he pushed my hair from my neck. A shudder rippled over my skin—cold and heat mixing.

"And what is that?" he asked, eyes hardening a little.

A flash of blue eyes and blonde hair. A man with wrinkled skin and a wife he could not bear to lose. The feeling of desire and heat in my skin faded to cold dread.

"I'm here to help someone back on my home island," I said, shaking myself from whatever spell he was trying to cast. "He needs something from the palace, a sort of medicine."

Niklaus's spell over the truth barely held together. It prevented me from revealing much to anyone, but Zaire was different. Rather than choking on my tongue, I could barely keep the truth back. Truth was a powerful tool in the Bazaar, I realized. Something that can be used against me, twisted to fit another's wishes. I fisted the material of my skirt, sweat sticking to my back.

He sat back a little, as if truly perplexed. But that expression faded almost as quickly as it fluttered across his gorgeous, scarred face. "I have many medicinal concoctions in my home. To which are you referring?"

"He said," I hesitated, my mind spinning, "he said I would know it when I saw it."

"Indeed." Zaire's silver eyes turned flinty, and he tapped one finger against his lower lip. "Very well. I will help you on your quest."

"You will?" I stuttered, jerking upright. "Why?"

"You are a fascinating creature, Hazel Blackthorn." Zaire stood and extended his hand. I took it cautiously, feeling that it was rough and rigid beneath my fingers. I wanted to pull my hand away but stamped down the urge.

"I'm only an illegitimate daughter of an unimportant noble-woman." I swallowed, my eyes drifting to Cassian. My guide stood rigid. Though he kept his gaze unfocused, I thought I saw him scowl at the king's hand.

Zaire leaned forward, looming over me as I sat rigid on the fountain, my hand trapped in his. "I feel we can be of use to one another. I will help you get what you came for before the festival ends, as long as you help me with something first."

I wilted.

Of course. I should have guessed. Just like Cassian had saved me for a price, Zaire would only help me if I fulfilled a request.

I breathed in sharply. "What could I possibly do for you?"

Zaire smirked and pulled me to my feet in a fluid motion, as if we were dancing. His grip on my hand tightened as he leaned forward, lips brushing my ear as if sharing a secret. That stranger lurking beneath my skin shuddered at the contact.

"There are places even I cannot go. Only someone like you could ever get what I need."

"What do you mean?" I whispered.

His smile turned wicked as he looked down at me with his liquid silver eyes. Zaire's tongue flicked out over his lips, wetting them before he continued, tucking my hand into his arm and guiding me through the grove of trees as he talked.

"Though this is not like any earthly kingdom, I am nevertheless a ruler here. All you see is under my command. The humans who wander, though they may not know it, are part of this empire. And yet, I was not here at its inception. It was once the home of the gods. There are places where immortals can't go, a sort of place reserved for those of you who are bound, at one point or another, to die."

"Immortal?" I squeaked.

Zaire's smile gleamed in the light glinting from the golden apples.

"In another life, I was different. But it doesn't matter. It was eons ago," he said, eyes stormy despite the pleasant smile curling his lips. "This place you must go for me—it is dangerous. I will not lie to you. You need to have your wits about you to navigate the Underworld successfully, and few humans fit the description."

"Underworld?" I choked, my throat burning at the word. I tried to pull my hand away. "You can't be serious."

Zaire shrugged, his fingers tightening around my wrist. "The Underworld is a place strictly for mortals. There is something I need there, something precious that was stolen from me. I ask you to retrieve it."

"I can't go to the Underworld," I yelped, a chill creeping down my neck. "Surely someone or something else could go for you."

"I'm afraid not." Zaire shook his head. "You are the only human I have ever met who can find their way. You are whole." He said it almost with envy, eyes scanning my face like he could see straight to my soul, complete and intact.

"What am I meant to get?" I asked. "If I agree to go."

My skin felt icy. This couldn't be the way to get what I needed. But Zaire was the King of the Bazaar. It bent to his will. I had wasted my first night and time was running out swiftly on my second.

"You only need to lead some of my men to a place near the Gates of the Dead. Don't look so alarmed. Cassian will go with you. I would trust him with my life—if I could die, that is." He laughed, the sound like sharp rocks clattering across marble.

I looked over at the intimidating man dressed in complete black. Cassian still leaned against the tree. He couldn't possibly have heard us, but he looked up from inspecting his nails and threw me a lazy smile. I curled my toes in my boots.

Tangling my free hand in my skirts, I considered what he offered. I couldn't go to the Underworld. It was dangerous. Mythic. Impossible. There was no chance I could survive, no matter what Zaire said. But... I absolutely needed his help. Nimuae's arena had taught me that much.

My mind followed every possibility. If I died in the Underworld, if I got lost for days and time ran out, I would lose Linus for good.

"I can't," I sputtered, my ribs tightening as I dropped his hand. "I don't know how you expect me to lead anyone in a place I've never been."

I would simply have to find another way.

Zaire's smile faded. His eyes grew dark, like storm clouds over the sea. My heart thumped, grinding to a halt. He reached out and gripped my shoulder, his thumb pressing against the side of my throat. Against the bruises fading there. A jolt of cold and fear ran up my spine.

I swayed as he spoke, my mind so foggy I couldn't remember where I was or who I was looking at. "Do this for me, Hazel, and I will make sure you find what you seek. What you *truly* want."

His words slammed into me like the hull of a ship. Electricity ran over my skin, cold and harsh, unlike the feeling of warmth Cassian's touch elicited.

"And once we get this stolen item for you, you'll take me to your palace?" I spoke slowly, tasting the words, not believing they were real, that they were coming from my mouth. They left without my permission.

I couldn't believe I was thinking of entering the Underworld, the Kingdom of the Dead. It was suicidal. But there was no other way to navigate this horrible labyrinth unless I had Zaire's blessing. I had to do what he said. But why? My mind cringed from the questions, begging like a dog to worship at the king's feet.

"We will celebrate your victory over wine in my great dining hall. The party will be so grand it may very well eclipse the ball on the last night of the Alignment." Zaire smiled.

He extended his other hand. Slowly, I lifted mine to shake it. Just like when I had made a deal with Nicklaus, a ripple of power spread across my body. The dizziness faded, but my mind felt foggy. What had I agreed to?

I watched him, studying the angles and planes on his face as if I could detect a hint of deception. But he seemed earnest, and if it were not for the scar, I would say he was an actual god. They could be benevolent in the old stories, couldn't they?

"As long as I am not going alone," I relented, my voice foreign to my ears. "And if you swear you will help me get what I need *and* leave without any harm."

But the words were hollow, and his grin deepened, making something cold knot in my middle.

"Excellent." He beckoned Cassian closer. "You can change into more suitable clothing and then you will lead a band of my finest men to fetch my stolen artifact. You are in the best of hands with my Captain at your side, and will receive the highest of rewards for your honesty."

Zaire finally let me go. I tried to smile. But all I could feel was a sickening cold sinking into my bones wherever he had touched.

Why hadn't I demanded answers? Why had I accepted his explanation about why he had me followed? But I couldn't open my mouth to ask. It was like something rooted me in place and stole my voice. A violation. I shuddered.

Cassian's deep brown eyes studied me as if he were trying to sort out a puzzle. Maybe he knew I hadn't been entirely truthful about what I'd come to the Bazaar for. Or perhaps he wondered why someone would be so stupid to agree to search the depths of the Underworld.

Cassian's eyes never left my face as the King of the Bazaar whispered instructions in a language I couldn't recognize in his ear. All I knew was that it sounded ancient.

I caught the last part, in my own language as Zaire gave Cassian a grave look. "Be careful, even I can't help you if you die down there."

TEN

A few hours after my meeting with Zaire, I stood next to Cassian at the yawning mouth of a pit blacker than ebony. The second night of the festival had drawn to a close. The third day dawned through the perpetual darkness, leaving the Bazaar abandoned and desolate. We saw no one on our trek to the strange barren land that held the pit, a gateway to the Underworld.

A groan escaped the crater. I choked on my whimper. Zaire had tricked or enchanted me. I would never promise something to a man like him if I was in my right mind. But that handshake—I had made another foolish agreement.

Eerie grey smoke belched from the crater's depths. An unnatural blue glowed faintly within, like when sunlight glints off of dark, fathomless water.

"Are we really going in there?" I whispered to Cassian.

"That's the plan." His shoulders were tense, but he threw me a nonchalant smile.

Behind us stood a trio of soldiers armed to the teeth in bronze armor, their helmets coming to a point in a twisting pattern. They looked as if they had wandered straight from the parchment of an ancient scroll.

I had changed into an outfit my aunt would have whipped my back for. The dryad, as I learned the women with green skin were called, had returned with her arms weighed down by finely crafted leather breeches. I was shocked when I realized I was actually expected to wear them.

But I had to admit, there was a strange sort of freedom in not being burdened down by corsets and petticoats and layers of tulle. The sable-colored breeches felt like butter against my skin, tucking into a set of black boots that reached up to my calf. A loose blouse and green crushed velvet coat were secured at my waist by a wide belt.

I fingered the golden embroidery on my long coat. Would Linus think I looked beautiful? Or would he react like my aunt or Veronica would, with a disappointed frown and hissing words?

"You'll need this," Cassian said, interrupting my thoughts.

He reached into his own coat and pulled out a dagger, the same one he'd been polishing in the orchard. He tugged me forward by the belt without a word. I couldn't breathe enough to protest. He tucked the blade into the belt. I tried to ignore the way his skin brushed mine—the smooth pads of his fingers tracing my waist as he cinched the small scabbard tight. My blouse was entirely too thin.

I darted my gaze from his bronzed hands. "If Zaire can't enter, what makes you think I can do what he asks?"

"No one is quite like Zaire, I'll admit that. But the Underworld is a place for mortals alone." His hands stilled on my waist. "If you wish to attract the attention of all kinds of demons and creatures of darkness, then certainly, we should have him come along, darling."

I huffed. "Are you being serious?"

It was impossible to tell. His face was always so impassive and marked by a subtle smile, as if he were constantly trying to smother his amusement.

"I promise we'll be fine. I will let no one harm you." Losing the infuriating smile, Cassian met my gaze with such intent, my cheeks heated. "You'll be the one who can find their way for once."

"Why won't you be able to?"

"I'm not quite mortal." He shrugged, flourishing his arm as if beckoning me to go first.

"You're immortal too?" I gaped at Cassian through the shadows scattered along his handsome face. Handsome? When had I come to think of him as *handsome*? I wiped the burning shame on my cheeks.

He made a non-committal sound in the back of his throat. "It's been so long I don't really know what I am anymore."

I held his gaze for a moment, as a twinge of sadness—even regret—flashed in his eyes. Cassian glanced away, seemingly unwilling to elaborate. He nodded towards the pit, breaking the odd spell.

A damp wind escaped the deep tunnel, pushing my hair back against my skull. It smelled of rotting flowers and dying wishes. I looked at Cassian for encouragement, a seed of doubt wriggling behind my breast. His lips, full and soft and an interesting dark pink, tilted up in a small smile. I faced the entrance to the underworld and stepped forward.

Darkness enveloped us in an instant, weighing me down. My boots sank a little into the soft dirt. My pulse quickened, and I wanted nothing more than to turn back. The only thing that kept me moving was the heat of Cassian behind me, and my desire to get this ridiculous mission over with. As soon as we were done, I could finally leave the Bazaar.

The darkness grew thicker and a frigid breeze cut across my skin like a knife. I sensed the tunnel drop away, leading into an immense underground cavern. I blinked in the low blue light, automatically searching for its source.

The soldiers behind us shuffled, their armor clinking uneasily. They filed behind us as if I were some general leading them into battle. The thought was so ludicrous I almost let out a snort.

The blue light lit the pitch-black obsidian walls of the cavern. Mighty stone formations erupted from the ground, piercing the air like broken teeth. Towers of pure darkness. Mist coiled around my ankles once more and I fought the urge to retch at the sight. Mist in the Bazaar was never a good omen.

"What is this place?" I asked, my voice a hoarse whisper.

"It's a trial for the dead," Cassian said, his voice low and almost shaky. "If they are whole and unblemished, they should be able to reach the Gates of the Dead and enter their afterlife."

"And what makes Zaire so sure I'm whole?"

"He's sure."

I pressed my lips together, holding my freezing fingers close as I studied the cavern. Snaking through the endless horizon of the massive cave was a hedge maze. It was at least ten feet tall, with thick leaves decorated by wickedly sharp thorns. It went on as far as I could see, sharp lines crossing the floor until deep mist obscured the rest.

My tongue felt dry and heavy in my mouth. What of the soldiers behind me? Would I be responsible if some terrible demon harmed them? Guilt and anxiety trickled down the back of my throat.

"We need to hurry, Captain," one soldier spoke, shifting his weight impatiently.

Cassian ignored him, placing one of his hands, warm and gentle, on my shoulder. "Are you ready?"

I looked into the opening of the sprawling hedge maze and the unearthly blue light. I tried to imagine Linus was beside me, encouraging me. If I could just get through this, then I would be one step closer to him. I shut my eyes and savored the image of Linus' blue eyes. But even as I tried to recreate them in my mind, they turned to pools of dark, earthy brown. My eyes flew open, and I stepped out of Cassian's reach.

"Zaire said I could find a path," I said, a little breathless. "And you're certain I'll be able to do it?"

"You're already in the Underworld." Cassian's voice was unwavering and strong. "I would say the fact we have made it even a few steps inside without being devoured by a ravenous guardian is proof enough. You're different here, Hazel. The Bazaar can trick and confuse you, but in the Underworld, you'll always find a way. I'm sure of it."

The seriousness of Cassian's expression never faltered; so confident in this odd mortal girl he didn't know. My heart sped a beat. Why did he believe in me? Why would *anyone* need me for something so important?

Cassian smiled cautiously, and for a moment, the chill in the air didn't hurt. I pressed my lips into a hard line and stepped into the maze.

It seemed ironic that there could be a maze within another maze. But the Bazaar and the Underworld felt entirely different, as if the Bazaar was a crossroads between world and planes, not really belonging to any.

I almost laughed at the thought. The Bazaar and I were quite alike in that respect.

I led the group of men through the maze, blinking away thick mist and darkness. Each man held the shoulder of the one in front. Cassian's hand was warm and heavy on my arm, sending a strange electricity skating along my skin whenever he adjusted his grip. I wrestled back a shiver.

The blue light was low but seemed to illuminate the very ground itself, guiding me through the towering tunnels of thorny branches. The only sounds were of rattling armor and footsteps.

We went on like that for a time, no one daring to speak and disturb the stifling silence that suffocated the hedge as if it were the hushed walls of a mausoleum. The impenetrable tangle of leaves shored up around us, reaching almost to the cavern's ceiling. My fingers brushed the leaves. They felt waxy and thick, and the edges were sharp enough to bite.

"How can you see anything?" Cassian hissed behind me, his free hand reaching out blindly. His fingers tightened around my shoulder, digging into my arm like a lifeline.

I glanced over, half expecting him to be joking. "What do you mean? It's dim, but you can still see a little way ahead."

Cassian laughed, but his voice was strained, uncomfortable. "I can hardly see my own hands. How do you know where you're going?"

I paused and looked behind me.

The other soldiers were grim and tense. I looked right at them but it seemed they couldn't tell. Each was staring in a different direction, unable to pinpoint where I was.

"I can see where to go. I don't quite know how to describe it. There's a blue light—you really don't see it?" I asked.

Cassian shook his head, turning his face in my general direction, but his eyes were six inches too far above my head. "As long as you know where to go, we'll follow you," he said, but his voice held a slight tremor.

He didn't even throw a sarcastic '*darling*' at me.

A light sheen of sweat dotted his forehead, and the skin around his eyes looked taut. I hesitated, troubled to see this usually confident and self-assured man look *afraid*. A jolt of pity surged through me. I knew exactly how he felt. The uncertainty, the isolation I had experienced my entire life—not just in the Bazaar. And that knowledge left me wishing I could vanquish the fear in him.

"Cassian." I hesitated, searching for something to say.

"Come on, darling," he smiled, and I scowled immediately even though he couldn't see it, "we need to get moving. It's not good to have the living stay in one place for too long."

Pressing my lips together, I fought the urge to abandon him. I couldn't afford to feel pity, not when he worked for Zaire and clearly held back secrets. He'd followed me, *terrorized* me, on the island and in the Bazaar. I had to harden my trusting heart.

I led the way, a little faster now that I realized the maze let me solve it. It was a strange sensation to know which path to take when it bisected, or to not hesitate at a crossroads. Was that how Cassian had felt when he worked his way through the constantly shifting streets of the Bazaar? No wonder he looked so uncomfortable. Just the thought of returning to my blind, helpless state was enough to send a ripple of freezing anxiety through my stomach.

"Wait," a soldier called, drawing the party to a halt. "Do you hear that?"

Silence.

Then a moaning sound.

The hairs on my arms stood on end. I pulled the velvet coat tighter around me like a shield. The sound repeated, closer this time and coming from a dark path to our left. The leaves in the maze rustled with an unseen wind. Or was it a hand brushing them?

"Careful," Cassian whispered, his breath tickling my ear. "Lotus-eaters. Don't let them touch you and don't look them in the eye."

He reached out his other hand and gripped my wrist. I wasn't sure if it was because he needed me to guide him or to keep me still.

"Lotus-what?" I breathed, the words hardly coming out.

Cassian's fingers gripped my wrist tighter, and he crushed me against his side just as the shuffling of dozens of feet grew louder.

"Don't move. Stay behind me no matter what," he whispered into my ear.

I stayed insufferably still, hardly allowing myself to breathe. Cassian's hand felt warm against my skin, and the smoothness of his palm was almost comforting, even in the Underworld.

The soldier behind me muttered a muffled curse.

I saw it then, the movement of dozens of bodies ambling through the maze. At first, I thought they were just people, wandering like us. Another band of searchers that Zaire had sent. But their heads listed to the side. They walked without seeming to be aware. Then I saw their feet.

Blood-caked and battered, like they had been walking for days on end.

I gasped and Cassian covered my mouth with his hand, his breath fanning out across my face. His palm tasted salty and a little like spiced ale. I breathed hard around his fingers. We stayed still as they parted around us mindlessly.

When one was only an arm's length away, I could finally see their features clearly. The lotus-eaters, as Cassian had called them, were more terrifying than Nimuae and Ragnor had been. Their skin was translucent and sallow. Dark veins crisscrossed their bodies like sickly sores. Their feet trailed blood behind them and their jaws hung slack.

The worst part was the silence, the sheer lack of sound. They didn't even breathe.

A soldier behind us cursed again. He flinched away from a woman with long, scraggly hair. Her head whipped towards him and her mouth opened, revealing grey, rotting teeth.

If it hadn't been for Cassian's hand, I would have screamed. Her eyes were milky white, totally without pupils or irises. Black veins webbed across them.

"No," the soldier murmured, stumbling back. He collided with another lotus-eater.

Suddenly all of them, dozens, swarmed him like a pack of rats. He let out a terrified scream as their hands gripped him, pulling and tugging and tearing.

I sobbed against Cassian's palm and bucked against him, trying to run. His grip turned painful against my face, the force of his hand cutting the inside of my cheek against my teeth. He dragged me back from the grisly scene, yanking us around a sharp corner.

"Hazel!" Cassian hissed, pulling his hands away. "We have to go! Which way?"

I shook my head, trying to cover my ears from the terrible sounds of agony and tearing flesh. The scuttling of hands and feet and clacking teeth was enough to send me doubling over, gagging violently.

"The girl is useless," one of the two remaining soldiers snarled. "We need to run!"

"Listen to me, Hazel." Cassian dropped to his knees, tugging my chin up. The warm brown pools of his eyes were so at odds with the cool blue and darkness around us. It was almost like he could see me. "You're the only one who can lead us through this maze. You can do this. You *have* to do this."

"And tell her if we don't leave now, the lotus-eaters will come for us next!" the same soldier who called me useless said.

I glared at him, even though his own scowl was fixed on the hedge instead of me. He reminded me of my aunt. The same proud, smug expression. The same doubt in his eyes when he appraised me.

Taking in a deep, shuddering breath, I pointed uselessly. "That way, to the right. I think we're getting close; the light is brighter."

Cassian nodded, barking my words to the two remaining soldiers, and they grudgingly fell into line. We ran, no longer content to walk through the winding maze. The screams of the fallen soldier echoed behind us, as did the scraping sound of the monsters dragging parts of him away into the darkness.

The whole time I ran, I imagined the bleached white hands of the lotus-eaters grabbing at my hair, tearing at my flesh, and ripping me apart. The memory of the agonized screams of that man spurred me on, long past the point where I lost my breath and my muscles burned.

Suddenly the light shifted from eerie blue to the cool grey of twilight. The soldiers blinked as if they could see too. We turned one last sharp corner of the maze and stumbled out into another vast cavern. Cassian's hand slid from my shoulder and brushed my waist.

"Janus," the second soldier said, his voice catching. "I can't believe he was foolish enough to let one of them touch him."

"You all knew the risks of coming to the Underworld. The lotus-eaters run free here, that is no secret," Cassian said, his breathing still fast. And yet, despite it, he sounded authoritative, sure of himself now that he could see. As if commanding soldiers were as natural as breathing.

"Where do we go now?" I asked, clutching the hilt of the knife in my belt. It seemed so pitiful against the monsters I had just seen tear a man apart.

"Towards the Gates of the Dead. That is where Zaire said the thief would be." Cassian turned towards the new cavern. It was dark, but not like the maze had been. Torches burned on the walls, glowing a strange green. "Take point," he instructed the quiet soldier. "We cannot be taken by surprise again."

The man nodded and pushed ahead, his helmet gleaming in the green light and his armor jangling as he ran into the depths of the cavern. The last soldier, the angry one, trailed behind Cassian and me, and glared holes in my back. Somehow, it didn't make me feel any safer.

"What were those things?" I asked. Another shiver crossed my skin, and I tried to rub it out. But the screams still lodged in my skull, replaying that awful scene over and over.

"Lotus-eaters," Cassian said, his voice grave. "They were once human, like many of us in the Bazaar. I'm sure you've noticed similar eyes in those you've met. Lotus-eaters are the result of selling more and more of your soul, piece by piece until there is nothing left."

"Nimuae mentioned something about lotus wine." I swallowed against the bitter memory of the wine I had drunk on my first night. "Is that how someone is convinced to sell their soul?"

Cassian shook his head, his forehead creased in thought. "No, not entirely. The wine is simply a potent drink meant to loosen the minds of those who enter the Bazaar. It is made from distilled lotus flowers, but is not nearly as strong as the real thing. Most sell pieces of their soul because they came to the Bazaar searching for treasure, for something specific to solve their earthly troubles."

"Someone tried to sell me knowledge, the kind that can end kingdoms," I recalled.

"I've never met anyone who could say no to Darius," Cassian said, sounding almost proud.

I whipped my head towards him. "You know Darius? He tried to cut me with one of those knives, but I got away."

"I know." He grinned. "Darius came to the palace complaining about some human who had burned him with hot oil after refusing to pay. I've never seen Zaire so intrigued, or Darius so irate."

I almost smiled at him. Almost.

"I still don't understand why Zaire sent you to find me." I sagged.

His smile slipped. "Zaire has taken a special interest in you. Sensed you long before you entered the Bazaar. You not selling a piece of your soul is... impressive. I've never seen a human in the Bazaar with their whole soul intact." Cassian turned his face away, towards the dancing green flames. "As you can see from the lotus-eaters, most come here searching for pleasure or glory. They find it almost instantly, and then they desire more and more, feeding off the intensity of that feeling. Until, well, until there is simply nothing more to part with and they become soulless, doomed to wander the Underworld without ever belonging amongst the dead."

I pondered the explanation. It reminded me of the way he had spoken earlier, like he could only dance around the subject. My suspicion that he had made a similar vow as me turned to conviction. I wanted to know why.

"Is everyone who comes to the Bazaar going to end up like that?" I asked, imagining all those people filling the streets, laughing, dancing, and looking so very alive. Were they doomed to the same fate?

"No." Cassian rubbed his jaw. "Some leave when they get what they came for. Others wander aimlessly until they either die or disappear. But everyone is here searching for something."

"And do they always find it?"

Cassian's eyes widened briefly, as if the question surprised him. He rubbed his face tiredly. A tattoo, the color of dark amber, lined the back of his hand. It was some sort of emblem with two crescent moons facing opposite one another. I'd never noticed it before, but it felt familiar.

"No, I would say we don't."

I watched him for a moment, wondering at the change of his words.

What could he be searching for? He was immortal, or at least close to it, like Zaire. But looking at Cassian and trying to compare him to the

King of the Bazaar felt wrong. Cassian was more earthly and tangible, whereas Zaire was starlight, danger, and wickedness.

He glanced at me, interrupting my perusal. I turned my face away to the dank tunnel ahead. *No.* I couldn't get distracted by Cassian. I had always been too empathetic to the troubles of others. Too trusting. Look where that had gotten me.

Not to mention that Zaire had been looking for me *before* the Alignment had officially begun. He had sent Cassian after me hours before Darius came to the palace complaining about his injuries. There was something Cassian wasn't telling me, something he held back. My skin tingled at the thought.

Why had Zaire sensed me? What did they want from me? And worst of all, I began to wonder if the trip to the Underworld had been planned before I ever accepted. My mouth went dry. I opened my lips to ask the thousands of questions streaming through my thoughts, to demand answers, but a shout stopped me.

"Master Cassian!" A voice, belonging to the soldier who had scouted ahead, reached us from further into the black cavern. "I think I've found its lair."

"Lair?" I breathed.

Cassian shook his head as if to say '*it's better you didn't know*'.

A rock settled in my gut.

"Then what are we waiting for?" Cassian pulled his curved saber from its scabbard and grinned. "Let's find the thief."

ELEVEN

I truly was in hell. The endless walking, not only in the depths of the Underworld but in the Bazaar itself, was like a punishment from the old gods. Every step forward ached like marching on broken glass. I would be happy to never walk again.

"Through there," said the angry soldier. Cassian called him Baltazar. "Finbarr said he saw the creature at the mouth of that cavern."

Baltazar pointed the tip of his sword towards a small cave that looked to be carved out by a set of wickedly sharp claws. I looked sideways at Cassian, who didn't seem fazed by the scattered bones or deep gouges in the walls.

We had emerged into a long, straight tunnel. The lair we sought was a mere gouge in the side. Further down, a soft light gleamed, like the promise of eternal rest. The temptation to run to it, to simply fall through the Gates of the Dead and leave my worries behind, was a pull that nearly staggered me.

But I had a job to do, and Linus and Nicklaus to think of.

"Do you have the chains?" Cassian asked Finbarr. The quiet soldier, who bore countless scars on his arms and face, nodded and set down a heavy-looking rucksack. He pulled out a set of chains, each link sliding and clattering against the cold ground, lining them at the mouth of the small cavern.

"What are we doing here?" I whispered to Cassian.

"Retrieving something dangerous that was stolen from Zaire. Marcel has been pilfering from the palace's vaults for weeks now. I thought I caught everything he took, but we got word he had holed up somewhere past the labyrinth in the Underworld with something my king cannot afford to lose."

"I thought you said I was the only one who could find their way through the maze that wasn't dead," I said.

Cassian rubbed his chin as Finbarr finished pulling out the chains and set them on the ground. He laid them in front of the cave's opening like a sort of barrier. Or a net.

"Marcel is clever. He found a way to get a recently deceased spirit to guide him through."

"How is that possible?" I shook my head.

"He killed a man who owed him a blood debt," Cassian answered, as if it made perfect sense. My stomach soured.

The chains glowed; links turned bright red, like the eyes of a hellhound. The smell of burning flesh filled the air, making my stomach turn even more. A loud hissing tore through the cavern and the chains melted, sinking into a liquid river. I flinched and slapped my hands over my ears. The cavern trembled and a web of golden lines appeared at the mouth of the cave.

"It's enchanted," Baltazar cursed. "Those chains once held the goddess Aikaterine! He knew we were coming."

"We can break the enchantment," Cassian said, his voice strong and commanding. "Hazel can do it."

"What?" I coughed.

Baltazar looked at Cassian as if he were mad, and I'm certain I did the same thing.

"No living human with an intact soul has ever been in the Underworld before," he said logically. "He did not create the enchantment with that in mind. She can enter the barrier without being harmed."

"That barrier melted those chains as if they were nothing," I sputtered, edging backward. "I can't break any sort of enchantment."

"As I said, useless," Baltazar grumbled.

I bristled at his glare and sharp tone. It was the same thing Lillianna had called me since I was pawned off to live with her after Mother died. It was what Jorgen had called me from the day I was born.

"I would never ask you to do something that would bring you harm," Cassian said, his gaze intense, making my belly flutter in a way that wasn't entirely unpleasant. Our eyes remained locked as I tried to think of an excuse, an idea.

My jaw locked.

Cassian breathed in deeply before turning to his men. "We will think of something else."

"No," I said through gritted teeth, surprising myself. "If it means I can leave this place, I'll try anything." The words bubbled up from deep within, born from years of resentment.

Cassian raised his brow, something like pride and interest crossing his face. I fixed a scowl firmly on Baltazar. The guard grunted and crossed his arms, lifting his chin in a silent challenge.

I stepped towards the barrier. The golden ropes of light hummed and shifted, like a spider web blowing in the breeze. The oozing metal of the once heavy chains puddled at my feet. I coughed against the stench.

"It won't hurt you. Nothing in the Underworld is designed for the living." Cassian nodded, trying to sound encouraging.

I met his gaze. His dark eyes were sure, unflinching, with a heady promise in them. I wanted to uncover the promise, the secrets in his gaze. I shook my head, turning my thoughts from him to the Underworld. Wrestling down the anxiety gnawing at my gut, I lifted a hand, fully expecting to lose the limb.

My fingers passed through the barrier with nothing more than a mere tickle. I dropped my shoulders, the knot in my chest loosening, and I walked through the veil.

Turning, I threw a triumphant smirk at Baltazar.

I didn't even get to gloat. Something in the air felt wrong. Every breath stung as if some invisible cord wrapped around my lungs. A low growl came from deep within the cavern. I choked around words that refused to form and stumbled to my knees. Each breath felt like inhaling ash. Doubling over, I clawed at my throat. I was going to die.

The grumbling sound echoed again from the cavern's depths.

Cassian bolted forward, hefting me into his arms and barked at Baltazar, "Take her back to the tunnel. Keep her safe at all costs."

"We need the treasure—not the girl," Baltazar complained

"Did you refuse an order?" Cassian's face grew fierce as he stared his soldier down. I groaned against the agony in my chest.

Baltazar turned white, and he grabbed my arm roughly, hauling me from Cassian's chest. I coughed and blood coated my lips. The golden barrier over the enchanted cave broke. Even as I wheezed and struggled, I realized something. Those golden ropes weren't only meant to keep us out. It was there to keep something *in*.

"Move," Baltazar ordered, dropping me to my feet and pulling my arm so hard, an angry red line of broken capillaries appeared on my wrist.

My lungs burned and seared as if a hot poker had been forced down my throat. I wanted to tell him to stop running, to let me go so I could breathe, but Baltazar was far too busy dragging me back to the entrance of the tunnel.

He dropped me unceremoniously, practically throwing me against the wall as I clutched at my throat, my vision turning black around the edges. I could see the smear of the dark cavern. Finbarr, the only other remaining soldier, screamed. Baltazar muttered something in a guttural language and drew his sword.

My eyes watered, obscuring my vision, but I saw a flash of gold and glossy black emerging from the cave. Another scream, louder and more painful this time. Finbarr slumped to the ground, writhing in agony. Standing over him was the dark, obscured figure of some sort of creature.

Baltazar lunged forward, running to his fallen comrade. Cassian crouched low with two swords clutched in his hands, his expression ferocious as he swung the blades like they were extensions of his arms.

I coughed and clawed at my throat, finally able to suck in air without feeling like I was being smothered. My vision cleared, and I blinked, rolling onto my knees. Then I saw Finbarr's face, lying a few yards away. It was burned beyond all recognition. Green poison leached into his skin and went straight to the bone. I bit into my palm to muffle a scream.

A snarl reverberated through the system of caves, rattling my bones. Baltazar roared, standing up straight and pulling a crossbow from his back.

Even before he loosed the arrow, I knew it wouldn't be of any use.

The beast was enormous, taller than a man with the body of a lion. The golden fur and mane rippled in the low light. Bright green eyes, the color of venom, glinted with vertical slits. Its tail, black and gleaming, curved over its back with a wickedly sharp barb. A scorpion. A lion.

"No!" I screamed as Baltazar fired the crossbow. The arrow ricocheted off of the creature's back like water from oil.

The monster snarled, its face twisting into predatory rage. The Manticore lunged at Baltazar. Its scorpion tail reared back as Cassian tackled Baltazar to the ground. Poisonous barbs flew faster than the eye could see, lodging with a thunderous crack into the cavern wall. The ceiling trembled above us, only shaking more when the beast let out a long, terrifying roar.

Cassian threw one of his swords to Baltazar, who caught it deftly. They rolled to their feet and crouched low, eyes narrowed and calculating. My heart sank to my toes. This was a fight the warriors could not win.

Everything I had ever heard about Manticores from sailors was fearsome. Their fur was impenetrable, their tails full of deadly poisonous barbs as long as a man's forearm. I touched my chest. The pain in my lungs. The poisonous cloud of air released from the cavern had suffocated me. What could it do if injected directly?

The Manticore swiped at Cassian with a massive paw, claws the size of daggers extended, ready to disembowel. But Cassian was surprisingly quick. He leaped out of the way, kicking off a cavern wall, and swiped back, his sword leaving a bright red mark on the creature's side.

"The arrows are useless," Cassian yelled to Baltazar, heaving for breath. "These are Zaire's scimitars, they're the only thing that can hurt a beast like this."

Baltazar nodded, his face a mask of determination. Those narrow spears of steel looked pitiful compared to the towering creature. How could metal stand against myth?

The Manticore shook out its mane, blood oozing from its side. But the wound was shallow and artificial, only angering it. It lunged again and both Cassian and Baltazar locked in a frenzied battle of dodging barbs, snapping jaws, and enormous claws.

My breath returned in a ragged gasp. The poison that had burned the lining of my lungs faded. I had to do something. I stooped low and scrambled on my knees over to Finbarr, lying in a heap only a few feet from the commotion.

I tentatively hooked my arms underneath Finbarr's armpits. He let out a low groan, and I almost dropped him. He was alive. I bit my cheeks to keep quiet as I linked my elbows under him again. Finbarr's face was a mess of bubbling skin and steaming poison. I tried to keep myself from whimpering and dragged him back another inch, digging my heels in to leverage my weight.

My feet slipped, and I slammed back against the rocky floor. I pushed my hair back and knelt, sweat clinging to my brow. Finbarr was dead weight, impossible to move more than a few inches at a time.

"Come on," I pleaded. "Help me!" I grabbed his wrist and pulled. My shoulders burned, but he slid a few more inches. The sound of steel clashing against impenetrable fur moved closer. I pulled harder; a desperate cry stuck in my throat. My muscles gave out, and I went down hard. My chin smacked against the ground, blood welling on the cut immediately.

Finbarr let out another pitiful grunt. I winced, brushing away a tear threatening to cascade down my face, and jerked at his arms again.

A horrible howl cut through the air. I looked up just as Cassian's blade sliced the Manticore's throat. Blood poured from its neck, matting down its mane. My stomach dropped, somewhere between fear and hope. But it didn't look injured enough to stop.

Cassian wiped at his lips, the back of his hand coming back red.

The Manticore dropped its head, shoulder blades rising as it stalked forward, teeth bared. Cassian cursed and fell back, pointing his sword at the monster's face. Blood drained from my fingers and toes. I saw what was about to happen.

"Look out!" I cried.

The monster pounced. Cassian was too slow. Its powerful arm connected with his stomach and flung him across the cavern. He collapsed into a heap. Everything stilled.

No.

The Manticore turned its eyes, burning with hatred and pain, on me. Claws scraped the cavern floor as it stalked forward. Muscles coiled under golden fur. I scuttled back, covering Finbarr's damaged body with my own as best I could. My fingers, ice-cold and shaking, closed around the hilt of the curved dagger Cassian had given me.

Cassian was down. Finbarr hovered on death's door. And Baltazar was nowhere to be seen. The Manticore hissed, green venom dripping from its fangs. I clutched my blade tighter and pointed the pathetic weapon, aiming for the creature's glowing eye.

The beast bared its long teeth, a growl reverberating in its chest. A chill, like icy fingers, wrapped around my shoulders and neck. It felt like the hand of Death preparing to usher me through his gates.

I wanted to close my eyes, to have the last thing I thought of be Linus or Adelaide or anything pleasant. But I couldn't bring myself to tear my eyes from the face of the thing that would kill me.

I wasn't brave, or strong, like Cassian believed. I was naïve and useless, just like always.

"I'm sorry." I whispered the prayer to Nicklaus and his wife. To my sister. And to Linus.

A blur of bronze armor flashed. The Manticore released a gurgling howl of anger and pain. A crunching sound replaced the roar.

I blinked as Baltazar's lip curled and he thrust his blade deeper between the creature's ribs. The beast shuddered and stumbled before it fell to its side and let out one last grunt before its jaw went slack and its eyes dimmed, cold and black.

Baltazar slid his blade free, wrenching it with a slick, wet sound. I swayed against the urge to vomit. Nausea bubbled, burning my throat.

Baltazar wiped the blood from the blade with part of his tunic and dropped his arms to his sides. "Why did you come back? You drew the Manticore further away from us," he hissed, baring his teeth.

"Where were you? Finbarr and I could have been killed!" I shouted.

"I saved you, mortal. You should thank me."

I cradled Finbarr's damaged face. "He is nearly dead, and you were going to let that thing attack us?"

"If it wasn't for you releasing the beast, Finbarr wouldn't be in this position!" Baltazar gripped his blade tightly. For a moment I thought he was going to run me through, but Cassian stepped between us, appearing from within the Manticore's cave.

"Enough." Cassian heaved for breath. He held his blade against the throat of a man I didn't recognize. "I told you to keep her safe, no matter what." Something akin to fury lit his eyes.

"She's alive, isn't she?" Baltazar threw his helmet on the ground and turned to his commander. "You should have known Marcel would have chosen the Manticore to guard what he stole, and we shouldn't have opened the barrier without a plan."

"There is no way to know the Underworld. Hazel helped us get this far."

Marcel, the infamous thief, struggled in Cassian's grip. But it was useless; Cassian was built like a stone, tall and dark and imposing. Marcel looked weedy, like he'd never grown into his lankiness. His face was pale, sweat staining the collar of his shirt.

"I swear I would have brought them back to Zaire if I knew what they were," Marcel protested. "I was just now going to return it to the palace vaults!"

"I've had enough of this." Baltazar drew out a short dagger, the kind used to cut out hearts and tongues. "I say we rid ourselves of this fool right now."

"No. Zaire wants him." Cassian pushed Marcel away, and Baltazar grabbed his shoulders. "Take him back to the palace while we search the cave."

Cassian's voice was tired but authoritative. Despite Baltazar's razor-sharp tongue, he conceded, as if the man draped in shadow could command him to do anything. The soldier's jaw was tight, his teeth grinding together like he wanted to say something but physically couldn't.

"What about Finbarr?" I asked, my vocal cords finally unfreezing. All three men turned their eyes towards me, Marcel with a sort of abject fascination.

"Is she alive?" he marveled, black eyes glinting like the scorpion tail of the Manticore.

"Quiet." Baltazar twisted Marcel's arms behind his back. "Finbarr is as good as dead; there's no use trying to save him now."

My jaw clenched and I skewered Baltazar with a disgusted look. "How can you be so callous?"

"The Underworld has claimed him, mortal. There is nothing your tears will do about that."

I looked at Cassian, pleading for him to do something. He pursed his lips and shook his head, looking at the heaped mess that used to be a soldier lying beside me.

Baltazar adjusted his grip on the prisoner, eyes hard and without feeling. "I will take Marcel straight to Zaire. The thief should be able to guide me if he wants his tongue to remain in his head," he said. "Be careful until you're back. Even Zaire couldn't save you down here."

"I know." Cassian's face darkened.

Baltazar turned and pushed Marcel roughly. He didn't even look when he passed by Finbarr and returned to the labyrinth.

TWELVE

Finbarr took another rattling gasp of air. I pressed my lips together, tears silently cutting down my cheeks as my shoulders shook. I gingerly patted his least-ruined hand, hoping he could sense some comfort through the pain.

Cassian faced the entrance to the cave.

"We can't just leave him like this," I pleaded, my voice cracking.

"There is nothing we can do."

I glared at his back, at his dust smeared robes that melted into the darkness. "You can't let this happen."

Cassian turned around, bronze skin ashen. "I don't enjoy his death, Hazel. But I am not a god. I am not Zaire. I cannot help him."

"You haven't tried." I set my jaw.

He looked at the ceiling and shook his head before turning back to the Manticore's lair. He entered without looking back at me. Anger replaced the sorrow coiling in my bones. I gently set Finbarr's head on the ground and chased after Cassian.

The lingering stench of death and decay clung to the small cavern, forcing its way down my nose and throat. I held my sleeve up to my nose to block out the eye-watering stink and pushed Cassian's shoulder with my free hand. He hardly moved.

"Stop ignoring me! We can go back to the Bazaar and take Finbarr to Zaire. I'm sure there is some way to heal him at the palace."

Cassian didn't look up as he rummaged through the collection of bones and strange items hoarded against the walls. "Even if we could get to the palace, an injury like that in the Underworld is fatal. He will die before we can get back to the entrance. If you checked his pulse right now, I am sure he would be dead, if not nearly dead."

"Why won't you even try to help him?" My voice cracked. I wanted him to show pity, to show any kind of emotion. Anything but that infuriating stoniness and loyalty to a mission that had killed two of his men.

Cassian straightened, looking down at me. Something seemed to flicker behind his eyes, a deep-seated emotion he was holding back. But it faded.

"Finbarr is injured beyond help. Now, if it were merely a scratch from a blade, he might make it. But a Manticore is a creature of the old gods. Even Zaire couldn't save him."

With a purse of his lips, he turned back to his work, rummaging through the plethora of looted items and bones notched with teeth marks. I glared at his coat and the black hair curling over the collar of his shirt.

My heart twisted, and a sound of fury lodged in my throat. I reached down and hurled a rock at his back as hard as I could. The small stone bounced off his shoulder and skittered away harmlessly.

"Why are you being so cruel?" I bit out the words, wishing I could kick the unfeeling, cocky man digging through a pile of femur bones. The same man who had seemed so steadfast to keep me from harm.

He twisted, closing the space between us in two long strides. I lifted my hand to slap his face, to scratch his eyes, but he caught my wrist. Cassian leaned forward, the warmth of his breath fanning across my freezing cheeks.

"You act like death is the worst thing that could happen. I envy Finbarr. He knew the risks coming here. He had the courage to die."

"Courage? You act like he chose this!"

Cassian's jaw flexed. "For some, there isn't a choice."

"What, like your king? If Zaire is so powerful, why didn't he risk his own life?" I spat. "Why does he need to send a human to do his dirty work?"

"Everyone is afraid of something, Hazel," Cassian said, the fire in his eyes dimming to something that looked like deep exhaustion. "Even him."

"Why did he really send you after me? Answer me that." I shot back, sure that this would be the time he caved.

Cassian opened his mouth to speak, but the words caught in his throat, causing him to choke. The tendons in his neck stood out, taut and white. He growled in frustration, flinging my wrist aside, and turned away. "Make yourself useful and look for a velvet bag, darling. Marcel has hidden it well."

"Stop calling me that!" I squawked indignantly.

He made a rude gesture over his shoulder and I turned, searching the darkness for Finbarr. I staggered, my skin on fire.

His eyes were open, glinting in the low light, glassy and still.

He was dead.

Using the tip of my dagger to push things aside, I searched for whatever it was Marcel had stolen. An object that was worth the lives of two soldiers. And I dreamed about plunging the knife into Cassian's back.

Something deep and painful twisted into my bones when I thought about Finbarr. He had died alone. Forgotten. Was that my fault?

The cavern was just as grisly a scene. Broken bones and piles of forgotten things. Torn clothes and dried blood. Everything here was cold and cruel. I was glad the old gods were gone. If Zaire was anything like them, humanity had made the right choice to forget them.

A moth-eaten rucksack caught my eye, breaking me out of my thoughts. It seemed more carefully placed than any of the other items in the Manticore's lair. A thick piece of twine secured it in place, something a monster with heavy paws could never have accomplished.

Warmth flooded my sore and exhausted limbs.

I tugged on the twine, and the mouth of the bag fell open. Deep green, like the surface of a calm and endless lake, gleamed from within.

A buzz started at the base of my skull, pulsing across my skin and through my fingertips. My reflection scattered across the facets of heavy-looking emeralds encased in gleaming curls of silver.

A temptation, more enticing than anything I had ever felt, rooted deep in my bones. The necklace begged me to understand its secrets, far more powerful than any of Darius' pathetic trinkets.

I pulled the necklace from the bag. The heavy ring of metal and fine jewels looked back at me. The moment the pads of my fingers brushed the smooth, ice-cold surface of the necklace, visions burst across the backs of my eyelids. I would have cried out, but my tongue stuck to the roof of my mouth as the images flashed across my mind, beautiful and so painful a shuddering gasp tore through my ribcage.

I saw Linus, bright blue eyes filled with adoration, looking down at me. He whispered how he loved me, how he would never abandon me like my father or leave like my mother. He held me tenderly, in a way he never had before. I wore a whirl of silk and lace, bright white and more beautiful than anything I had ever seen.

Veronica and Aunt Lillianna stood behind us, fingers dabbing at happy tears clinging to their lashes. The whole town had gathered to celebrate my union with Linus. Everyone was so happy for me, so excited that the island's greatest treasure was marrying someone worthy of her.

Jorgen stood beside me, congratulating me and admitting how wrong he had been to punish me for my mother's mistakes. Jorgen said I was worthy of my mother's name, of his and Linus' too. Hazel Black-thorn was no longer a curse on anyone's tongues.

My chest burned with longing as I clutched the necklace to my skin, desperate for the vision to be true. Blistering tears clung to my lashes and rolled down my cheeks. I whimpered.

It had to be true. I *needed* it to be true.

Because this necklace was showing me what it was to be loved.

"Hazel!" Cassian's booming voice barely scratched at my conscious-ness. "Don't put that on. Drop it."

But I didn't care. The emeralds bled into my eyes, begging for me to fasten them around my neck.

Cassian collided against my side, knocking me over. I gasped, the sound tearing my throat as the visions faded from my mind. *No.* I whipped my head to search for the necklace. It lay a few feet away, whispering and begging for me to wear it. I scrambled, clawing my fingers into the rough stone floor.

"Stop! Look at me!" Cassian demanded, using the same commanding voice he did on the soldiers. His hands shot out to grab my ankles. But all I felt was an incessant itch in my skin, like I was being burned from the inside out. I had to get to the necklace.

I would die without it.

I kicked hard. The bottom of my boot collided against his nose with a crunch. He grunted, cupping his face. I dove for the necklace, rolling over ragged bones and broken wood. But the pain that flared across my skin as they pierced my arm was nothing compared to the burn I felt without the necklace.

My hand closed around the metal, and the visions returned. I let out a cry as the beautiful, gold-tinged world displayed across my mind again. It had to be real.

The golden world tilted and swirled again.

"No!" I screamed.

My breath whooshed from my lungs as Cassian tackled again. His weight crushed me to the floor. He braced one arm against my shoulders, pinning me with his body, and wrestled for the necklace. I bit his arm, trying to kick at his hips with the heels of my boots. But he was stronger than I was and wrenched my hands away from his face.

"Look at me!" he yelled, his voice cutting through the spell, only a little. "Don't put that on. You need to let go of it."

"Get off!" I wailed, thrashing underneath him.

Cassian reached for the necklace in my fist, his hand clasping my wrist. I fought harder, desperate to keep seeing the world that I wanted so badly. He dug his elbow into my forearm, trying to get me to open my hand.

He was so intent on getting to the hand that held the necklace he didn't even realize he'd let go of the other. I fumbled for my belt, fingers sliding over the hilt of the dagger.

The necklace whispered encouragement. Whatever it took to keep it.

I yanked the blade out of its sheath and slashed blindly. Cassian hissed and rolled away, hands clutching his face. My trembling fingers closed over the silver again, so cold it burned my palms. I crouched and held both ends, desperate to feel the weight of it against my breastbone.

But Cassian wasn't done yet.

He lunged forward, one large hand capturing my wrists and the other grabbing painfully at my chin, tearing my eyes from the beautiful piece of jewelry. I sucked in a shallow breath when I saw his face.

Blood dripped from his nose, which looked purplish and swollen. On his cheek, where I had cut him, was a line of deep crimson, slicing through his bottom lip. Realization jarred me, and almost of its own accord, my hand opened and the necklace clattered to the ground.

"It's alright, Hazel," he breathed, speaking softly. "Just focus on me."

Tears, hot and shameful, spilled over my cheeks. I turned away to hide them. I'd never laid a hand on someone before. Not even to fight back at Jorgen when he would lash me with his belt. Never to hit Veronica as a child when she would pull at my hair or kick my ankles. I'd never even held a knife before.

My face reflected a thousand times in the emeralds at my feet. I didn't recognize the person looking back at me, greedy and wild. I pushed Cassian away and crawled until my back hit the cave wall. I pressed my fist to my mouth to smother my sobs.

Cassian pulled himself to his feet, his hands held out like he was afraid I'd launch another attack. I pressed my forehead hard into my knees, wiping at my eyes and nose with the backs of my hands.

He stayed silent when he picked up a dark blue velvet bag from the ground, not too far from the burlap rucksack. He placed the necklace in the bag, careful not to let the silver touch his skin.

With the necklace gone, the whispers faded, along with the visions it had given me. There was a hole punched in my chest, the edges raw and ragged.

Carefully, Cassian eased himself to the floor next to me.

I sniffled and turned my head away. He was silent for a few moments as I tried to control my tears. But it was impossible. With each passing moment, the images of Linus and my family turned black and crumbled to ash, acrid and sour.

"Hazel," Cassian said softly, lifting one hand and gently brushing a lock of hair from my face, letting his gentle touch settle on my back. "I don't know what you saw, but it wasn't real."

I laughed once, lifting my head enough to look at him. "Oh, I know that perfectly well."

His face was passive except for the slight furrow of his brow, and his eyes—they were the worst. Pain and pity reflected on me. I wiped angrily at my cheeks, dropping my gaze.

There was blood on my fingers. My arms. On Cassian. My coat was relatively clean, so I tore at the fabric and busied my hands and thoughts with swiping at the blood from my scratches and bites.

Finally, I looked at the cut on his cheek and the blood staining his mouth from his broken nose. I reached out, gently dabbing at the cut on his lower lip. He breathed in sharply, capturing my arm with one hand.

"Hurts?" I asked.

A small sound slipped between his lips, but he shook his head. I knelt between his legs, carefully wiping at the blood. Each wince that crossed his face hit me like a blow.

"Hazel." He reached up again, snagging my wrist, his eyes searching my face. He watched me like I was breaking glass seconds from shattering.

"I'm sorry about your face," I said, my voice scratchy and dry.

Cassian shrugged, and one of his warm hands splayed across my back. I didn't flinch. I looked down at the rag in my hand. Blood stained the once dark green fabric. I shrugged out of the coat, despite the cold. I couldn't stand the color any longer and threw it across the cave.

"I'm fine. I heal quickly," he said, his fingers pressing a little firmer into my back. "Are you alright? I didn't mean to frighten you."

"No." I bit my lip hard. "I just wanted it to be real," I whispered.

I was afraid he was going to ask me what I saw. His face was grim, almost like he understood. His hand moved rhythmically, stroking my back as I fought off another wave of tears.

"The necklace," he said, his voice like warm honey, "is powerfully enchanted so that the wearer is impossible not to love or admire. But it is also a curse. Whoever wears it becomes obsessed with the devotion the necklace promises them. They're filled with a desire and hunger that can never be satiated. No matter what you saw, reality is always preferable to dreams. If the necklace showed you something, *someone,* then they don't belong in your life. It plays on your desires, the things you long for most that can never be."

"Why would Zaire have something like that?" I wiped roughly at my cheek and tried to control my shuddering breath.

"He's a collector, just like the Bazaar. Anything of power or magic is something he wants so others can't have it." His jaw tightened, but all traces of ire vanished as he asked, "Can you walk?"

I nodded and let him pull me to my feet. His hands were gentle and careful. I didn't mind the way they felt as he kept one against my back, guiding me from the cave. No one, not even Linus, had touched me like that.

My cheeks burned with humiliation at the thought.

"I found the necklace here. I'm not sure what else was inside the bag." I pointed to the pile of broken boxes and the burlap sack.

Cassian crouched and rummaged through the bag. He cursed, pulling away as if bitten. A vial of crystal-clear water laid in his palm, and next to it a sprig of deep, bursting burgundy fruit. He took the strip of fabric and wrapped the berries gingerly.

"What is that?" I asked. My voice was hollow, lifeless.

Cassian looked over his shoulder, eyes flickering like we were being watched. His lips pursed, his face a thousand angles and emotions I couldn't read. "Nothing, just another thing Marcel stole from Zaire. We should get moving."

THIRTEEN

I led us into a dead end. Twice.

Even though I could still see the faint blue light guiding us where I wanted to go, we never made progress. Images from the necklace flashed across my mind. I was cold, tired, and worst of all—I felt hollow.

After a while, sweat clung to my skin despite the frigid air. My legs burned; my lungs couldn't get enough air. I was all but running. Cassian trailed close behind, squinting and breathing hard.

"What's going on?" I stopped suddenly, a sensation like a thousand spiders buzzed along my arms. "We aren't making any progress."

"What do you mean? Can't you see the path anymore?" Cassian strained to see in the dark.

I pointed to a patch along the cavern wall that was darker than the rest. An opening to a tunnel. "That's where the Manticore was. We've been going in circles. The path keeps leading us back here."

"That's impossible." Cassian's jaw tightened. "We've been walking for hours."

"You don't believe me? It's right there—can't you smell the poison?" My voice grew shrill, almost hysterical.

Cassian raised his hands defensively. "Maybe we're not meant to leave yet. We should wait, see what the Fates might want."

I growled and kicked at the ground. A rock skittered, echoing off the walls of black stone. Cassian stood silently, which almost made it worse as he witnessed me frustrated and cold and broken.

"I guess there's never a choice is there?" I said bitterly.

Cassian hesitated before he spoke, "Something feels off. I know you don't like the idea, but the reason why we keep returning is important. I need you to trust me, Hazel. But first, we should rest, you're exhausted."

Trust him? How could I?

There was no use in fighting anymore. The Bazaar, the Underworld, and Zaire—they would all get what they wanted from me. I clenched my teeth hard even as my shoulders sagged.

Cassian sat and rummaged through his pack. He produced a bed roll and a strange looking flint and steel. I sat down across from him, my back against the stone wall. He unfurled the bedroll and then struck the flint.

A bright golden spark illuminated his face in a flash before a flame began to glow. The fire grew into a comforting blaze, warm and bright. But it did not need to consume wood to burn. The fire floated above the ground a few inches, burning without tinder.

The golden light complemented his dark bronze skin and made his hair gleam like liquid onyx. His eyes looked into the flames, troubled and brooding. My fingers trailed the circle of my engagement ring, but my thoughts were nowhere near Linus.

Cassian glanced up and our eyes met across the flames. My mouth went dry. He motioned for me to sit on the bedroll next to him. I did, but only because my tailbone hurt from the cold ground. I leaned my chin on one hand, watching the fire burn silently.

"You shouldn't be so hard on yourself for what happened with the necklace, Hazel," Cassian said.

I looked away from the fire, my eyes swimming with spots and memories. "Why not? I almost tore your eye out."

Cassian smirked, and a line appeared on his cheek. I wanted to trace the line with my finger, but clamped my hands together.

What is wrong with you? I scolded myself. *He let Finbarr die. He works for Zaire. He protects you because his king told him to.*

"*Almost* is better than *did*. Besides, I'm fine. I heal quickly, see?" He pointed to the cut on his cheek from my knife. It was no longer red and bleeding, but soft pink like a fresh scar. His nose was a little crooked still, but it looked like it might slip back into place at any moment.

I pressed my lips together to keep them from trembling. "I'm sorry. If I had known what I was doing..."

"I know," Cassian said. And it did seem like he knew, like he believed me. "But you broke from the enchantment. That says you are stronger than you know."

The muscles in my back tensed. "I don't want to talk about this anymore."

Cassian leaned back and stretched his legs out. He looked almost normal lounging by the fire, his dark hair curling over the collar of his shirt. Not like a person who had lived for many centuries and worked for a man who took the place of gods. I didn't understand how he could be so relaxed in the Underworld while lotus-eaters and other monsters could appear.

"Do you miss your home?" Cassian asked, steadfastly keeping his eyes on the fire.

The question took me by surprise, tugging my thoughts from the necklace and the Underworld. I studied his profile for a few seconds before he finally turned and looked at me.

"Of course, but what makes you think I'd want to talk about it?" I skewered him with a glare. "You haven't explained what Zaire wants, or why he sent you after me. Not really."

"And you haven't told me what you're here for." Cassian grinned like a cat.

"Enough games," I said forcefully. "I need to know what Zaire wants and why he sensed me. If you want me to trust you, you'll tell me."

His smile faded, but he nodded and faced the flames again. His eyes reflected the golden light, and I thought I saw images dancing there, memories of his past.

"I can't say much. I am sure you understand about oath enchantments." He paused meaningfully and my teeth clicked together.

He continued, "But I can say this. You're of great value to Zaire. He thinks..." Cassian's tendons strained, and he seemed to choose his words carefully. "He believes you are the key to keeping his power in the Bazaar from falling into the hands of the gods."

Silence. The only sound was the *drip, drip, drip* of water through the system of caverns.

I laughed, a full body giggle that shook my shoulders and made tears leak out of my eyes. Cassian gave me a bewildered look, which somehow made my laughing fit even worse. I doubled over and gasped for breath; certain I was going insane.

"How can *I* be the key to Zaire's powers?" I asked between gulps of air. "He is the one who overthrew the gods."

The idea of me, a mortal and a bastard, no less, being the key to an immortal king's power, was absurd. I was a half-decent seamstress with no fighting skills or magical powers. Useless.

Cassian looked like he wasn't sure if he should laugh too. "There is much I'm not able to say. Zaire overthrew the gods when we first came to the Bazaar. They were already weak since humans stopped worshiping and began to hate them centuries earlier. It was easy enough for Zaire to imprison them and take their land for himself."

I stretched out my legs, mirroring Cassian. "Why would Zaire need my help? The gods are gone. What else does he want?"

Cassian hesitated. I could tell he was afraid of sharing too much. Was it loyalty to Zaire? Was it an oath enchantment similar to mine? I wanted to trust him so badly. Friends for me had always been few and far between. Only Adelaide on the island and Saskia in the Bazaar.

And even their loyalty was fragile.

I felt tired. Bone deep and painful from a lifetime of carrying my burdens completely by myself. "Please. If you can tell me, if you can help me understand. I just want to know," I begged.

Cassian's eyes softened, and he scratched the stubble on his jaw. "The gods stir now and again. Zaire will always be at risk of losing his kingdom. That's why someone like you who has..." His neck bulged again like he was being choked, "—certain qualities you have are attractive to him. You can see clearly where others cannot. Maybe see *weaknesses* in the gods that he can't."

He said 'weaknesses' like he wanted to use another word. I tried to decipher the meaning, but it was too abstract. The gods were far away, long before my time. Then another thought crossed my mind.

"You said he overthrew the gods when *we* came to the Bazaar. Have you been with Zaire this whole time?"

He made a pained sound in the back of his throat, the corners of his eyes pinching. I was afraid I'd pushed too far or reached for answers he couldn't give. But his shoulders slumped, and he pressed his thumb to his lips.

Speaking faintly, he said, "Yes, even before the Bazaar. I've known him for a long time."

I couldn't imagine that Cassian was over a thousand years old. To me, he looked to be somewhere around his twenty-first year. Only two older than me.

"Why do you stay here? Don't you miss your home?" I asked.

A look so full of pain I thought it might cripple me, twisted Cassian's mouth in a rueful smile. "I miss it more than anything. But my old kingdom is gone, lost to sands and time. Everyone I knew was dead long before I figured out what I was doing. What I had become."

"You're here because you have to be?" I asked.

"In a sense. I can't leave the Bazaar unless Zaire allows it. We agreed long ago to never leave each other." Cassian grimaced into the flames.

"Why would you agree to that? You sound as if you wanted to go home."

"I made mistakes when I was mortal and let him down. To atone for what I did, I promised Zaire anything. It took a few centuries to learn what *anything* entailed."

"Forever," I whispered, and he nodded. "But what could you have done that was so terrible? I can't imagine you doing anything worse than a flippant remark."

Cassian chuckled and tossed a small pebble at the floating fire. "I was a prince. I had a duty to keep my people safe, and I failed. I was selfish. People suffered. My family suffered."

I held my breath until my chest ached. Cassian stared at the fire; his face contorted with misery.

I licked my lips. "Does helping Zaire keep control of the Bazaar make any of that better?"

Cassian's eyes fluttered, like he had forgotten I was there. "I don't think I will ever know the answer to that question." He cleared his throat and ran a hand down his face. "Enough about my past. That's all dead and buried."

"Oh."

Another awkward silence stretched between us, as deep and as wide as the North Sea. He had finally told me more, gave me hints of what Zaire really wanted. But then Cassian had slammed a door between us. I wrapped my arms around my legs.

"I miss it, you know." He whispered, his breath brushing my cheek. "Clean air and sand. Sunsets and rises."

Was this his own form of apology?

"I guess you don't get many of those in the Bazaar."

He snorted. "Nothing changes here, darling," he drawled, looking delighted as I scowled at the endearment. "The moon and stars never dim. The same battles are fought every day. Mortals come and go, but I stay the same."

Something in my chest, that hard part of my heart that never really softened, melted a little. I traced the profile of his face with my eyes. His strong jaw, sharp and covered with dark stubble. His coal black hair curling over his forehead and ears. His high cheekbones and fine nose. He looked like a prince. A fallen one.

"You regret choosing to stay immortal with Zaire, don't you?" I whispered.

Cassian turned to look at me so half his face was bathed in shadow. I imagined it reflected the war within himself. Part of him loyal to Zaire, part of him tired and hungry for something different.

The air between us stilled and I noticed how close we sat. How his arm brushed mine when he moved or the way his body blocked the cold of the caverns.

"Sometimes I do. I'm not quite immortal, not quite human. I heal quickly. I can theoretically live forever. But Zaire controls my destiny. He can decide if I keep my immortality or if I regain the ability to die." Cassian's voice was soft and a little husky as he traced the tattoo on the back of his hand. It sent a shiver down my spine.

"Doesn't that drive you mad?" A bubble of heat rose in my chest. "Why don't you force Zaire to let you have your mortality again?"

Cassian hesitated, and then a soft smile spread across his full lips. A rush of warmth, not from my frustration, flooded my limbs. "Zaire likes control. Though we are tied together, he is desperate for loyalty. He keeps my fate to himself. He knows what I want, so he makes sure I'll never have it."

His words reminded me of Niklaus' warning from what felt so long ago. Zaire was just like the Bazaar, keeping control through confusion and brutality. Cassian and his soft, sad smile stirred a different story in my mind, a kinship, someone who had experienced the same oppression I had. Maybe I could trust him. Just maybe.

"And what do you want?" I asked.

His smile faded as he watched me, his eyes troubled and unsure. "I want…"

His gaze dropped to my lips, and he breathed in sharply. My mind went blank as he lifted one hand, the one with the tattoo, and traced the outline of my jaw. Slowly, as if afraid I might try breaking his nose again, he leaned closer. So close I could feel heat pouring off his skin.

My fingers tightened in my lap.

Suddenly, his hand fell away. A strange surge of disappointment settled in my stomach. I had done something wrong; I was sure of it. I opened my eyes, my lips, to apologize, but Cassian drew one of Zaire's scimitars, leapt to his feet, and crouched in a defensive stance in front of me.

I followed the line of his sight and saw exactly what had set him off.

An entrance to another cavern appeared from the mist, carved into the black rock. Columns and facades of incredible craftsmanship glimmered like polished obsidian. Flanking either side of the arch were two giant bull statues.

No, not bulls exactly. Powerful eagle wings sprouted from their enormous backs. Giant hoofs capped each leg. Long wiry beards framed their frowning mouths. Worst of all, the creatures glared down at us with cruel human faces.

And then the statues began to move.

FOURTEEN

"A mortal," a booming voice spoke, jarring the cavern. "We have not had a living human wander to the gates in eons."

Stone scraped together. Dust rained over our heads. I scrambled backward, scuttling until my back hit a wall that hadn't been there a moment ago. We were trapped.

The pair of statues pulled themselves from their pedestals, towering at least two stories above us. Their bull tails flicked as they lowered their human heads to inspect Cassian and I closer.

"What do you want?" Cassian stepped further between me and the statues, sword point raised. It looked pitiful against the towering giants of stone. I reached out and grabbed his hand, shocked at how instinctual the desire was. He squeezed my fingers once.

"We would ask the same of you," the left statue spoke, a grating sound tumbling from his lips. I realized it was laughter.

The right statue leaned down further, its head clearing Cassian easily. Stone ground and popped with its movements. I froze, my neck cramping as I looked up at the beast hewn from dark obsidian.

"This is the girl that the master seeks," the statue said, stone eyes blank and cold as he swiveled his head to Cassian. "The man is a servant of Zaire. Lord Arae will not appreciate his presence."

The left statue made a sound of agreement. "I suppose Lord Arae will not kill him. Perhaps if he puts that irksome scimitar down, we will have a civil conversation."

Cassian grit his teeth. "You serve Arae?"

The left statue released a rumbling sigh and returned to his pedestal. "Yes, child. He longs to speak with the girl. He will not kill you if you do not provoke him further."

Cassian paled, his hand crushing mine. "She will go nowhere without me."

The other statue joined its twin and settled back against the stone. It watched me with blank grey eyes, ignoring Cassian's spitting words. "Our lord comes now from the gates he guards so well. He is curious about you, human. Do nothing foolish."

And with that warning, the statues froze again. I stayed perfectly still; my eyes glued to the figures carved into the wall.

"What were they?" I sputtered.

Cassian cursed and lowered his scimitar. "Lamassu. They are servants of Arae, the God of the Dead."

"God of the dead?" I gaped. "He wants to speak to me?"

A cold breath of air curled around my shoulders and licked up my spine. The empty archway between the two guardian lamassu grew darker. Shadow accumulated around it, so black it was an endless void.

"Indeed, Hazel. I ask a favor of you." A silky voice emerged from the arch, along with a man. Darkness and shadow cloaked him like a robe, moving and spinning with the breeze in the air. His skin was dark blue, like midnight. Long black hair tumbled down a set of broad but lithe shoulders.

It reminded me a little of the shadows that clung to Cassian.

"Arae," Cassian said through gritted teeth. "What business do you have with her? She is on a mission from Zaire."

The God of the Dead smiled. His lips were full and tinged an even deeper blue than the rest of his skin. His eyes sparkled like black diamonds. And then he looked right at me. My blood stopped flowing, my heart slowed to nothing, and my skin prickled with cold.

"I am well acquainted with Zaire. But it is his prize I am concerned with. Come, walk with me for a moment, child." Arae lifted an arm in invitation.

Cassian rumbled, "Do not touch her." He raised his scimitar point towards the god. The lamassu growled, their faces animating once more in the stone.

Arae raised a sleek, dark brow. "No harm will come to Zaire's prize. You have my word, prince."

Cassian blanched at the title. "Hazel, you don't have to go with him. He's a god. He has a score to settle with Zaire." His gaze was urgent as he stared at me, imploring. Anxiety etched lines into his forehead. But did he worry about me, or something I represented?

An overwhelming urge to look at the god washed through me. I swiveled my head, scrutinizing his face, otherworldly and soft. His expression remained passive and his brow smooth, but there was a tug low in my belly. Something shifted in my mind, something I didn't understand. Like a moth to flame, I *needed* to speak to him. I felt it.

"I mean only to talk with you, Hazel. There are things I wish you to know that will help you on your way." Arae folded his hands, his dark robes of smoke and shadow swirling hypnotically.

"It's all right. I want to talk to him." I slowly pushed Cassian's sword so the point rested in the dark dirt at our feet. He looked at me like I was mad. Perhaps I was.

"Be careful not to move, prince." Arae turned towards the tunnel he had come from, flanked by the lamassu, a smile tinging his words. "Or my guardians will be forced to crush you underfoot."

Cassian scowled at the god's back. Slowly, I uncurled my fingers from his, immediately feeling the emptiness his touch had filled. He set his jaw, ready to protest, but the lamassu growled on their massive pedestals.

"I want to go," I whispered. He looked indignant for a moment, eyes flickering to my lips, as if remembering we had been interrupted. My stomach twisted.

I had to get away for a moment, to feed that strange urge to commune with a god, and to hide. I didn't doubt for a moment that if the lamassu had not appeared, I would have kissed him. Betrayed Linus. Loathing curdled my blood.

I gave Cassian an apologetic look before I drifted after Arae.

Zaire's Captain stood before the two hulking lamassu statues, his face plastered with fear, almost like he was silently begging me back to the safety of his side.

Arae walked quickly. The tunnel pitched down sharply, descending towards the Underworld. My balance shifted, swayed like I was on a ship. I braced my hand against one wall, catching my breath. Veins of gold ribboned through the black walls. I followed the shadows leaking from Arae's clothes.

The floor was of polished diamond and precious gems. Shadows clung to Arae, but light seeped from the gems, reflecting dozens of colored spots across the tunnel. The god flourished his arm. A throne emerged from the ground, cobbling itself together from gold bars and nuggets of other precious metal. The God of the Dead sat and scrutinized me, his blue skin a rich indigo in the low light.

"You're a god," I said after a long pause, wincing immediately at how stupid I sounded.

Arae smiled indulgently. "I am. The last remaining free god. Zaire did not dare march on my domain, not when he is as vulnerable as any mortal in the Underworld."

"Cassian can die down here?" I asked. Part of me worried he'd antagonize the lamassu, simply to free himself of his burden of immortality.

Arae made a thoughtful sound, perhaps wondering why I immediately thought of Cassian. "The Prince of Shadows could die in my domain, yes. But he holds a kernel of my power, stolen long ago by Zaire. It would take much to fell the Captain of Zaire's Guard. But it could be done in my lands."

"The shadows on him are yours?" I asked.

"Indeed." The god's face darkened. "Zaire, while unwilling to enter my kingdom, showed his power in other ways. He took part of my powers over darkness and light and granted them to his Captain. Forced, rather. Another reason he would be so hard to kill."

"I don't understand." I shook my head.

Arae waved his hand sharply. "That child is wreathed in darkness, girl. More than you could imagine. He cannot free himself so easily."

I sensed he was done rehashing the past.

"What do you want from me? You mentioned a favor." My throat was bone dry.

"On the contrary," Arae reclined further into his regal throne, "there is something I owe you."

I expected to feel fear, cold and feral. But, looking at the kind face of the God of the Dead, I felt nothing but a sense of serene calm. He seemed so at odds with the nature of his calling. But death was inviting and fair, alluring in the face of a cruel world filled with torment and injustice.

"What could you owe me?" I wrinkled my nose. "If anything, I trespassed where I didn't belong."

Arae made a thoughtful sound low in his throat. "You do belong here, Hazel."

"I'm not dead." Blood drained from my face. Images of Finbarr's glassy eyes and the other soldier the lotus-eaters had ripped apart screamed through my mind. No. I did not belong here.

"Decidedly not. But there is something strange about you. I see why Zaire is so desperate to have you. Given your blood, you should not be able to enter my home. And yet here you stand, alive and well."

"My blood?" I scratched at the base of my head. More riddles, always riddles. But this one left my skin itching.

"Indeed. You are a walking contradiction. Zaire could use your abilities quite well. My siblings, the other gods, are hungry for their old lives. I hear them sometimes, whispering and plotting in their prisons. Zaire fears them and what they will do when they are free."

"The other gods are going to free themselves?" I shuddered.

Though Arae looked pleasant enough, I sensed power simmering below the surface. He could snap his fingers and I would wilt like a dying plant. He could command armies of the undead. What would the other gods be like after centuries trapped by a usurper?

"They are trying to find a way. I'm sure eventually they will succeed. Zaire will use you as a failsafe."

"How? Do you know what he wants from me?" I stepped forward, hoping I might finally learn an actual truth in this strange world.

Arae shifted and his smoky robes billowed. Images of funeral pyres, gravestones, and weeping filled my mind. "Not entirely. You are still a puzzle to me. But I will tell you this, something I believe I owe you for ridding my kingdom of that beast, the Manticore. But perhaps I also wish to see you succeed over Zaire."

I held my breath as the God of the Dead leaned forward. His blue skin and black eyes reminded me of the sky at dawn and dusk, liminal and stuck between worlds. "Do not trust the king. Fulfill no more of his demands. He wants something from you, this is true. But I foresee that there are others beyond him that also desire your abilities."

Fear bloomed behind my breastbone. "What abilities? What others?"

Arae regarded me, black eyes eternal and knowing. "Your resistance to the Bazaar is not because of your intentions towards good. It goes deeper than that. Your ancestry is responsible, and exactly what Zaire needs to cement his power over my fallen brethren."

"My ancestry?" I squeaked. *My blood.*

Arae raised a brow. "I see you are unaware of your father's identity. It is not my place to reveal it. I value my kingdom and my freedom here."

"My father? He was a sailor," I said numbly. I couldn't feel my pulse in my throat anymore.

"Perhaps. Perhaps not." Arae shrugged. "But listen to this advice, child. Zaire wants possession of you more than anything. If he gets you on his side, and *by* his side, everything you love will crumble and wither. The usurper has plans for you that are beyond even my knowledge."

I stepped forward, hands reaching to clasp the edge of his throne. "Why does he want me? What is going to happen?"

Arae stood in a flash of billowing shadow. He leaned close to me; his breath sickly sweet, like a field of dying flowers. "My tongue is tied, so I cannot say. The Fates forbid it. But I offer you this advice: beware, girl. Zaire and the gods have plans for you yet."

Night Three

FIFTEEN

My thoughts swam with indigo skin and secret plans. Cassian walked silently behind me until we finally left the hedge maze and emerged from the pit leading to the land of death. The blanket of stars and endless night was welcome after the confines of the Underworld.

Cassian took me to the tavern, guiding me as easily through the streets of the Bazaar as I had the tunnels below our feet. He did not ask questions about Arae. I was glad, because I wasn't sure who to trust, or what to think, after the god's confession.

After Arae had finished his message, he'd disappeared beyond the Gates of the Dead. The lamassu dismissed us, vanishing as if they'd never been there. Cassian and I had found our way out of the Underworld easily. We encountered no more lotus-eaters or monsters. Only the bloodied breastplate of the fallen soldier remained in the labyrinth.

We stopped at the main door of the tavern and I leaned heavily against the wall, rubbing my eyes. The pleasant scents of spice and incense filled my nose, replacing the odor of death and decay.

"Zaire will demand to see you once he knows we've returned," Cassian said softly, almost apologetically. "You should rest for a while until I return with word from him."

He held my gaze as if asking a silent question. Memories thrummed through my body. His eyes in the golden firelight. His expression when he told me of his past. The fierce protectiveness when the lamassu appeared.

I looked away, mumbling something about being tired. He nodded slowly and turned, leaving for the palace with the emerald necklace securely in his pocket.

I would be glad to never see it again.

I shuffled to my room and collapsed on the bed. The sounds of laughing voices carried to my ears. I rolled onto my back on my cot and clutched my necklace. Zaire had to keep his word about helping me. Arae was wrong. The King of the Bazaar would lead me to his vaults, and soon I could return to Linus.

The thought of him brought a jolt of pain to the hole in my chest. I closed my arms across my ribs, trying to hold myself together. Cassian said the necklace showed the wearer a vision of what they desired most, but that couldn't come true.

Linus needed money. We could be together if I only finished this task and returned to Nicklaus. The necklace was a cursed object. It simply played on my greatest fears. Linus loved me.

But even as I let my eyes close, knowing full well I'd not fall asleep, a part of my soul felt like it withered and died.

After a few hours of restlessness, I wandered the stairs to the main floor. I couldn't seem to shake the visions from the necklace. In snatches they stole across my mind, confusing memory with fantasy. I could not tell which were real and which the necklace had planted. I shut my eyes against the sight of Linus pulling me to his chest, swearing his undying love.

A haunting thought sunk my heart lower. Linus hadn't fought for me at my aunt's ball, yet Cassian had been ready to spar against the lamassu, even though he could have died. If the positions were reversed, what would the outcome have been?

I slumped in a chair near the fireplace. It was always warm in the

Bazaar, but since the Underworld, a constant chill rooted deep beneath my skin, winding and fusing with my essence. I enjoyed the blistering heat on my back and slipped down in the rough wooden chair, my fingers tracing the lines of Linus' ring.

A blur of dark fabric roused me from my misery. Cassian stood above me, two plates of food weighing down his hands. He wore only his loose black shirt tucked into dark breeches; the collar hanging open a little to expose his throat and hints of his chest. I looked back at the table, fingers clamping hard on my ring.

"Saskia sent me to bring you food," he said and slid into the chair next to me.

I tried to ignore the way his knees brushed mine. He was too tall for the humble tavern furniture and looked too grand and fine to be seen in such a place. And yet there he was, dressed simply with his hair dangling in front of his long, thick lashes.

"When are you taking me to see Zaire? I'd like to leave this place as soon as possible," I said, my voice hollow. Cassian pushed the plate towards me, his knuckles brushing mine almost subconsciously.

He cleared his throat and shifted. "I know the effects of the necklace must still be bothering you. Eating will help, but I brought you something as well."

Cassian reached into his pocket, and for a moment I was terrified he would bring out that horrible ice-cold necklace that spun lies, deceit, and heartbreak into silver and emeralds.

But he pulled out something small and simple, a sort of talisman strung on a gossamer silver chain. Two crescent moons, facing opposite one another, backed by a starburst and decorated with tiny diamonds, dangled from the chain. It glowed with the same silver light as Zaire's eyes and the Bazaar's permanent midnight sky.

I hesitated, my fingers a few inches away. "What is it?"

"Consider it a healing charm. Its purpose is to guide your soul in the direction it should go." His eyes softened, as if he understood too well. He reached across the table and turned over my palm, pressing the dainty talisman into my hand. I swallowed hard as he closed my fingers around it.

"I can't accept this. I know everything in this Bazaar comes at a price," I said, the words tasting as bitter as the Manticore's poison.

Cassian let out a low sound. "Can't I simply give you a gift? No strings attached. I only wish for your safety." His eyes bored into mine, too soulful, too meaningful.

I pulled my cheeks between my teeth and studied him. His skin was like copper. The dark tattoo on the back of his hand matched his talisman. My stomach twisted and the ring next to my locket sank right into my bruised and battered heart.

"I don't trust you. I don't even know you," I said.

Cassian flinched. Maybe that was unfair after everything that had happened in the Underworld, but he was still a servant to Zaire. And he knew more than he could share.

I set the talisman down. It was a beautiful piece, exquisite. And whenever my fingers touched it, a warmth spread through my limbs. But I couldn't keep it. It felt like a betrayal to Linus. To myself.

"I know the last necklace you touched was not a pleasant experience." Cassian grimaced. "But I thought you could use a good luck charm. These crescents collect light throughout the moon's cycle. In the Bazaar, the stars are bright and the moon never fades. It can show you where to go. Like my shadows show me where to go. I thought that maybe with a bit of moonlight, you won't struggle so much."

Cassian's fingers traced the gentle curve of the twin crescent moons as if remembering something. His eyes were far away, the silver talisman reflecting in them, glinting off of the deep amber brown.

"But I won't need to find my way through this maze anymore." I kept my hand on the table beside the necklace. "I held up my end of the bargain. Aren't you here to take me to Zaire to get what I need from the palace?"

He looked to the side as if the fireplace was vastly interesting. My heart sank, settling somewhere deep in my stomach.

"Zaire does not know that I'm here," he said, voice throaty and deep. A little thrill ran across my skin when his eyes met mine. "And he won't be able to see you for a few more hours. He is taking care of Marcel."

"And how long will that take? I need to return home." I pushed the necklace and food away. His face fell.

"I'm not sure exactly. But you will get what he promised you. Zaire is many things, but he is not a liar."

"Can't you take me to the palace? I can find what I need on my own from there." I kneaded my forehead with my thumb and forefinger. Cassian shook his head. A sigh ripped from my teeth and I stood, ready to stomp up the stairs to my room.

He caught my arm. "I can't take you to the palace. Zaire is very particular about his home. Besides, taxes are being collected from the vendors during the Alignment. It is not something you need to see. Trust me."

"And why not? Or are you going to give me another riddle or avoid answering my questions?" I pulled my arm from his grasp.

He looked up at the ceiling in exasperation, pushing a curl of hair from his forehead. I noticed his face was completely healed. His broken nose looked normal again and his cheek was without blemish, not even a pink line from where I had sliced him with my dagger.

"The Bazaar is a dangerous place, and it is run particularly. You know the currency of trade here. Souls keep this place alive, and once gave the gods their power. Collecting them is a brutal affair."

Nausea roiled my stomach. "Is that what is keeping Zaire alive?"

Cassian lifted a brow and nodded. He looked tired; I realized. I had been watching him for days now. I thought he was an overly confident man. But I saw it etched in every line of his face, every facet of his eyes.

He was silently begging for something to happen. Something *different*.

"Zaire will send for you when he is ready."

"Why? Why can he order me about, and you for that matter? I did his task. I went to the Underworld, all so I could get the wa—what I came for," I stammered, choking on the invisible hand of Niklaus' oath; the force of it turning my vision black.

Cassian didn't flinch. He stood there for a moment before he scooped up the necklace and put it in the pocket of his loose black shirt. I ignored the lines of his chest and arms.

"Come with me," he said softly, extending his hand. "I think I might have something that could help you."

I hesitated, staring at his smooth palm before glancing at his face. His eyes were warm and open. He was a servant of Zaire, sent to gather information. But the spark in his eyes, the defiant set of his jaw made me wonder... did Cassian have a will of his own? Or did Zaire truly control him like a puppet? And I still wanted a friend, someone to help *me* for a change, so badly the desire stole my breath.

Maybe it was a mistake, but the thrumming of my heart begged me to go with him.

"Where are we going?" I relented and set my hand in his, stubbornly ignoring how my stomach flipped. There was nothing for me to do but wait for Zaire to bother to summon me again. What was the harm?

"Somewhere that will help you understand this place better. And maybe yourself."

Sixteen

"Watch your step." Cassian helped me through crumbling stone streets. After leaving the tavern, he had led me through the streets of the Bazaar for almost half an hour, refusing to give in and tell me where we were headed.

No one noticed as we slipped between a crack in the stone coated in ivy. Everyone was distracted or deep in the depths of the merchant's stores and shops, too busy seeking power or sin to rest.

Torches clung to the winding streets lined with ancient olive trees, twisting and bending like a canopy around the roads and growing into buildings. The torches burned without any hint of fuel or someone to tend them. A familiar shudder rippled across my skin.

Ionic columns, reminiscent of ancient empires, supported roofs decorated with friezes and statues in various states of disrepair. Villas with cracked red-tiled roofs surrounded squares where the reaching roots of olive trees twisted and lifted the paving stones.

It was entirely abandoned.

Not a single voice could be heard. No peals of raucous laughter echoed through the streets. There were not any vendors trying to lure people to buy their wares, dangling cursed fruit dripping with power and consequences. The torches burned on, blazing determinedly despite the loneliness; small spots of warmth against cold, broken memories.

"What is this place?" I asked, my fingers reaching to clutch my locket.

Cassian helped me over a toppled column, its round, carved body lying broken and decrepit across the steps of what looked to be a temple. He led the way up those stairs.

"This is where the Bazaar first began," he said, breathing sharply as we continued to climb over fallen stones and avoided thick, grasping roots. "Over time, it has grown and taken much more, becoming what you see today."

"Why does Zaire have this hidden away?" I peered into the ominous black of the decaying temple. Nothing but a pervasive coating of dust looked back at me.

Cassian stepped forward, as if the eerie silence and whispers of secrets in the air did not frighten him. "He does not want others to wander where the gods did. Zaire is always trying to control their magic, especially that of the old king Irra, head of the Thirteen Ancients. The scimitars Zaire and I carry were once his."

Cassian slipped into the darkness, disappearing. I staggered after him, a breeze at the back of my neck feeling too much like the breath of those savage gods. Another set of stairs, coated in thick grime, greeted us from behind a lonely altar.

His voice continued, soothing, like he was reciting tales I heard as a child when my mother was still alive. "Once the gods were forgotten by mortals and too weak to win the war, Zaire destroyed any trace of them and their ways. He hated them, despised them. So, he sealed off this portion of the Bazaar, where they once ruled. Where everything started."

Immense statues towered above us, glaring down at the altar and looking as if they could come to life and snap my bones without a second thought. We slipped into the small staircase and followed it for a dozen steps.

"Why are we here?" I whispered. My skin tingled uncomfortably, like someone watched us.

"Like I said, I think I know something that can help you." Cassian shrugged one shoulder and turned back to the almost endless-looking staircase. The air was cool and smelled of earth. The stars above slipped further away, plunging us into darkness.

I blinked against a blaze of light. Cassian held aloft a torch, one that had been anchored to the wall for so long I'd thought it was a part of it. The staircase ended, depositing us in a massive underground chamber.

In the depths of the temple sat rusting braziers, shields, weapons, barrels, casks, cauldrons—a menagerie of treasures and objects piled high. All were slightly blackened and charred, as though someone had tried to burn the items but hadn't been successful.

"What is all of this?" I asked, brushing my fingertips across the surface of a brass shield. Black soot clung to my skin like a disease, and I wiped it away. Beneath the smudge of soot, the shield looked remarkably intact, as if the fire had done no damage at all.

Cassian nudged a dismembered spear with the toe of his boot. "The remnants of the gods that Zaire tried to destroy. This was their palace, their temple, where mortals once came to worship or make sacrifices. Zaire gathered together many of their items and set them ablaze, but they would not burn. The Three Fates, the spinners of destiny, wouldn't allow him to sever their threads so completely."

"Why would he try to destroy a bunch of rusty old weapons?" I drew my fingers away, curling them back from the shield that glinted at me as if it could see into my mind and draw out my deepest fears.

"They hold the powers of the gods. They were the weapons they wielded to cause wars, disease, and famine. Zaire tried to destroy them and this city, and when it didn't work, he sealed off this portion of the Bazaar."

His voice was earnest, almost pleading. Like he wanted me to read between his words to a truth buried beneath them. But I didn't understand and couldn't ask.

Cassian picked his way through the towers of objects and unending dust. It swirled around his legs, wrapping around his ankles, and plumed towards his chest. He came to a stop near the far wall and set the torch into an empty sconce. The licking flame set alight thousands of strands of cobwebs in a dance of flame and embers that died out in a flash.

Leaning against the wall was a large oval item half-covered in a dusty sheet. Gilded edges of curling metal peered out through the grime. He wrapped his fingers around the edge of the sheet.

A chill ran across my shoulders. "I want to leave, Cassian."

The unnaturally cool air numbed my fingers. The dust cramming my lungs made me feel like a caged animal. I folded my arms, clutching them close to my body. It was foolish following him. We were alone, and I was totally at his mercy.

"I promise it will make sense soon." Cassian flicked his eyes between me and the oval object once before he yanked on the cover. The dingy sheet sailed to the ground in a shower of dust. I squinted and shielded my eyes against the harsh glare of the torch reflecting in the face of a mirror. It was tall, immensely so, at least three feet higher than Cassian.

I coughed and stepped back, clutching at the wall.

"Wait," he pleaded. "This mirror is the artifact of Ismene, the Goddess of Magic and Prophecy, one of the many treasures Zaire wanted to shatter. It will show you the truth."

"The truth about what?" I wheezed. My eyes watered as facets of light reflected from the mirror. The surface glimmered and moved, like something or *someone* was trapped inside. I gasped and backed away, my spine hitting the wall.

"About what you refuse to see. Maybe the truth I'm bound to be silent on." My chest seized, and our eyes locked. "It will show you what you need to know, but not everything in the glass will be as it seems."

I coughed again, but lowered my hand from my eyes. "If I look in the mirror, I'll get the answers I've been after?"

Cassian nodded, but kept his eyes firmly away from the glass as if he were afraid to see what would stare back at him. "I wanted you to—I thought there were things you needed to know," he said, a look of nervousness crossing his features.

I hesitated. Was this a trap?

But Arae's words stuck in my mind. I wondered if the mirror would show me who my father was. That could be the key. Maybe Cassian was doing his best to show me the things Zaire had forced him to keep secret. Warmth slowly replaced the chill on my skin at the thought.

Excitement burned in my throat, and I paced towards the mirror.

My eyes adjusted to the glittering light and the swirl of colors dancing across the perfect, unblemished glass. My breath caught in my lungs, unable to expand when images formed into solid shapes and ghostly voices reached my ears.

And then I wasn't in the Bazaar.

~

"How long do we have to wait to tell my parents of our engagement, Linus?" Veronica huffed; her arms crossed under the bosom of the low-cut garnet dress she wore. They stood in the offices of his father's shipping company. Outside, the ports bustled and sailors shouted. The sun was bright and islanders walked about in light linen and held parasols to shield their delicate skin from the sun.

It was summer. But which summer?

Linus pinched the back of his neck; sandy hair longer than it had been during the festival. "Just until I can get things sorted with someone," he said, voice tight.

He wore a light linen suit, but his waistcoat was open and the white shirt below rumpled and unbuttoned. Veronica looked to be in a similar state of disarray. Her hands moved greedily over his arms.

"Your father? Why would he oppose our marriage? I am from one of the wealthiest families on the island," Veronica purred.

"It is nothing. We will tell everyone during the festival at your parent's party in a few months. Won't that be grand enough for you?" Linus's smile was drawn and did not reach his eyes, but Veronica beamed, throwing her arms around his neck and capturing his mouth in a fervent kiss.

The images changed, the colors draining from the glass like low tide from the shore. Linus and I were on the beach during the height of summer. The air was thick with warmth but cut by the perpetual wind that buffeted the headlands of the island. We sat together on the beach in the sun, his blonde hair long enough to brush his eyebrows and the tops of his ears.

"What is it?" I asked, looking up at him with adoration. The expression in my wide brown eyes startled me. I looked at him as if he was water in a dry desert or shade at the height of summer. I would give anything if he only asked.

His eyes were distant. "Nothing. I was just thinking of where we will go once we are married."

A detail in the image sent skitters of pain down my skin. He wore the same linen suit he had with Veronica in his father's offices. Rumpled. The buttons not matching. But I remembered this afternoon well. We'd hardly touched hands. Two days before this picnic, he had proposed. The excitement etched across my face was heartbreakingly trusting.

His lips looked a little swollen, rimmed in red around the edges. Lip paint I didn't wear. He had told me he'd come from a busy meeting in his father's blisteringly hot office. The Hazel in the mirror didn't dare question it. Nor had she questioned the disappearances, the brief talks, or the long nights together, followed by days without speaking.

Stupid, foolish girl.

I wanted to shout at the version of me trapped in the looking glass. But she would not listen.

Images raced across the glass once more. Whispered words and kisses under the moonlight. It seemed obvious then, though the Hazel in the mirror was swept up in the romance of it all. Swept up in the attention, the promise of love and affection she so desperately craved.

But the kisses were not all for her, nor were the soft words of promises and devotion. They were tangled with images of Veronica, of Linus embracing her in the dark of night, of words whispered between them of love and desire.

All at once, the light dancing in the glass changed. A dark shape formed, hulking and monstrous. I saw myself running across the sky in a beautiful ball gown.

Running.

Running.

Running.

And then I was falling. I was a shooting star trapped in the velvety black sky as the monster wrapped its talons around me. I was lost in the depths of the Bazaar. Hopeless.

Zaire appeared on the silvery surface and stood behind me, his gaze wicked and sharp. One hand grasped my waist and the other wrapped around my throat as the shadows melted off him.

The beast and the man were one. I was its prey.

The new Hazel staring at me in the glass looked as if a part of her had died. I'd lost something precious and important. Blood bubbled from my mouth, coating my teeth red as I grinned and leaned into Zaire's touch. The emerald necklace rested against my breastbone, complementing an extravagant dress. Zaire traced the gems with his fingers and smiled, his lips pressing against my ear, eyes flaming with desire.

He held a goblet of crystal-clear liquid to my lips as he whispered, "And now you can never leave."

SEVENTEEN

"Hazel, are you alright?" Cassian's deep voice ripped me from the visions.

"What was that?" I whimpered and jerked back, my calves bumping into a box of dusty weapons.

Cassian glanced once at the mirror, his face going slack and hard all at once. His eyes scanned whatever images appeared to him before he threw the sheet over the oval of shining, terrible truth.

"The mirror shows you what it thinks you most need to know. It is not always pleasant." Cassian grimaced, a light sheen of sweat dotting his forehead.

The sight of Veronica and Linus entwined burned through my mind, and turned my heart to crumbling ash. Bursts of darkness, images of me falling, and part of me dying at the cold hands of Zaire.

A ragged gasp burst from my lips. "Why would you show me this? It's a lie!" But my voice cracked, losing all conviction. He held out a hand as if asking me to take it, to trust him. I recoiled, willing the tears to stay back for just a little longer.

"It may not be exactly how it seems, but the mirror doesn't lie. It can't," Cassian said, his voice unrelenting.

"No. You're wrong." I shook my head, pushing my hair back, but it tangled around my knuckles and sent stings of pain across my scalp.

"What did you see?" His eyes flickered to the covered mirror as if his curiosity would overtake him. I reeled at the thought of him seeing me like that, draped over Zaire with glassy white eyes and blood-stained teeth.

I stammered, my mind warring between the two terrible visions. And I decided. "That can't be true. Linus would not have done that to me."

"He is the one who gave you that ring?" Cassian pointed to the necklace dangling against my chest. "I saw him at your aunt's party. You came here for him, not for yourself, isn't that right?"

I didn't like the way he looked at me. It was the same expression he'd worn when he wrestled Zaire's necklace away. Seeing straight through me again. Knowing too much.

"Yes." My voice was a hoarse whisper in my hollowed-out chest. "I came here for him."

"You would do anything for him, sacrifice your own life, and he cannot even give you a real ring." Derision dripped from his words as he glared at the chain against my breastbone.

"What do you mean?" Tears of hurt shifted to burning ones of anger and blame.

He reached out, one long finger hooked under the chain, drawing the locket and ring up to the low torchlight. "This gem is fake. It is only glass colored red. That man does not care for you, he never has. You should not waste so much time and energy here on him."

"How would you even know?" I jolted away, barely registering the chain of my necklace snapping and tumbling to the ground. My breath came shallow and hard. I had to leave. I had to get far away from the mirror and that image of myself: dressed in power but empty inside.

Cassian didn't flinch at my acidic tone. "Tell me why you really came to the Bazaar. Everyone has a reason."

I grit my teeth. I knew it. Zaire had sent him here to learn about Nicklaus and our deal. I took another step back.

"To get the money Linus needs for his company, so we can marry." I wanted to sound angry, but I sounded fearful. My vow kept me from mentioning Nicklaus, and I was glad about that. To keep something from those knowing eyes of his. From Zaire's hungry teeth.

His mouth pulled in a hard line. "You came to get a treasure from the palace vaults," he said without question. I held back a gulp, wondering how long it was until he figured out precisely *which* treasure. "I know what price anything of Zaire's fetches on Earth. And I know you're doing this all for a person who does not care for you."

My teeth clicked together, and I stepped forward, jabbing my finger into Cassian's chest as hard as I could, wishing I could bring myself to hit him. "You have no right to say that! Linus loved me first. He wanted to marry *me*."

Cassian's nostrils flared, and his eyes flickered to my lips. "You forget I was there at the party. I saw everything. What if he doesn't want you even if you had money? Would you still fight so hard?"

"That's all he needs." I curled my fingers into tight fists. "He only needs Veronica for her dowry. If I take care of that, he will choose me!"

Linus had to love me, or what else did I have?

"And you're so sure of that?" He laughed once. "If he really loves you, should money matter? He's a whelp of a man for refusing to stand up for the woman he supposedly loves. He should strike down all who come against her, against *you*." Cassian's voice was hoarse, like the words affected him more than they should.

I flinched at their weight; at the way they pierced through the thoughts I had been trying to hide for days. Against the memory of Linus kissing another in front of me. Of him letting me go into the cold, dead night.

If someone loved another person, truly and as completely as they claimed, would money matter?

I turned sharply and snagged the torch from the wall before making my way up the staircase, towards the pale starlight glaring down on the decaying temple. Cassian's heavy footsteps followed closely. I could practically feel his breath against my neck as I burst out into the night.

"Hazel, wait—"

"What do you know about love?" I turned to him suddenly, and he nearly ran me over. "You live in a world full of lies, deceit, and selfishness. You've never loved anyone. You're as old as Zaire and just as cruel."

My voice trembled and my lips quivered as the weight of what I had seen crashed over me. What were the lies and what was the truth? It was impossible to tell in the Bazaar and under these wicked stars.

"I am trying to help you!" he cried. "Whenever someone like you comes along in the Bazaar, they are always used. You are too trusting, too desperate for someone to validate you. You would give your very life for it."

I gasped. The image of the necklace against my skin and Zaire caressing me as if I had given him something precious leaped into my thoughts. I clenched my jaw. I was not like the other people in the Bazaar. The money, the power, the water—none of it was for me. I didn't want it. And now, I had no one to fight for.

"You know nothing about me," I laughed mirthlessly, but his words cut like the glass knives the merchants carried. He was splitting my skin, seeing right through me with his deep eyes.

I hated him for it.

The torch burned out, and I grabbed the handle, aiming it at his aggravatingly attractive face with a cry. It sailed through the air, arcing for his head. Cassian stepped aside easily as the torch clattered to the stones. He narrowed his eyes and moved forward, capturing my wrist and hauling me against him.

"Let me go!" I demanded, writhing in his grip. He didn't flinch, only leaned closer.

"For eons, I have seen lovers and friends tear one another apart. I saw your precious fiancé when I was on your island. Saw how he cast you aside like dirt. He has been using you selfishly and you are too naïve to see it. You are wasting your time and your energy on a man who is not worth a single one of your thoughts. Who is not worthy of *you*, Hazel."

My fingers itched to beat at his chest, slap his face, maybe even break his nose again. But his words froze my limbs. I was no one, a bastard child. How could Cassian say someone was not worthy of *me*?

A trick. A lie. Always lies.

Cassian hesitated, choking on his words, on an oath he'd made with Zaire. Frustration and anger burned in his eyes. I studied their depths, searching them like I did the mirror. They were ageless as the night sky and glittering with the same tortured light. There were secrets buried there, of pain and hurt that went on for centuries. I could feel his heartbeat slamming against his chest.

"Why do you care what I came here for? Or for who?" I asked, letting my arms go slack.

Cassian's breath slipped from his lips sharply. "I know why the necklace affected you so much. I know what the mirror showed you. You don't deserve to feel that way over a man who does not care for you."

Cassian's fingers slowly uncurled from around my arm and slipped away. A thick wind smothered the flame of the torches in the ragged square, dropping shadows over us like a curtain. His chest heaved with unspoken words.

I didn't know what to think, besides how badly I hated him for knowing my worst flaw. The weakness I wished I could banish, like Zaire removed any memory of the gods. My need for someone to love me, though I knew I was not worth it.

"You don't know anything about Linus." My voice trembled. "And why I came here is my business. I came here for love."

"A love that is a lie," Cassian hissed through his teeth. "Linus, Zaire, Arae—they are all using you, and you cannot seem to see it."

"And you're not?"

He flinched, and my heart sank.

"It's not like that. I don't want you for the same reasons as Zaire."

I pressed my trembling lips together. "Then why do you want me?"

Cassian's nostrils flared, and his eyes dropped to my mouth. My skin heated. He tried to speak, choked, and then tried again.

He sighed harshly, raking his hands through his hair. "I want you to trust me. To trust that I will get you out of here."

I opened my mouth to argue, to scream, to do *anything*—but his body pressed against mine again, and the fierce beating of his heart echoed my own. My skin burned where we touched.

His hands moved slowly, cautiously, until they cupped my neck and the back of my head. And then he was everywhere. His fingers sank into my skin, anchoring me to him as his lips skated across my neck, my collarbones, brushing past my ear. I shuddered, my eyes closing despite everything. My mind went blank. I was nothing besides a swirl of anger and pain and desire.

"Let me show you," he rumbled, tugging me closer until I thought I was going to break. "You deserve more than this. You deserve everything."

His lips trailed up my neck, tasted the skin behind my ear. My breath stopped as his stubble scraped against my skin. Shivers wound through me like sparks. He buried his fingers in my hair, tilting my face towards his. His breath tickled my cheeks, tasted sweet on my tongue.

A knot lodged in my throat. Why was he doing this? What game was he playing?

Cassian's lips brushed mine. Once. Twice. I wanted to sink against him, fall for his pretty lies. But my gut twisted.

"Stop it." I pushed hard at his chest, staggering back. Tears finally spilled over my cheeks, their salt stinging the invisible wound gaping over my heart. "Tell Zaire I want to meet with him as soon as possible. I'm leaving the Bazaar."

We stood there for a breath, his eyes hurt and hungry, mine shuttered and burning. Finally, I turned away and stalked down the steps. Cassian did not follow me.

I disappeared through the crack in the wall and fled through the Bazaar, back to the tavern, betrayal and fear rising like bile in my throat.

Night Four

EIGHTEEN

Saskia found me in my room, sitting on the plush wool rug. Her golden eyes were sharp, as if she understood everything that had happened without asking a single question. Perhaps she didn't need to. She was a siren, and they knew a thing or two about humanity's deepest desires.

"You went to the Citadel," she stated, joining me on the floor. "I can smell it on you."

I lifted my chin from where I had tucked it against my knees and regarded her with red, stinging eyes. "Cassian showed me a mirror."

"Ah, the Mirror of Ismene. I thought Zaire had destroyed it long ago." Saskia leaned against the bed frame next to me, her legs stretched out and her arms folded loosely across her chest. She rested a hand on my shoulder gingerly, as if she had never touched a human before, and worried I would feel slimy.

I rubbed my face with one hand, feeling numb and raw and a thousand other things. "It showed me things I don't understand. I can't help but think Cassian is tricking me."

Saskia made a thoughtful sound. "I've known Cassian a long time. He is Zaire's oldest and most loyal companion."

"So I can't trust him? Whatever he showed me, everything that mirror held, is a lie?" My voice was ragged and hopeful.

"No," she said quietly, eyes flickering around the room before she dropped her voice. "Taking you to the Citadel could get him killed. He must be trying to tell you something important. Something Zaire doesn't want you to know."

"Why is he doing this?" I whispered.

The siren shifted. "I say this because I care for you. Leave the Bazaar now. Come with me to the gates. You are not safe here."

My breath stuttered. "Why?"

"Zaire has always been mad with power." She licked her lips, eyes burning bright gold. "But things are different this Alignment."

"Different how?" I shook my head, drawing my knees tightly to my chest.

"During the last Alignment something happened. Something to frighten Zaire and push him towards desperation." Her voice lowered, the words rushed and nearly frantic.

"Saskia," I choked, "what are you trying to say? Zaire promised he'd help after the Underworld."

"Forget the palace. Return home. The gods are stirring more and more since the last Alignment." She dropped her voice further. "A god escaped its prison three decades ago. I don't trust Zaire with you."

My stomach turned to ice. "A god escaped last time?"

I heard Arae's words again; Cassian's too. Something about using me to cement Zaire's rule above the gods. My heart felt bruised.

"Because I am a siren, Zaire cannot control me with oaths or enchantments. I tell you this at the risk of my own life." Saskia curled her lip in distaste.

"Zaire wants my help to find the god?" I shook my head.

The siren shrugged. "I truly do not know. But none of this is a coincidence. You must leave before things get worse."

"Thank you again for all your help, Saskia, I couldn't have survived here without you. But I can't run from this."

"Are you truly leaving?" The siren sat forward, eyes wide.

"Zaire is sending for me." I tried to ignore the panic fluttering in my belly. "I can't turn back now."

Saskia clenched her jaw. "And you're certain this is wise?"

I laughed. "No. But I am so close. Zaire made an oath. He will keep it."

"If nothing else, Hazel, listen to Cassian." She rubbed her jaw. "After taking you to the Citadel, I believe he has the same fears as me."

I couldn't reply, only nodded tightly. Saskia helped me to my feet.

"I am happy to help you, Hazel. I hope you get what you need from Zaire and can leave this place."

Hooves clattered outside and the breathy sounds of a team of horses filtered in through the windows. The sound was so alien that for a moment I forgot where I was. I peeked my head out of the window.

A midnight black carriage waited in the street in front of the tavern doors. Dark horses shuffled their massive hooves and snarled at passersby that wandered too close to their silver manes.

I pulled back from the window, my heart rate picking up at the thought of getting home. "I'll miss you," I said to Saskia. She waved her hand dismissively, but I thought I saw her eyes shimmer with something more than just their usual golden light.

Saskia nudged me towards the door. "Go on. If the Fates will it, we will meet again."

I stepped out of the tavern, bustling with life and patrons, and into the Bazaar, the canister and Niklaus' bag of coins securely in my pocket. A man dressed in a dark blue livery stepped down from the carriage and swung open the door. A beautiful velvet interior lined the luxurious vehicle. It was finer than even the governor's carriage on the island.

Thoughts of home and Linus crushed my chest as I accepted the servant's hand. The door swung shut, and I parted the curtains with my fingers to wave a last goodbye to Saskia. Her amber dress shimmered in the lamplight as she watched me forlornly, hand lifted in farewell.

I leaned back against the cushioned seat, my bones aching with days of weariness. The mere thought of a simple carriage ride to the palace was enough to make my skin itch with anticipation. I had struggled for hours, days even, to reach that infernal building, and now I was being escorted in the finery of the King of the Bazaar right to its doorstep. The irony was painful.

The carriage jolted forward, the echo of the cobbled stone beneath the wheels resounded off of the buildings in the square. I peeked out the window as the Bazaar whirled by, a blur of brilliant colors and beings and things.

The carriage rode faster, hastening speed as we left the familiar tumble of buildings and climbed steadily upwards, towards the palace sitting regally on the hill. The tangled web of streets and aimless humans faded until all that was left was an endless meadow of darkness and the single ribbon of white road climbing towards the lonely palace.

The sparkle of silver paper caught my eye, resting stoically against the opposite seat. A smooth cream envelope bearing the seal of the mysterious king winked in the dark interior of the carriage. Berries and crescent moons. Both images were tantalizingly familiar.

I hesitated for a moment before I reached out and snatched up the package. I unfolded the letter, plucking the tissue-thin paper from the envelope, and held it up to the window to read.

My dearest Hazel,

You have waited patiently for your reward, and I thank you again for the aid you have rendered me. It is most appreciated.

For your efforts, I invite you to my traditional ball to be held at the palace at the close of the Alignment on the final night of the festival. Inside the package, you will find a gown fit for someone of your station.

I look forward to dancing with you.

-Zaire

I sat back, feeling exposed and cold. This was not our deal. Once I helped Zaire, I was to be given whatever I asked for and escorted from the Bazaar. But he wanted me to attend his ball, a party that would rival any earthly gathering by tenfold. And it wouldn't happen for three more days.

The sweet ambrosia in the air turned to ash in my mouth and I tugged at the ribbon on the package. It unfolded to reveal a gown that most certainly did not fit my station.

A full silk dress of soft sage green fell in waves to the floor. Translucent layers of silver taffeta covered the skirt, framing a slit that reached above the knee. The bodice was tight-fitting and steel gray, decorated with embroidery and studded with jewels. The sleeves were slashed open and as long as the train of the dress, so it almost represented a cape of embroidered silk.

Admiration faded to nausea as my fingers ghosted along the shimmering fabric. I knew this dress. I had seen it in the mirror with Zaire's hands running greedily along my skin.

The carriage rolled to an abrupt halt. I stuffed the dress back into its packaging and tied off the ribbon hastily. The servant opened the door and silently helped me down.

The moment my foot hit the ground, I was enveloped in an almost smothering presence of finery. A large circular driveway wrapped around a five-tiered fountain. The entrance to the palace itself sat further down a long stretch of marble, surrounded on both sides by intricate rows of columns.

The servant remained mute but led me down the long courtyard. His heels clicked on the marble floor, sending whispering echoes off of the columns. I clutched the package to my chest and scurried after him.

All thought fled my mind the moment the grand doors to Zaire's palace swung open.

A foyer of white checked marble sprawled before us. The ceilings were high, almost cavernous. A vast dome sat in the center of the entrance and a circle of windows at its apex let in milky moonlight. Columns braced against the weight of the roof, and each surface was trimmed in brilliant gold. A shiver wracked my body as the cold, sterile air of Zaire's home wrapped around me.

"Through here," the servant said, the first words he had uttered. "Zaire awaits you in the dining hall." His eyes were glassy and around his wrist I noticed the thin, almost imperceptible outline of golden shackles.

I trailed behind him, my mouth agape at the splendor. The package weighed against my chest; the paper crinkling under my sweaty palms. The servant led me further into the palace until he stopped in front of a set of open bronze doors.

"Hazel Blackthorn, my king," the servant announced, bowing so low I thought his nose might scrape the ground.

I straightened my back and entered the dining hall, ignoring my pounding heart. At first, all I could notice were the rows of windows facing the Bazaar in intricate arches. More gilded marble adorned every surface, and a plush azure rug stretched the length of the room, atop which rested a long table of richly oiled wood.

And then I saw Zaire at the head of the table with Cassian sitting at his right. Blood roared in my ears as Cassian dared to look right in my eyes. He nodded politely, as if nothing had happened between us. I didn't realize my fingers had impaled the delicate wrappings of the dress until Zaire made a noise of displeasure.

"Hazel, how wonderful it is to have you in my home. I promised we would celebrate your victory in the Underworld with a feast, did I not?" Zaire grinned. His face was flushed, empty glasses of wine at his side. He was drunk, or at least very close to it. My guard raised.

"While I appreciate the gift," I smoothed the wrapped dress in my hands before I thrust it at his chest, "I am afraid that this was not part of our deal. You promised if I did your bidding in the Underworld, you would give me what I needed. I do not plan on staying for the ball at the end of the Alignment."

I avoided Cassian's intense gaze. It burned through me. Memories of his lips on my skin and his hands in my hair.

Zaire lifted a dark eyebrow but made no move to take the dress. "Nonsense. You cannot leave yet; we have barely begun to know each other."

I opened my mouth to protest, but Zaire clapped his hands and a flurry of servants emerged from hidden doors, arms laden with platters of food and drink. Words stuck in my throat as Zaire gripped my hand tightly and pushed me into the chair at his left, directly across from Cassian. The dress sat wrinkled and abused in my lap.

More servants with glassy eyes fussed over me, filling my glass with bubbling champagne and setting platters of aromatic dishes in front of my crystal plate. Zaire clapped again, and the servants lined against the wall, completely silent, their eyes trained on the horizon.

I swallowed, thoughts racing. "Your invitation is appreciated, but I really need to get back home. Staying that late would not be wise."

"Ah." Zaire tapped his lower lip. "But you are my special guest. How can you refuse? I can guarantee you've seen nothing like the ball at the end of the Alignment. There are creatures from all across the Bazaar from every land and time you can imagine. Magic is everywhere on this rare night. It is almost... sensuous, wouldn't you say, Cassian?"

Cassian's eyes locked on mine, his nostrils flaring at the word. I refused to look away first. I couldn't forgive him for what he'd shown me, or his cruel words at the Citadel.

"I am sure. I need to get back to my fiancé."

Cassian made a sound very much like a snort.

My eyes burned as I glowered across the table. Linus wasn't even my fiancé anymore. Maybe he never was.

No, there was still love to fight for. I had Niklaus' wife to think of. I balled my fists in my lap, blinking away traitorous tears before they could rise.

"Hm." Zaire made a low sound in his throat, like a laugh. "I know of your situation back on your island. I am sure that whomever you are waiting for does not miss you."

My mouth parted in a gape, and I speared Cassian with an accusing eye. There was only one way he could know that.

Zaire remained stoic, his silver eyes glinting.

"I have lived many lifetimes, Hazel. I know your island home and its people well. They are small-minded fools with no regard for the world beyond their shores," he said, his voice like diamonds tumbling across velvet. "But that is not what I wish to discuss. We are celebrating after all."

I swallowed and tore my eyes from his intense gaze and the cold fire raging behind his smile. Zaire snapped his fingers, and a servant swept by, filling his glass of dark wine. I looked at the girl, not much older than I. As she set the bottle of wine back down, I saw golden chains, so fine they almost looked like thread, wrapping around her wrists. I studied every servant lined against the walls as Zaire took a long drink and Cassian speared some kind of meat with a fork.

"Are they all mortals?" My voice cracked.

Zaire smiled lazily; his eyes hooded as one elegant finger trailed the mouth of his goblet. "Indeed. But that is not so pleasant a topic as I think your lovely ears deserve to hear. Cassian told me of your success in the Underworld and your bravery with the lotus-eaters and Manticore. It seems you are more powerful than you give yourself credit for."

I looked at Cassian again, my stomach churning. Did he tell him everything that had happened? Did he share what we spoke of by the fire or Arae's visit? Every warm thought I'd ever had about the man withered.

"I'm sure he exaggerates." I bit down on the inside of my lip. "Why do all your servants have chains around their wrists? Why are they mortal?"

Cassian looked away, chewing his food mournfully. Zaire did not seem to notice the tense air between us. He simply took another long drink from his glass, eyes blazing with something very much like triumph.

"It matters not, Hazel. They are fools who owe me a debt. They come to me begging for refuge from their creditors in the Bazaar." Zaire devoured me with his eyes.

The smells of the food turned putrid.

How could he speak of them like this? And then I glared at Cassian, at his guarded dark eyes. He knew keeping mortals as slaves was wrong, and yet there he sat, being waited upon by them.

"I would like to leave the Bazaar. Now." My voice cracked. "You promised you would let me retrieve the medicine I need if I helped you in the Underworld. I'm going home."

Zaire's smile slipped. "I said I would give you what you *needed*. And I must tell you that you are home, Hazel."

Silence.

Anger flared in my chest, and I stood, throwing the package on the table. "That is not the same thing, and you know it. What I need is the medicine I told you about."

Zaire's eyes turned to slits. He snapped his fingers again and before I could think, a set of guards emerged and grabbed my shoulders, forcing me to sit. Thin golden chains sprouted from the arms of the chair, lashing me to the seat. I gasped as they cut into my wrists and ankles, holding me in place.

"You may deny it, Hazel, but you belong here. Like I do." Zaire stood; his hands folded behind his back. The stars shone brightly down at the palace, like prying eyes waiting to see a show.

"As soon as Cassian told me of your success, I knew I chose well. You are a remarkable human. You have been tempted and learned hard truths in your time in the Bazaar, and yet here you stand," he said, two fingers coming up to trace his mouth. "I know what awaits you once you leave. Your fiancé will remain with your cousin. Your sister will soon wed someone worthy, and you will be forgotten and alone. All the money in the world will not change these things from happening. The Fates have willed it to be."

My jaw tightened and my face burned hot with shame. "How do you know about my cousin or my sister? Did Cassian—"

"Did Cassian tell me? He did, not that he needed to. I saw everything almost the moment I met you. You may use the god's old toys to see the truth, but I have their powers. I can see what has happened, what is, and what might be only by looking at a person."

Cassian made no move to protest or defend his actions. He only looked at me with sympathy etched across every line of his face. I struggled against the chains holding me in place, but it was useless. Betrayal burned hot and shameful. How could he?

"I know what you wish to say. You think I am wrong, that you belong amongst those pathetic people on your island. But you belong here. You belong to *me*," Zaire growled, leaning forward and catching my chin in his hand. "I will show you how precious you are to me; how much I desire you to stay. I can give you the revenge you seek."

I shook my head, pulling my chin from his hand. "No."

His silver eyes turned dark grey. He ignored my snapping teeth and captured my chin again, roughly tilting it up. "Oh, my Hazel. I will so enjoy breaking that spirit of yours."

A muffled curse sounded from the hall. The doors flew open and guards dragged someone into the dining hall. I glared at Cassian, every ounce of hurt and anger I could muster thrown at him.

"What is the meaning of this?" A velvety voice demanded from the open doors. "I have paid my taxes and then some during this Alignment. I demand to know what you are holding me for!"

"Ah, Darius, so glad you could join us." Zaire stood, releasing my chin. My spine stiffened as I struggled to turn my head far enough to peek over the back of the chair. I caught sight of long black hair and a face riddled with bubbling, scarred skin.

"You," Darius snarled, lunging at me. In a flash Cassian was out of his chair and standing between us, one of Zaire's scimitars leveled at Darius's chest.

"Do not touch her," Cassian warned.

"She is the mortal girl who denied me my payment! She attacked me!" Darius wailed as he thrashed against the two guards. They moved him to the head of the table, dropping him unceremoniously on his knees before Zaire.

"I heard of your bravery with Darius, Hazel," Zaire purred as he prodded the kneeling man with the toe of his boot. "He wronged you, did he not? Took you away and tried to extricate payment unfairly. He dared to touch you."

"That is a lie!" Darius tried to stand, but Cassian moved faster, the tip of his sword against the other man's throat. My heart hammered in my chest. Why was Cassian defending me so fiercely from a man in chains, but not from his king? But then I looked at Zaire's hungry expression and my stomach curdled.

"You have been hurt and used countless times, haven't you?" Zaire moved to caress my neck. I shuddered, wanting to slap his hands away, but I was helpless and chained in place. "We are so alike, my dear. We have both been taken advantage of, cast aside, and betrayed." Zaire looked at Cassian accusingly.

I had no time to wonder at the anger in both of their eyes.

"Kill him." Zaire waved to one guard. My eyes widened just as Darius let out a scream of protest. A bronze dagger emerged from his chest. Blood leaked from his mouth and sprayed the floor.

A choking gasp tore from my throat. I heaved. Zaire stepped back, using a handkerchief to wipe the blood from his shoes.

"Why did you do that?" I gagged as the guards dragged Darius from the room, blood trailing behind him. Zaire's eyes were cold and hard as he took his seat again. Cassian straightened and sheathed his sword. But he didn't meet my eyes.

"A gift for you, my dear." Zaire settled into his seat and downed the rest of his wine. "To show you I will kill anyone who gets in the way of us."

"Us?" I sputtered, trembling so hard I thought maybe the earth was shaking the palace. "There is no us! Let me go. I want to go home."

Zaire didn't flinch, didn't look wounded as tears streamed down my cheeks. All I could smell was the iron tang of blood. So much blood. Cassian's face looked pained, but he made no move to free me.

"Call me any name you like, but we are the same. Darius wronged you, so I killed him. How often have you wanted to take your revenge on those who harm or shun you on your foolish little island? It is pathetic, my dear, to defend them so."

"I am no murderer!" I spat, anger warming the shock out of my system. "How can you claim we are the same? You are a blood-thirsty king and a liar!"

Zaire's lips dragged over his teeth in a lazy smile. His quicksilver eyes, burning with a hunger so intense it frightened me, turned to Cassian. "Shall you tell her, cousin, or shall I?"

Cousin? I breathed in sharply as Cassian grimaced and moved to retake his seat. He steadfastly ignored the smear of blood on the floor that silent servants scrubbed clean.

"What is it you want me to share?" Cassian asked, his voice clipped.

"You look at me as if I am repulsive, Hazel. But I have always acted out of self-preservation and the greater good. My cousin was once a prince, you see, and I was the son of the Vizier."

"Zaire." Cassian's jaw clicked. "It is better to keep family matters private."

"Nonsense." Zaire reached for his glass again, brimming once more with deep purple wine. His eyes flashed like a madman. "If you are to understand my plans for you and see how alike we truly are, you have to know my past."

"I don't care!" I protested. But Zaire snapped his fingers and my lips stuck together. I struggled against the enchantment. My lips burned, fused like hot metal. I glared at Cassian, letting hate coil around my heart.

"My father banished me and marked with a traitor's scar when some gambling creditors of a rival caliphate imprisoned me." Zaire's fingers ghosted over his jagged scar. "My father was never kind to me, nor my sisters. He threw me away like a dog to the mercy of our enemies."

"Please, cousin. This is not something that needs to be dug up from the past." Cassian's hands clasped the edge of the table, knuckles white.

"And you," Zaire snarled to Cassian, his face ruddy from alcohol and malice, "you did not stop him from the endless beatings. My sisters and myself, every day decorated with bruises and broken bones. You, the *prince*, did nothing for us. Nothing for *me* when I was thrown into the desert!"

"I did not know!" Cassian protested; his face shadowed. "You were a mercenary. You were a traitor to my father the moment you made deals with our enemies to save your own hide."

Zaire breathed in slowly, his chest heaving as his face rearranged into a pleasant smile. "I should thank you and my father both. If I had not been banished, I would not have scoured the sands searching for my revenge. Broken and alone, I found my salvation: the Bazaar and the gods."

Cassian stared firmly away, his ears burning red. I wanted to scream, but the sound didn't escape my throat. Zaire reclined, his feet resting on the table as he drained his glass yet again. My skin prickled.

"But Cassian atoned for his sins. He helped me gut my father like the pig he is. He watched as his uncle's blood stained the waters of the wadi that monster lounged around day after day. And we escaped into the Bazaar and I became greater than the gods ever were."

I breathed raggedly through my nose, sweat stinging my skin. Cassian made no move to look at me or his cousin. Murderers. They were both as cruel and wicked as the other.

"Why do you tell her this?" Cassian asked through gritted teeth.

Zaire grinned and leaned his elbows on the table, one of his hands trailing my arm. I struggled against my binds and the sight seemed to send a ripple of feverish hunger through the King of the Bazaar. He stood behind me and leaned down, teeth nipping at my neck. A scream died in my chest.

"To show my future queen the lengths I will go to secure her freedom, as I did mine." Zaire dragged my hair off my neck. "Another gift for you, my love."

A weight against my chest. Cold metal and visions. A muffled scream pressed against my throat even as the necklace from the Underworld called forth my worst desires.

Visions of smoke filled my eyes. Linus kneeling at my feet and begging for forgiveness. My island razed to the ground for how they treated me and my mother. I saw Zaire at my side, our eyes matching silver as I glowed with power. He wanted me to be his queen, to become like him. Just like the mirror had warned.

Hot tears dripped down my cheeks. *No!* I tried to scream. *I am nothing like you.*

"What do you want from me?" I choked, squeezing my eyes shut as Zaire freed my lips of his magic.

"I can give you whatever you want. You have already proven your strength and tenacity. The necklace has chosen you. You deserve its powers, unlike any human who would frivolously use it for money, like Marcel. I will give it to you, and anything else you crave."

I opened my eyes, fighting back the visions.

Zaire knelt at my side, his face completely inhuman.

"In exchange for what?" I asked, my fingers growing cold. They ached to reach out and stroke the necklace around my neck like a collar. I wanted to see the way Linus would look at me, the way he would worship me. I imagined myself coming home with it.

"All I ask is that you join me," he whispered. "That you realize you were only ever at home here, with me."

The stars glittered through the windows in the facets of the emeralds, watching me like they watched Zaire. His lips grazed my shoulder as he moved to set the necklace against my skin once more. I trembled at his touch.

"I know what it is like to wish to be loved and accepted," Zaire said against my skin. "I understand as no one else could." One hand caressed my leg and then trailed up my side. I was frozen in place; the necklace playing on my greatest pains and wishes.

"Be my queen. Rule at my side." Zaire's silver eyes narrowed as he tugged me forward, his hungry lips searching for mine.

"No!" I snapped my head to the side. Zaire staggered, his hand brushing the necklace to the ground. Without the magic seeping into my bones, revulsion crawled wherever Zaire touched. I no longer saw golden immortality, only visions of myself looking cruel and cold—just as I had in the mirror.

Cassian stepped forward, brown eyes blazing with something that looked worse than anger. Zaire cursed and stood at his full height, towering over me like the statues of the gods in the Citadel.

"Very well," he growled, hands smoothing his doublet. "You need more time to consider my offer and how generous it is. You will stay in my palace until the ball. Three days and two nights to come to your senses. Then you will make your decision."

"What decision? I will never agree to stay here with you!"

For a moment, I was afraid he would snap my neck like I was nothing.

Zaire laughed and pushed his hair back. "If you return to the island, even with that medicine and earn your fortune, you will still be a bastard. You will never be accepted, no matter how much money you have. Only here can you truly be yourself. You will be and always have been *nothing*. Unless you have me."

"Why do you want me to be your queen?" I seethed, remembering Saskia's words. Her fears.

He grinned mockingly. One rough hand tilted my chin. Then his fingers dug into my jaw, forcing me to look into his eyes.

"No human could retain their soul here. I have not met one in a thousand years. There is only one reason for that. I suspected it on the eve of the Alignment, but I know it to be true now. You and I would be more powerful together than apart."

"What reason? What are you talking about?"

His grip turned painful, cutting my cheek on my teeth. "Think, Hazel. I am sure you know. I will have your decision by the ball." Zaire glowered, leaning close enough to consume me.

I tilted my face up defiantly, breath ragged. "And if I refuse?"

Zaire laughed, cruel and sharp. "I have many ways to convince you. You will see, my love."

I grit my teeth at the endearment. Zaire gave me one more scorching look before he motioned to his guards and they stood beside him.

"My cousin will show you to your quarters. I have more taxes to collect before the celebration. Until then, you will be confined to the grounds, unable to leave. And be sure to wear that gown, unless you want to displease your king."

NINETEEN

I kept my composure until Zaire disappeared into the halls of the palace. The golden chains fell from my wrists the moment he left and, with a ragged breath, I stood. My chair toppled, clattering to the marble floor.

"Hazel, please—" Cassian reached out, but I turned and fled, running blindly. The guards in their bronze armor only followed me with their eyes, watching as I tore through the beautiful halls in my tattered clothes.

I slammed into a wooden door leading outside. My fingernails scraped across the grain and I twisted the handle roughly. Even though I knew it was useless, I ran. My borrowed boots stumbled over the immaculate grass of an elaborate garden.

Fountains bubbled and willow trees swayed. A deep green lake gleamed in the moonlight. I ran until I reached the edge of the garden, tantalizingly close to the white road leading back to the Bazaar. And then I collided with an invisible wall.

I crumpled to my knees at the edge of the lake and the palace grounds. My shoulders heaved as I fisted my fingers into the plush grass. It was useless. I would never return to my island to help Niklaus or see Adelaide again. Zaire would turn me into a monster.

Tears dripped down my cheeks and rolled off the tip of my nose. I shuddered back a sob. The grass beside me shifted. Cassian knelt, one of his large hands tentatively reaching out to touch my shoulder. I scratched away from him on the shore until my boots dipped into the glassy green water.

"Are you alright?" he whispered, standing tense, his body perfectly still.

A growling laugh rattled from my chest. "Of course not! Your cousin is blackmailing me. And you told him about me, about Linus, and the mirror in the Citadel."

Cassian's face fell, his dark eyes reflecting the starlight. "I had no choice. Zaire has me followed everywhere. If I don't freely tell him what I do, he will find another way to extract the information. I can only hold back so much before he tears it from me, one way or the other. It is not as if I want him in my head."

"You could have fooled me." I pushed his hand away as he tried to reach for me once more. I would have welcomed drowning in the deep pool at my boots. "You let him *murder* his father. You went to the Bazaar with him willingly, and yet you act as if this has all been done to you. All this time, you've been helping him, doing his bidding. And now you're going to lock me in the palace. I hate you."

I fell silent, that brief rush of anger washing away any energy I had left. I felt like the mortals wandering the Bazaar, empty and without purpose.

Gingerly, Cassian reached into his pocket with the hem of his loose shirt and dropped the emerald necklace on the grass. I looked at the sky. Each temptation was harder and harder to resist. Soon I wouldn't have the strength to push it, and Zaire's offer, aside.

How could I be so weak as to have part of me desire what he offered? Love and immortality at any price.

Cassian sat beside me cautiously, dropping the necklace into a velvet box. I turned my face away, winding my arms tight around my legs, holding myself together. I wished the gesture could heal the cracks in my heart.

For a moment, I thought Cassian was going to ask me to wear the necklace as well. Become Zaire's queen and let him take whatever power it was I offered him. But instead, Cassian wound his arm behind his head.

His muscles flexed as he released the necklace. My eyes tracked its arc towards the surface of the still green lake. It made a hollow splashing sound. The ripples were the only disturbance on the surface for a breath. Suddenly, a white hand shot up from the depths, a flash of sharp nails and desperation.

Then the box, and the necklace within, disappeared into the waters.

"Why did you do that?" I gasped.

"My uncle was not a good man. I don't regret helping my cousin escape from his tyranny. But I have spent hundreds of years at Zaire's side, trying to make up for the man I was." Cassian's face tightened. "I was a spoiled prince, too blind to the suffering of others. I did nothing when my own cousins were beaten or banished. But I have changed, and so has Zaire. All I have done since we left our mortal lives is try to reign in his anger, his total lack of empathy."

I licked my lips. My eyes stuck on the lake, on the bargaining chip Cassian had just plunged into the darkness. Zaire would be irate.

"Why did you stay with him?" I shivered as the lake rippled again. "He took control of the Bazaar from the gods and uses human souls as they did. He's a monster, and you're helping him."

"Guilt is a powerful tool. I should have done more when we were mortal. I should have seen more." Cassian sighed and ran his hand along his jaw before turning to face me. "My only purpose these past centuries has been to preserve some of my cousin's humanity. And maybe some of my own."

"You told him everything," I whispered, my chest aching differently than when I'd learned the truth about Linus.

Cassian's eyes flared, and his jaw clenched. Leaning closer, so close I could see the deep bronze ribbons hiding in his brown eyes, he said, "Zaire has no humanity left. He is too afraid of losing his power to change for anyone, least of all me. That is why I volunteered to follow you on the island, to guide you through the Bazaar and accompany you in the Underworld."

"To hand me over to your cousin?" I whispered.

He cringed and bit down on his lower lip. "At first, I saw you as a chance to save myself. A way to give Zaire what he wanted so he would finally let me go. But when I saw you that first time at the ports, so vibrant and full of hope—I couldn't do it."

"How could I save you?" I asked, unsure if he was telling the truth. Cassian had always helped me in the past. Whether it was for Zaire or for my benefit was another matter entirely.

He winced, and a flash of golden ribbons appeared on his throat. His oath of silence. "He won't let me tell you."

Anger flashed, and I stood, wishing I could throw myself into the lake and let that creature drag me into the depths. "Why did you follow me, then? After spilling every secret about me to your cousin, after knowing you're bound to secrecy, why? Is it to torture me?"

"No." Cassian stood too, his tall form and broad shoulders blocking out the light of the moon. "He can't see as well in the Citadel, with the power of the old gods still rooted in its stones. He doesn't know every-thing we said."

My cheeks burned.

"He knew about Linus."

Cassian sighed. "I'm here to tell you I didn't mean to hurt you."

"Get out of my way," I growled, shoving past him. Or I tried to, at least. It was like hitting a brick wall. Cassian hissed something through his teeth, words in a language I didn't know. A second later, his hands grabbed my arms, anchoring me in place.

"I'm going to help you leave the Bazaar."

A trap. It was a trap. But my heart leapt.

"You can't defy Zaire. He knows everywhere you go. He'll have you killed, or worse," I choked.

"I know." Cassian pinched his eyes shut. "But until you came here, I had forgotten what it was to be mortal."

"What do you mean?" My voice was small. I wanted to fight against his grip, push him into the lake. But my skin prickled and my body tightened with traitorous hope.

"Hazel." A pained sound slipped through his lips. "I can't stand by and let him corrupt you. That's why I showed you the mirror. I wanted you to know the truth about Linus so you could come to your own decisions without Zaire using him against you."

My pulse quickened at the reminder. "Maybe the necklace keeps preying on me because I can't face the truth about Linus. Maybe Zaire is right and I belong here."

"You're stronger than that necklace." Cassian's fingers tightened on my arms, dragging me closer until our chests brushed. "You don't deserve to risk your life and everything you have for a man who uses you. Zaire has been doing the same thing—using your desire for love against you. If you don't realize these tricks, he will succeed. You don't have to be trapped here like me."

"How can I let Linus go? How can I let everything I've ever wanted go?" My voice broke at the thought. My dreams of being free from the island, from judgment, and loneliness faded to ashes.

What was left?

"You pick up the pieces and decide what you want for yourself. I won't let Zaire have you," he said with such heat I wanted to blush. "You have a family to return to and promises to keep."

I blinked up at him in surprise. He wasn't asking me to abandon my promises, even though he didn't know about Niklaus. Cassian wanted me to get the medicine, even though I no longer had Linus to return to. My throat tightened.

"What can we do?" I watched him carefully, waiting for deceit. "There is no way I can leave the grounds and even if I could, Zaire wouldn't allow the Bazaar to let me go."

Cassian dropped my arms but offered me his hand. I hesitated, wiping the last remnants of my drying tears away. *Please be telling the truth.* Slowly, I set my palm in his, unable to deny that I liked his warmth. I might have been entranced by his scent—rich spices and dark wood—had it not been for the pain twisting my heart to shreds.

"I have a plan; one I've been trying to put together since before the Alignment. But first, I have to take you to your rooms. We can't let Zaire suspect anything. Once the ball begins, we will get you the medicine you came for and escape the palace grounds. If that is still what you want."

"It is," I answered slowly.

Not for Linus. For myself. To keep a promise to a kind stranger who offered to change my life.

Cassian nodded. "The night of the ball, I can distract Zaire long enough for you to get to the vaults. Then I will be there with Saskia when you exit the tunnels to take you to the gates and back to the mortal lands."

He put his hand on the small of my back, guiding me towards the doors. The inside of the palace was cold, contrasting with the warmth of the Bazaar. Cassian steered me up a massive staircase, towards a tower jutting out of the castle. He stopped outside a carved oak door.

The nearest guards were at the base of the staircase, waiting for Cassian to return. But my eyes searched the endless hallway and winding staircase anyway, waiting for some guard to jump out and foil the plan before it could even begin.

"The door will lock from the outside once I leave. Zaire will send servants in for meals and have you watched closely."

"Will you be here?" I asked, my chest tight.

He shook his head. "I don't know when I'll see you again. Zaire is suspicious. He has me busy with collection of taxes from the merchants, but I am sure he will ask me to fetch you when the ball begins. I will send word to Saskia to help me. She has her own reasons to escape Zaire."

"Won't Zaire know what you're up to? He has you followed. He could kill Saskia." My heart thundered. The kind siren had offered me shelter. Advice. She didn't deserve the wrath Zaire was capable of.

"She can hide my thoughts from Zaire for a time with her powers. Her siren blood is hard for even the King of the Bazaar to navigate." His face softened as he leaned around me to twist the handle. "The guards will report on us to Zaire. You should go inside."

He swung the door open, but I didn't turn around. "Why are you helping me? This whole time you've been keeping me safe—why?"

Zaire's explanation of their past life was only a fraction of the experiences Cassian had lived through. Years of habit couldn't be so easily broken; I knew that firsthand. His warm brown eyes locked onto mine, and for a second, I almost regretted asking the question.

"As soon as Zaire shared he sensed something odd in the mortal world, I volunteered to watch you. I knew you were important to him, that he would use you for something that could change the Bazaar forever. I didn't really understand what that would mean until I met you myself. You showed me being mortal isn't what Zaire made it out to be. Not all are cruel and selfish." Cassian reached out tentatively, twining our fingers together. "You were so passionate, so desperate to help those you love. I couldn't let Zaire turn you into what we are, so I tried to protect you. Guide you towards the truth."

"What does he want from me?" I pleaded, holding his hand tighter. "Saskia said a god escaped during the last Alignment. Does it have something to do with that?"

He made a growl of frustration low in his throat. "I wish I could tell you. I've made an oath that I can't break. Just know he will turn you into a monster if you let him and use your powers shamelessly." Cassian's fingers slowly brushed my jaw and my heart stilled. "Let me help you. Trust that I have always tried to protect you."

"I want to, but I don't know if I can." I swallowed hard, not sure if I was making a mistake in putting my faith in his plan. "I don't know why you want to help me."

Cassian's mouth lifted in a half-smile. His voice was low and sent an unexpected shiver down my spine. "I think you do."

I thought he might kiss me. He was only a breath away, so close I could smell some type of woody oil clinging to his skin. I could see dark bronze flecks in his brown eyes as he flicked his eyes to my lips and back again. He seemed to search my face, waiting for me to say or do something.

"I—" the words stuck in my throat.

I wanted to tell him I felt something mixing with my anger and hurt and betrayal. Something that could soften and grow, given time. But I still felt a horrible loyalty to Linus, even though I knew he'd never loved me. But Cassian was so different. He listened to me, challenged me, and believed in me. I'd never had that before.

I didn't know what to say, what to do. I was frozen with indecision.

He threw a glance over his shoulder and the moment broke. Cassian pushed my hair from my face, his finger tracing the outline of my widow's peak briefly.

"I have to go; Zaire will be waiting for me. I'll be back soon," he promised, pressing his lips briefly to my knuckles.

When his hand slid from mine, I felt something cool in my palm. But before I could look, he gently pushed me back a step into the room that was to be my prison. His eyes were steady, and I tried to believe that maybe our plan really could work. He gave me a careful, almost shy smile before he shut the door. His boots echoed against the stone walls as he retreated from the tower. I opened my palm.

My mother's locket looked back at me. Next to it was the small double crescent moon charm. Cassian must have picked the necklace up in the Citadel after the chain had broken and added his gift. My fingers traced the moon's curve.

Before I could think, I fastened it around my neck and let the familiar weight slow my heartbeat. The fake ruby ring was nowhere to be seen. The lack of it didn't hurt as much as I thought it would.

I sat heavily on the gigantic bed in the center of the room and stared at the canopy above me. Golden constellations were stitched into midnight blue fabric. Even indoors, I couldn't escape the Bazaar's watchful stars. Like the eyes of the gods.

Could Cassian be trusted? Or was he simply helping his cousin in his plot to keep me here, to use my soul for his own purposes?

I shut my eyes and wrapped my fingers around the locket. Only one truth remained: I had to get to the spring and leave the Bazaar before it trapped me forever.

Night Five

Night Six

Night Seven

TWENTY

With each passing hour, my anxiety grew until my fingers had scratched a long line of red onto the back of my hand. Three days of silence. Two nights trapped in the room in the tower. Servants came periodically to bring me meals and silver-wrapped gifts from Zaire. I hardly touched the food and left the presents in a heap flung by the window.

The last night of the Alignment finally arrived. I had slept little over the long, agonizing hours. Worry gnawed at my stomach. I was running out of time and hadn't seen Cassian since the garden.

The dress Zaire had given me days before felt too heavy as I paced the room, trying the door handle every few minutes, even though I knew it was useless. Tulle and silk fluttered while I walked. The dress was a perfect fit, as unsettling as the thought was. It made me look like a princess, not the daughter of some sailor and a dead, disgraced mother.

I stilled at that thought. Arae's words about my father sat like a rock in my chest.

A soft knock sounded at the door, and I jumped, smoothing my loose bronze hair. I tried to keep my pulse under control as the knob turned. A head of dark hair poked through the door and I immediately pictured Zaire ready to force me to be his queen.

Cassian slipped inside and I sucked in a sharp breath. He wore a black tunic embroidered with silver fleur-de-lis and tiny crescent moons. His signature black shirt was open at the collar, tempting my eyes to wander across his chest. He wore dark boots that reached his calves and one of the curved scimitars in a decorated scabbard at his side.

"Are you ready?" His voice was like water rumbling from the edge of a cliff as his eyes scanned my dress. I nodded mutely. He extended his arm, and I wound my hand through it, feeling the smoothness of the velvet brocade brush my fingertips.

We stepped into the hallway and the door slammed shut behind us, as if by some unseen hand.

"Did you find Saskia?" I couldn't quite keep my voice even. Part of me still felt that he would betray me. Trick me. Use me. But I dared to hope.

Cassian's boots echoed hollowly off the elaborate marble staircase. "She knew something was wrong when there was no word of a human returning through the gates. I told her of our plan. She will help us."

The bodice of the dress dug into my ribs and I wished I could loosen the ties. "How will we leave the palace without being seen?"

"First, we must get you to the vaults. I trust you know what you are looking for. While you're gone, I'll distract Zaire," Cassian said, his breath tickling the hair at the nape of my neck.

We reached the end of the staircase in no time at all. Our shoes clicked on the polished floors, reverberating in the empty grand hall and off its delicately painted ceilings. A murmur of voices spilled out in the distance, accompanied by lamplight shining bright orange on the bleached white floor.

"How are you going to do that?" I whispered, my dress of silver tulle and sage green tightening until I couldn't feel any blood in my face.

Cassian's hand splayed on my lower back, guiding me relentlessly towards the row of doors flung open to the ballroom. "I can't say much right now. Trust me, Hazel."

I wanted to dig my heels in or flee before Zaire trapped me permanently, like an insect in a terrarium. But guards in their bronze armor studded the hall every few feet. Watchful eyes glinted beneath the brims of twisting helmets. Wickedly sharp sword points grinned in the starlight, desperate to taste my blood on their steel teeth.

Trust. I had to trust him.

Cassian leaned towards me again, his scent of spice and leather comforting. "When you're inside, keep your eyes forward. Ignore everything and everyone but Zaire. There isn't a single creature that belongs to the Bazaar who wouldn't love to capture a human with an intact soul."

"Wait." I hesitated, falling back a step. I didn't want the only quiet moment I'd had with him in days to end so soon. "How will I know when to go, or how to navigate the vaults?"

Cassian's eyes darted towards the guards that leered from the shadows. They shifted on their feet but kept to their posts, just far enough that they could not hear us whisper.

The music and voices drifting from the ballroom grew louder, mimicking my heartbeat. The cold from the marble floors seeped through my shoes and up my legs.

"Listen carefully, Hazel." Cassian's arm tensed, the muscles bunching beneath my resting palm. "Once I get Zaire out of the ballroom on the pretense of a commotion in the Bazaar, you will head for a secret panel at the back behind the tapestry of the pomegranate tree. The tunnel will lead you to the hidden vaults. Most of the passageways are traps designed for thieves. But if you have this, it will guide you." Cassian pressed his fingers to the double crescent moon charm hanging on my necklace. A thrill of heat radiated from the pendant and through my skin.

"But you won't be with me?" The very thought sent a jolt of panic through my veins. Cassian cleared his throat and drew his hand back.

"I can't." His brown eyes turned dark black. "Once you're gone, Zaire will notice, and I have to be with him to know what his next moves are."

"But you could protect me if you came. We could leave the Bazaar together." I held my breath, not sure when I'd decided I couldn't imagine life on the island alone. Without Cassian.

His eyes stayed dark, but a hoarse chuckle melted from his lips and curled around my heart. "I want nothing more than that."

A guard standing before the ballroom doors coughed.

Cassian straightened and adjusted the long black coat he wore over his tunic. "We have to enter the party or the guards will get suspicious."

I nodded, but my dress weighed thirty more pounds at the thought. Before I could pause or try another way to get Cassian to stay outside for just another moment, we entered the ballroom.

The floors were a creamy marble, inlaid with delicate patterns of twisting vines and bursting petals. A dazzlingly bright chandelier made of a thousand colored bits of glass cast a flurry of light across the party-goer's skin and clothes. An immense dome adorned the ceiling like a crown jewel. Towering glass panes let in the silvery starlight as if allowing a window to the old gods to seethe over their usurpers' celebrations.

A wall, coated with tapestries as large as the windows, was set back against a raised dais. My eyes locked on the one of the pomegranate tree. Bronze braziers burned in a circle at the perimeter of the dais, casting sparks and embers into the air like tiny fireworks.

Cassian kept walking, his head and shoulders upright and relaxed. He looked so calm, his face serene. If we had not just spoken, I wouldn't have believed he was about to betray the person who had been at his side for a millennium.

Voices faltered as we passed. People and creatures of all kinds parted before us without hesitation. My skirts were a whisper on the floor, my heartbeat a wild drum in my chest. Once my eyes adjusted to the color and smells that choked my senses, I noticed Zaire standing tall and expectant in the center of the dais.

He wore a silver velvet doublet stitched in a delicate diamond pattern and studded with tiny crystals. When the lamplight glinted off his clothing, he shimmered. The light, though soft on his clothing, was harsh on the sharp planes of his face. His eyes glinted cold, hard, and lifeless. And his scar stood out angry and haggard against his skin, a reminder of a life he could not fully escape.

"Hazel, my love." Zaire dipped into a low bow. His cold lips brushed my knuckles when Cassian handed me over. "You look as ravishing as I imagined."

"I can't say the same for you," I hissed.

Zaire did not seem displeased. Instead, his eyes roved my figure for a few moments before his lips parted in a wolfish grin. "How did you like your accommodations? Once you are my queen, your rooms will be far finer than the ones in the tower. I will fill them with any trinkets you desire," he purred.

I stiffened as one of his slender, stiff hands snaked around my waist, tugging me to his side with more force than was necessary. "I am not your queen."

I would have winced from the ice in his sneer if it had not been for the group of guards bursting into the ballroom, swords drawn. Cassian met my eyes, nodding imperceptibly, just as Zaire released me and blurred across the room to meet them.

"An uprising, sir," Baltazar, the guard who had accompanied me in the Underworld spoke. "There is talk of a mob trying to break through the gates to the mortal world."

A ripple of voices shattered across the crowd, interrupting the soft music.

Zaire's lip curled in disgust and he spoke so low I could barely hear. "This is not new. Many who have bound themselves to me and do not have enough souls to pay their taxes try to escape when the veils are thin. Round them up, send them to the dungeons, and *extract* what I am owed."

Baltazar nodded, face pulled into a determined grimace. He pulled a short knife from his hip, one of the glass blades that the merchants used to collect pieces of mortal souls. Zaire dismissed the group of guards and they shouldered past the gawking party guests and back into the Bazaar.

"Zaire." Cassian stepped from the dais and bowed to his cousin, whispering in his ear. "There are more reports of Marcel's companions and others who could not meet the quota this season. They are rallying against you and wish to take your throne."

Zaire's eyes flashed a murderous silver. He leaned his head close to Cassian, eyes skimming the crowd as if to search out those who would dare betray him. "They will try, but they will fail now that I have her."

Zaire fixed his hungry gaze on me.

I tried to keep my face unreadable, but Cassian's jaw twitched. He had planned for the rumors of an uprising to take Zaire from the ballroom. But his cousin seemed even more intent on me, as if I could solve the issues threatening his control.

He turned from Cassian and flew up the steps, one hand digging into my side as he pulled me to stand with him at the center of the raised dais.

Sweat slithered down my spine. What could we do now?

"Honored guests, loyal subjects." Zaire lifted his voice so anyone in the ballroom could hear. The room quieted with a reverent hush. "I am pleased to welcome you to my home at the close of yet another Alignment of the seven planets."

A roar of approval rippled through the crowd. Among the guests, I saw animal-headed humanoids, dryads, rabisu, selkies, sprites, and creatures that should not exist but did. Zaire's grip on my ribs tightened, and he tugged me further under his arm. I stiffened at his touch, revolted. Cassian stood stoically, moving to wait at Zaire's other side, his face an impassive mask.

"We have gained many souls these past days, enough to carry us through to the next Alignment." Zaire's voice was clear, like a rushing river smoothing even the most jagged of rocks. It was hypnotic and melodic, lulling everyone with a sense of contentment. Even me. I swayed and would have fallen over if it weren't for Zaire's arm holding me so tightly.

The sound of heavy chains sliding through brackets clanged behind the dais. The wall behind us shuddered, and I jumped as a heavy metal door fell hard against the marble.

A pair of guards wrestled a man forward. His hands were bound in front of him, the ropes so tight his fingers had turned a sickly purplish-black. A heavy canvas hood covered his face, muffling his groans of protest when the guards forced him to kneel before the King of the Bazaar.

The onlookers pressed forward eagerly; eyes alight with the flames of the lamps above. I cringed back instinctively, only to bump into Zaire. He steadied me, running a finger along my spine before stepping forward. His eyes held a savage gleam as he paced the perimeter of the dais, scrutinizing the man who knelt hunched over and bleeding.

"For any of my subjects who dare refuse their tax of souls reaped from wandering mortals, let this stand as a witness. Any who defies me," his lips parted with animal ferocity, "any who betray me will not only suffer the pangs of mortality, but will die painfully and slowly. Let this be a warning to all."

My breath snagged in my chest, and for a terrible moment, I thought Zaire knew. But instead of reaching for Cassian's throat, he continued his slow survey of the pitiful kneeling man. The king gripped the man's face through the heavy burlap, eliciting a pained yowl from within the hood.

Zaire's eyes glinted with pleasure. "The power of the old gods is as strong as ever," he spoke again as the crowd's fervent roar died down. "And yet there are still some of my subjects who would steal from me, and who would deny me what I am owed. They scorn my protection, my hospitality, and loyalty for their own greed and selfish gain."

A chorus of hisses emulated from the crowd. They pressed closer still, eyes wide and hungry, as if they knew what was about to happen. My pulse beat against the side of my neck so quickly I felt light-headed. I wanted to press back into Cassian's chest, but I stood rooted to the spot, a black pit gnawing at my gut.

Cassian flickered his eyes at me for a moment. *Be ready,* the look seemed to say. My blood turned to fire.

"The kingdom of the old gods was born from such selfishness and greed, of taking and wanting and ruining. Under my reign, all prosper and I grant all immortality. And in return for this great gift, for this kindness the old gods hoarded for themselves, all I ask for, above all, is your loyalty."

Zaire's elegant fingers curled under the hood before tearing it away unceremoniously. A clump of dark hair went with it. Marcel squinted up through swollen purple eyelids. His lips were split, his mouth bloody and missing more than a few teeth. He looked to be on the verge of death.

Marcel moved to crawl away, back into the blackness of the dungeons. Zaire laughed and gripped Marcel's hair, jerking his head up and exposing his throat.

Any trace of lingering humanity vanished as Zaire's eyes seemed to glow. He looked to be etched out of the same marble as the gods in the

Citadel. I could see a glimpse of what life was like when they ruled, and it terrified me.

"One of my most trusted advisors, welcomed at my court for the past two hundred years, has betrayed me. He has stolen and lied and tried to run from justice. Not only that, but he took what is most forbidden and sacred," Zaire said, his voice booming with fury and power.

Marcel croaked and writhed. "I only wanted the necklace—the fruit was a mistake," I thought he muttered.

But that didn't make sense. Zaire sent me after the necklace, not fruit. Marcel was delirious with pain and blood loss.

Zaire's calloused hand blurred across my vision, connecting with Marcel's face. A thud echoed through the silent ballroom, and Marcel let out a groan of agony. The crowd hissed in pleasure, as if this spectacle excited them.

My ribs seized, strangling any breath from my lips. If Zaire was this irate over Marcel stealing a few trinkets, what would he do when he discovered what Cassian was taking from him? I glanced over my shoulder at him, a question in my eyes.

I couldn't let him die for me.

"Kill him!" A chant rose from the ranks of beings that were perhaps at one point mortal, but now resembled nothing but hungry vultures. My hands balled into fists and dug into my skirts, desperately seeking something to hold on to. I was powerless to stop the brutal scene before me.

I was nothing.

Zaire's lips curled into a smile. "Nowhere, in this realm or another, is safe from my wrath."

He spat the words like a curse, and each one lodged like an icy knife in my skin. It was like he was speaking directly to me. He was cultivating a sense of fear, of omnipotence to his subjects. Even in the land of death, you could not escape the powerful and fearsome Zaire.

He would find *me* no matter what.

"And for his crimes, he will die here in the palace at the peak of the moon's cycle, right as worlds merge and mix. His soul will be damned to wander for all eternity between planes, never to be at rest."

"No!" Marcel's broken voice burst from his lips, jagged and desperate. I could hardly see the whites of his eyes between the swollen lids. He had seen the maze first hand and would fear that fate more than anything.

Marcel scooted forward, crawling on his bound forearms to bow at Zaire's feet. "Please, do not kill me, my lord. I will do anything, give anything! Take my riches, take my soul!"

Zaire snarled and kicked at Marcel like a nipping puppy. "I do not need a broken soul. You should never have tried to take them!"

The light from the brazier roared ever higher, glowing a wicked red, like the eyes of hell. The flames in the semi-circle of braziers shed light, bearing witness to the awful scene. Zaire raised his hand, weighted down with a heavy bronze dagger. But I could only focus on one thing.

You should not have taken them.

Them, not *it*.

My mind grasped onto the small morsel of information even as I had the sense to close my eyes. The dagger connected with Marcel's chest. A horrible, wet sound greeted my ears. Slowly, I opened my eyes as Marcel slumped over. A few muffled groans were all that escaped his ruined mouth before his eyes faded to black.

I retched, smothering a scream, and backed away from the pool of blood slowly leaking out from Marcel's body. A halo of crimson. Zaire pushed his hair away from his face and wiped the dagger on a handkerchief before he stashed it at his hip.

The crowd cheered and beat their chests, stomping their feet. Ear-splitting bellows rent the air. I slapped my palms over my ears and backed up, one of my shoes slipping on sticky red blood.

Marcel's blood slowly sank into the dais, traveling on tiny ridges, painting a picture of a double crescent moon in scarlet.

Zaire walked through the bloody picture and gripped my hand, forcing our fingers to intertwine as I tried to swallow down the urge to vomit. "There is no way to escape my justice, not even in death."

His nails dug into my hand. I winced and cringed from his cool breath on my neck, searching for Cassian. He stood at the foot of the dais next to Marcel's body, his jaw tight but his face blank.

No. This was wrong. We couldn't move forward with the plan.

Zaire's nails bit into my palm and I sucked in a breath as he grinned at his subjects. "Before we begin our festivities, I would like to introduce my future queen to you all. I am sure many of you have heard rumblings of the mortal girl who scampers across the Bazaar with an intact soul."

I scowled at Zaire, the word *queen* tasting like iron on my tongue.

He continued, "With her at my side, we will usher in a new era of prosperity and power to the Bazaar, and raise ourselves higher than even the gods!"

And with that, servants spilled from the shadows, their arms laden with heavy trays of strange and aromatic foods. Music swirled from a stage in the corner, a mix of brass and string instruments I had never seen. Guests cheered and lurched for the food or the dance floor. The air seemed to sparkle with golden light while dresses twirled across the marble. The only thing that ruined the spell of magic and perfection was the heavy tang of blood and wildness in the air.

Zaire swept me from the dais, my struggles useless against his stone-like grip. I threw a desperate look at Cassian, searching for a hint of a new plan. But he could only watch as Zaire led me to the floor. The music swelled and shoulders, skirts, and faces swirled. Colors and smells burst across my eyes and tongue, overwhelming me. I raked my eyes over the crowd, desperate to spy a familiar head of curling coal black hair and deep brown eyes.

Zaire pressed me close, nearly crushing the breath out of my lungs while he led me in an impossible-to-follow waltz. "And how did you enjoy the entertainment this evening, my queen?" Zaire purred, his lips grazing my shoulder when he stepped around me.

I narrowed my eyes, my teeth grit so tight I thought I heard them crack. "You're a monster. And I have not agreed to be your queen."

And I never would.

The necklace was gone. His one bargaining chip over my free will had sunk to the bottom of that lake. Zaire only laughed, the sound producing a thousand goosebumps across my skin. His fingers skated along my collarbone before he forced me to twirl out and then back against his chest. I fought each step of the dance, desperate to exercise my control.

"You will, my love. Tonight, I guarantee I will offer you something you cannot refuse."

I kept my arms as rigid as possible, trying to generate as much space as I could between our bodies. But the dance swelled to its crescendo, and amid the crush of people, all I could feel was his stone-cold form against mine.

"My king," Cassian's rumbling voice emerged from a web of shadows. I hadn't seen him approach with Arae's magic cloaking him in darkness. "Amadeus is here to report on the stores of lotus flower."

"Ah, I suppose we should get this taken care of." Zaire sighed and pushed one of my hands into Cassian's before purring in my ear, "Dance with him, my queen, until I come back."

I shoved away from Zaire's chest. My skin crawled and each second that passed. The weight of time itself. A moment later, he was gone and Cassian surrounded me. I tilted my head back to look at him, his expression turning my heart to stone.

"What is it?" I whispered, glancing to where Zaire stood on the bloody dais with a wizened old man in white robes.

His fingers dug into my waist, as if anchoring me to him. "Get ready. I knew my first plan may not work. Things could get messy, and you need to be prepared to run."

"What do you mean?" I squeezed his hand tighter, and he tugged it to his lips, gently brushing my knuckles in a tender caress. He didn't answer, just kept looking at me like it was the last time he'd ever see my face.

A deafening boom shook the palace. Walls and windows trembled. Chandeliers and ornate lamps clinked against one another, creating a cacophony of bell-like ringing in my ears. Zaire straightened, looking over the crowd to the arched windows.

Frightened whispers rippled across the room. Cassian twisted, pushing me behind him, a knowing look on his face. It did not surprise him in the least. Whatever caused the earth to shake was his doing.

"Cassian." Zaire snapped his fingers, beckoning his cousin forward. "Identify that sound immediately. We are celebrating." His voice was commanding, but a forced smile curled his lips, clearly for the benefit of his wary subjects.

But Cassian never got the chance. The windows trembled in their frames and dust rained from above as something heavy collided with the side of the palace. A roar, the kind that can strike fear into the hearts of warriors, split the silence.

Zaire transformed. One moment he was the picture of a collected and powerful king, the next he was a soldier, crouched low with one of his curved scimitars in his grip. His eyes turned to steel. His lips curled back over his teeth.

Glass shattered. Screams filled the ballroom. I staggered and fell to my knees, pain radiating through my bones. A hiss split the air in two, so loud I thought my ears might bleed.

A beast the size of a merchant ship slithered into the ballroom, bursting through the broken windows. Golden-red scales, like blood tinged with molten metal, rippled across a muscular body. Wings topped with curved black horns folded over the back of the creature. Snapping jaws, two muscular front legs, and a tail that whipped over its back.

"A wyvern," Cassian breathed into my ear, his hands wrapping around my waist. He hauled me over broken glass and fallen bodies to the dais.

"This one and Zaire have had a feud for the past six hundred years. Wyverns hoard treasure, especially what is left of the gods. It causes Zaire endless annoyance as he constantly battles it and collects the artifacts it steals," Cassian said, panting for breath.

"This was your plan?" I wheezed.

The wyvern hissed, a guttural sound that echoed in its cavernous chest. Its eyes narrowed to sharp slits, bright green and deadly. Zaire appeared just as menacing, the starlight reflecting off of his skin and clothes.

"This is your chance, I won't be able to keep him distracted long," Cassian spoke, hardly above a whisper. Not that it mattered, a naiad to my left let out a piercing scream. The ballroom descended into chaos as palace guards pushed forward to defend their king.

Cassian urged me towards the tapestries hanging elegantly against the far wall. Someone's shoulder collided with mine, sending me careening to the floor. All I saw was a blur of legs and shoes aiming for my head. Two firm hands heaved me to my feet.

"Go! Right behind the tapestry of the pomegranate tree, you'll find the door to the vaults. Run as fast as you can. Let the pendant guide you. Once you have what you need, keep going down the tunnel lined with ivy and stones carved with runes. That will lead you to the main road where Saskia will be waiting."

I started forward, my slippers slick with some of Marcel's slowly drying blood. But I didn't sense Cassian's sure presence beside me. I twisted and caught his arm, shouting to be heard above the turmoil, "You're not coming with me?"

Surely, with our plans completely blown apart, he would change his mind. He would come home with me.

He shook his head, brown eyes grim. "Zaire will suspect me in an instant if I am gone."

"I can't just leave you here!"

A wry smile curled the corner of his mouth, and I fought the wave of heat that stole over my cheeks at the sight, the flutter in my stomach. "I'll be fine. Saskia knows where to meet me; I'll be there when you escape. I'll get away."

"How?" I sobbed.

His hands tightened for a moment on my waist, as if he wanted to keep me there. I met his eyes and saw an edge to them. He opened his mouth to speak, but hesitated. Instead, he pulled me tightly against his chest, crushing me there with his powerful arms. An embrace that ended far too quickly. When he let go, it left me feeling alone and cold.

"I'll see you soon."

The promise didn't do anything to soothe my anxiety.

"But—"

I wanted to ask how I would find him again. Where would he be? How could I be sure Zaire wouldn't hurt him? But the wyvern's piercing screech sliced through the air. Guards surrounded Zaire, swords drawn and pointed.

Cassian's face hardened again, shadows growing thick around him. He pushed me once more towards the tapestry. "Go!"

And with that, he turned, lost in the panicked crowd. I wrestled the strange urge to cry and wrapped my fingers around my mother's locket and Cassian's pendant.

I pushed past a few bird-headed men and collided with the wall, my fingers searching for the edge of the woven tapestry. Golden pomegranates stared back at me accusingly as I shoved the heavy fabric aside. My fingers caught on a small brass handle. I pushed as hard as I could, opening the rusty hinges. For a moment, I was thankful a raging serpent thrashed about the room, or the screeching hinges would have given me dead away.

A cold, dank wind met me when the door swung open. I took a shallow breath and threw myself into the darkness of the vaults.

TWENTY-ONE

I thought I knew what total darkness meant. I'd spent two days locked in my aunt's cellar when I was ten for breaking one of Veronica's porcelain dolls in a fit of childish anger. Even then I'd had little shafts of cold island light stuffed through the wooden slats to see by. But the sheer obscurity in Zaire's hidden vaults was unlike anything I had experienced.

Alone, beneath the palace of the Bazaar, I could not make out a single shape in the inky darkness. It was oppressive, weighing like a thick burial shroud. My lungs tightened painfully at the thought of finding my way through, stumbling and helpless—no better than a blind man. I reached my arms out to feel along the cold, slick wall to my right.

This must have been what Cassian experienced in the Underworld maze.

I felt a pull in my stomach, urging me into the darkness. I took a deep breath and hoped I could trust Cassian's gift.

Trailing my fingertips along the frigid stone, I descended deeper into the belly of the palace. A few hundred steps later, a break in the wall led to another tunnel. Hesitating, I reached out, feeling for the other side of the new hall. Cassian's pendant turned ice cold, burning with frost. I yelped, brushing at my skin, and felt my way back to the original tunnel. The pendant grew warm again, easing the bite on my breastbone.

I counted my steps again. Time crawled by. Dust choked the air. When I had been walking for what felt like a quarter of an hour, I had to stop. Placing my hands on my knees, I gasped for air, sweat sticking my long hair to my neck. The air was thick, almost impossible to breathe.

I gritted my teeth and straightened, straining hard to see in the blackness. The vaults were as much a part of the Bazaar as any other street I had walked. Despair only makes the roads and paths to change and confuse.

Though nothing changed, not the heavy air or impenetrable darkness, I thought I heard a sound, soft and enchanting. It was like a summer's breath and smelled of honey and spices. The necklace burned hot.

My chest lightened, and I quickened my steps. The rushing sound of water, gentle and almost elegant, became louder. A steady light, warm and golden and full of life, grew. A cold sweat broke out across my back. My mind went blank, and I started running, desperate to reach the end.

A brilliant light flooded the tunnel, so golden and alive it almost burned. I fell forward a few awkward strides before catching myself against a set of stone steps.

Sounds that didn't belong underground rushed through the open vault. The exotic warble of colorful birds in large leafed trees. A rushing river and the sound of fish leaping from the surface. A perfectly crisp breeze, cool and warm all at once, blew across the scene. I had no words to accurately describe it.

The dark, cold tunnel opened to a staggering scene of natural wonder. It was like Zaire had carved a piece of the god's garden free and shuttered it up in the vaults. Grass and wheat stalks grew wildly. Pepperings of wildflowers adorned the field, their colors so brilliant it was like they were gemstones.

A hill rose steadily, trees falling away until only one thing resided at its crest. A brilliant natural fountain, crystal clear water bubbling up beneath a beautiful pergola. The stone steps led the way to the top.

The smell of clean, fresh air pushed through my lungs and nestled in my throat. I staggered forward, half-running, half tripping, as my blood pulled me forward. My skirts billowed around me and I raced up the steps before dropping to my knees at the lip of the fountain. The sounds of the ancient garden stilled as I peered into its depths.

My heart twisted, strangled with an emotion I couldn't place.

I saw myself in the reflection of the gently bubbling water. The spring was bottomless, going on for eternity. My fingers uncurled, desperate to brush the surface and see if the water tasted as sweet and perfect as it looked.

Then I remembered from that night in the inn so long ago. Niklaus and his warning. *Whatever you do, do not let the water touch your skin.*

I snatched my fingers back.

How had he come to know of this fountain or that it could heal? Had he reached the palace thirty years ago during the last Alignment? I pressed my lips together, studying the surface. The beautiful garden and rippling water shuddered with power. With magic.

Determination coiled around my shoulders. One good thing would come of this nightmare. I would keep my promise and free myself.

I drew back from the water and dug through the heavy pocket of my dress. The silver canister was still intact, one of the few things I had from the beginning of my time in the Bazaar.

I unscrewed the cap and gently lowered the lip into the water. Almost as if it were eager to save a life, it rushed into the bottle, filling the space in an instant. Careful to dry the edge and cap in the soft grass at my knees, I tucked the canister back into my dress. The slight weight dragged my skirts down on one side, but my chest swelled.

I had what I came for. It would save Niklaus' wife and give me a future with...

A bitter taste coated my mouth. Linus was not in my future. But at least I could bring peace and happiness to a couple that truly loved each other.

Climbing to my feet, I turned, ready to leave the vaults and find Saskia. But as I stepped forward, my slipper caught on something. A vine, so elegant and dainty I had mistaken it for a blade of grass. I shook my foot free and knelt to inspect it.

The vine led to a cluster of dense, short trees. A bright color, a smudge against the green, caught my eye. A bursting, bruising purple sprig of berries growing in tight clumps around the edge of the fountain. No. They were too large to be berries. They almost looked like budding pomegranates. The bulbs dangled dangerously close to the water, but never quite touched.

I wasn't sure what it was, if it was the color or the magic of the place, but I had the urge to take a piece with me. A way to prove I had bested Zaire. And perhaps Niklaus would need the fruit for his wife if he was wrong about the water.

I plucked a sprig of the heavy looking fruit, their skin waxy and deep. They reminded me of something, though I couldn't quite place it. A wisp of memory. I wrapped them carefully in a scrap of tulle from my dress and tucked it beside the water in my pocket.

Straightening, I scanned the beautiful scenery for my escape. At the far end of the large vault, a dark shape loomed. The tunnel leading out. Ivy and scratches adorned the walls on either side as I raced to the tunnel, holding my skirts up so I wouldn't trip. Cassian's charm burned as if to tell me I headed in the right direction. The markings on the walls seemed to glow blue as I passed.

This tunnel was not half as dark as the one before. The familiar aroma of spices and excitement in the air hinted that I was close to the tangled streets of the Bazaar.

The scents grew stronger. A hint of starlight gleamed in the distance. I ran, the heavy canister in my pocket clanging against my leg. But I didn't care. I had to see Cassian. Saskia. I had to know that they were safe.

I burst into the Bazaar. The tunnel deposited me at a silent bend in the river next to a crumbling building near the Citadel. I had never been so happy to see the familiar limestone paths. A siren with dark brown skin and bright gold eyes stood beside a horse and cart. I grinned; my eyes curiously damp.

"Hazel!" Her voice, smooth and wild as the sea, wrapped around me and I fell into her embrace.

Her lean arms enfolded me, tentatively patting my back. I sucked in a shuddering gasp of air. I was free. We were going to get out of here, and I could live my life with my sister—as an equal.

"I can't tell you how happy I am to see you." I pulled out of the awkward-looking siren's hug. "Where is Cassian?"

Saskia's bright smile faded a little, her expression slipping. "He isn't with you?"

"He said he would be with you."

Saskia shook her head, golden eyes turning amber with concern. She stepped towards the cart and ushered me with a jerk of the arm. "We have to go. If he is not here there is no time. The gates will close in only a few hours."

The world ground to a halt. I swayed on my feet, blood rushing past my ears and draining from my face.

"No," I gasped, my chest burning with panic. "We have to go back or Zaire will kill him!"

The walls of the crumbling Citadel beyond gleamed at me like a reminder. Zaire knew without a doubt what Cassian had done. That I was gone. He did not take betrayal lightly, and if Marcel had shown me anything, it was the King of the Bazaar's brutality.

My stomach twisted. I thought I would be sick all over my slippers.

"You can't," Saskia said, her voice commanding. She caught my wrist, and I tugged feebly. "I knew Zaire would not let you go so easily, and now there isn't time. Cassian must have known what he was doing when he sent you on your own."

I followed her pointing finger. Two hazy blue lines sat on the horizon, growing closer and closer together. The gates.

No. It couldn't be, he wouldn't do this, not when he knew the consequences. But I remembered the way he had looked at me when he said goodbye. And I knew.

Cassian had never planned on making it out of the palace alive.

TWENTY-TWO

"Hazel!" Saskia hissed, her hand latching onto my arm. "You can't go that way. The palace guards will be patrolling, especially with the wyvern attack."

I hovered at the entrance of the vaults. After begging, Saskia had finally agreed to help me get Cassian, as long as we were back to the gates before they shut. This was going to be her last night in the Bazaar as well. Zaire would never let her live knowing she had helped me escape.

She let go of my arm and closed her molten gold eyes for a moment. "Zaire will know where you have gone. He will expect you to re-enter through the vaults. We need to go another way; one he would not expect."

"What other way is there? The main entrance doesn't seem like an option."

I knew my voice was sharp and tense, but I couldn't help it. The thought of Zaire gutting Cassian like he had done to Marcel sent a cold sickness through my limbs. Guilt pricked at my skin, my heart. I should have trusted him sooner.

"There is a passage through the Citadel, in the ancient temple of Caelus."

"Why is there a tunnel through the Citadel? I thought Zaire cut it off to smother any memories of the old gods." I shook my head, eyeing the cracked pillars and ruins peeking above the walls that sealed off the ancient kingdom of long forgotten deities.

"Zaire claims to hate the gods, but what he longs for more than anything is to be one," Saskia said, her lip curling like the words had an unpleasant taste to them.

She led me through the entrance Cassian had used, tucked in a small gap in the wall. We crossed through the crumbled city. The grand temple that housed the ancient treasures of the gods rose before us. A centerpiece in a broken crown. Toppled pillars cast broken shadows across her brown skin.

Saskia kept going, leading us further into the Citadel, past the grand temple and old villas with cracked tile roofs. I kept looking over my shoulder at the faint blue lines, like a veil, slowly drawing closer together with each minute that passed.

A much smaller temple, but no less fine than the one in the main square, sat lonely on a small escarpment. This one was made of white marble with silver accents at the base of every pillar and on every statue. The roof was open, though it looked intentional and not the result of decay and time.

We crept inside.

The walls within were littered with cracked mosaics and paintings of old gods. I saw their mighty forms surrounded by storm clouds and lightning. Below their palaces in the sky sat the mortal world, brown and flooded and sickly.

Saskia moved with purpose, her hands working over the plinth of a statue. The arms were missing, but it was clearly a depiction of the old sky god, Caelus. His eyes were hard and cold, glaring down into mine and crackling with thunder.

Saskia leaned forward, using her weight to press against a notch in the plinth. A grinding sound reverberated at the bottom of the statue. Dust flew as a gaping hole opened at the base. I coughed and waved at the air. A ramp led into a packed earth tunnel.

"This will lead us into the throne room. Taxes have been collected, the ball is being wrapped up, and now all are paying tribute for another three decades of immortality gifted by Zaire for their loyalty. Cassian will surely be there."

"Alive?" I choked on the word.

Cold amber flashed in her eyes, and her mouth tightened. "Perhaps. There is only one way to be sure. Now go." Saskia pushed me in first and then followed.

I bit back a sob that threatened to tear from my throat.

The thought of leaving Cassian forever hurt worse than anything I'd felt before. Even worse than learning the truth about Linus. I dug my nails into my palms. *Focus.* I would be of no use if my sentimental thoughts reduced me to a puddle of tears.

The packed dirt smelled of earth and humanity. It reminded me of home. I set my jaw and squinted through the darkness. Up ahead, a pinprick of light glinted, like a keyhole in a door. Saskia's skin and eyes glowed softly. I studied her shoulder blades as she strode ahead of me, her hands wrapped around the hilts of two long golden daggers.

I knew so little of her life before the Bazaar, or after for that matter. What did Cassian mean to her?

I cleared my throat and quickened my pace to walk alongside her. "How do you know so much about the palace? And about Zaire." I forced the words out before I could choke them back.

Saskia stilled, her muscles coiled under her dark skin, like a snake ready to strike. Her eyes blazed for a moment, as bright and as liquid as the sun. But just as quickly she seemed to sag, to dim.

"You know I have been here many centuries. When the mortal world grew too dangerous for my kind, I entered the Bazaar," she said, her silky voice thick with emotion. I was afraid to speak, so I only nodded. "There was a time I thought I was in love with Zaire. Though I never knew a siren could feel such a thing. My old home was gone, and Zaire had created a new one, one that seemed perfect. I would not be hunted; I would live forever with him. Revenge appealed to me. Zaire's mission appealed to me. I wanted to hurt the humans who entered our world, steal their souls, and use them to feed my immortality."

My blood chilled. "But you don't deal in souls, you told me yourself."

The end of the tunnel approached quickly. A rotting wooden door, entirely forgotten, sagged ahead, with only a tiny amount of light slipping through a rusting keyhole.

"I was different all those years ago." She grimaced. "Zaire... he convinced me that humans were base creatures that did not deserve his kindness or respect. I was inclined to agree. Being chased at harpoon point will convince anyone of that." She smiled drily. "But as the years wore on and more and more was asked of those who called the Bazaar home, I began to question him. Why should we harm others to keep ourselves alive? I left his side at the palace, though he did not seem to care."

"He just let you go?" I shook my head, shuddering at the thought of the siren, someone I considered a friend, torturing others at the behest of Zaire.

Saskia looked away, an old hurt clearly surfacing. "He did. Maybe I began to refuse mortal souls as payment to get back at him, to make him notice me. But over time, I realized what he was doing was wrong; that it was murder. I doubt Zaire actually cared for me at all."

I was quiet for a moment while Saskia rested her hand on the doorknob. She looked so old then, not physically, but her eyes were worn down from eons of pain, suffering, and wandering. I did not envy her immortality at that moment.

"I am glad you are not like him anymore, Saskia."

She smiled weakly, her grip tightening on the daggers. "The sooner we leave this place, the better."

She turned the knob, and the door creaked and groaned, hinges straining under rust and grime. The corridor was empty, lit only by a dying torch. Bars shone black and firm on the walls. The smell was putrid. The air reeked of stagnant water and human refuse. It was the dungeon.

Saskia stepped out and grabbed the torch, moving with purpose, like she knew this place like the back of her hand. She ushered me down one tiny branch of the dungeon to where the floor lifted into a raised platform. Chains looped into brackets on the wall. I shuddered at how expertly Saskia navigated the prison.

"Through this hidden door is a passage that leads to the throne room. We will have to grab Cassian and fight our way back. If we are quick, we might slip back to the dungeons before they know which path we have taken. It is our only chance, do you understand?" Saskia asked, her words a command. She drew one of her daggers and flipped it in her hand, the hilt pointed at me.

I nodded and accepted the blade. "Saskia, when we leave the Bazaar, I hope you know you have a place with me in the mortal world. I will not let anyone harm you."

"Thank you, Hazel." A small smile flickered on her full lips. She squeezed my hand with her own before she took a breath. She squared her shoulders, golden eyes narrowing.

And then the siren pushed the door open.

TWENTY-THREE

Saskia and I slipped from the tiny hidden passageway and entered the shadows of the throne room. A wall separated us from the finely decorated room, hemming us in a sort of servant's channel. We crawled through it, ducking low to avoid being seen through the arches.

A massive crowd, bigger than the one at the ball, pressed in tightly. Zaire lounged on a vast marble throne, looking regal and cold. But his face showed hints of true rage. Beside him sat a basin of crystal vials filled with sparkling liquid. One of his guards slowly distributed them to a line of waiting subjects.

I tightened my fingers around the canister in my pocket.

"What is that?" I whispered.

Saskia crouched low, movements fluid. "The elixir of immortality. Zaire grants each citizen of the Bazaar a portion after they have paid their taxes each Alignment. It lasts for three decades before you must take more."

She ushered me to follow, and we skirted through the servant's corridor. Shadows, deep and long, hugged our figures. No one noticed us or the flash of Saskia's dagger. A hushed silence filled the air, one tense and fraught with anticipation.

Saskia stopped, back pressed to a column, and I dragged my eyes across the crowd.

I studied the heap of vials, a cold finger dragging down my spine. The potion looked familiar. *Smelled* familiar. A heady feeling of magic and brightness. Except it looked wrong somehow. A gentle violet hue tinged each bottle. The finger on my spine turned to lead.

"Saskia," I hissed. "Can you still die even if you are given that elixir from Zaire?"

She gave me a strange look, like that was the last thing she was concerned about. "Yes, he dilutes the water and keeps the pure form for himself and his most trusted companions. The weakened version grants eternal life, but does not prevent injury or heal deadly wounds. If you are stabbed with a sword as a subject of Zaire, you will still die. But you will not perish from old age or sickness as long as you continue to serve him."

That didn't make sense. I wasn't sure why.

"And do his subjects know this?" I asked.

Saskia shook her head. "No. I learned that during my time at his side."

My skin tingled, even as I searched the room for Cassian. "What does he dilute it with?"

"I never asked. My kind is extremely long lived, so it did not matter to me." She shrugged, clearly done with the conversation.

I pursed my lips and followed her narrowed gaze.

The wyvern attack had not damaged the colossal throne room, but creatures of the Bazaar huddled together and watched the domed glass ceiling warily. They pressed forward, eager for their own vials of water. For the safety Zaire swore.

Something flitted across my thoughts, something Zaire, Cassian, and Marcel had all hinted at. But I could not quite grasp it. Not as an indistinct murmur rumbled through the crowd, and I choked back sobs. I searched for a familiar head of messy black hair. Anything to hint Cassian was alive. As we crept through the shadows, darting behind columns that obstructed our view, a sickening thought soured my stomach. Had Zaire already killed him?

"There!" Saskia pointed.

We reached the back of the room where Zaire's throne rested. The columns we hid behind were so large they took at least fifteen paces to cross. Together, we huddled in the immense shadows and peered around the edge.

At the base of the throne's platform, kneeling between two guards, was Cassian. His nose looked broken, his face bruised in a tapestry of purple and black. His hair hung limply in front of his eyes, and his doublet and shirt were torn open. A bright red cut slashed from the base of his left eye and curled under his jaw. Like Zaire's scar.

A traitor's mark.

Rage slammed against my ribcage. Clawed at my throat.

"No!" Saskia hissed when I tried to dart forward, throwing me back against the column. It was so dark in the shadows that no one could see us, not even the guards marching by to patrol the crowd. I fought against her, red blinding my vision. I would kill Zaire. I would sink this blade straight into his dead, black heart.

"Zaire branded him like an animal!" I fought to keep my voice quiet.

Saskia's eyes glittered with wrath. I had never seen her like this. Her fingers trembled, her mouth curled over her teeth, which were deadly sharp. She looked like the siren sailors feared in the dead of night. Beautiful and deadly and hungry for still beating hearts.

"Revealing yourself now helps nothing. We will get our revenge another way."

I clasped my dagger with one trembling hand. "But—"

Saskia clamped a hand over my mouth as the pair of guards skirted close to our column. Zaire said something, and the crowd clapped. I stopped fighting, sagging against her as she slowly lifted her fingers.

"We have to cause a distraction," Saskia muttered as the guards passed to complete another circle, eyes narrowed. "We need to get through the crowd."

I ground my teeth together, my eyes raking over the scene. Cassian knelt, head listing, held up by two guards. Soldiers flanked the crowd clustered under the glass dome ceiling. More sentries blocked the other exits. The only free spot was the tiny passage through the servant's corridor to the dungeons. We could never drag Cassian there without notice.

Zaire stood and walked down the stairs to glower at his cousin at the base of the stone dais. He pulled out his long scimitars, curved and wickedly sharp. I sucked in a breath.

"I have been betrayed twice in only a few days. My cousin allowed my queen to escape, the very thing that would have assured the Bazaar's future before that meddling god—"

Zaire stopped himself, lips sealing shut in a snarl as he set the edge of the blades below Cassian's chin. Cassian breathed hard; eyes narrowed with hate. A bead of bright red blood appeared at his throat and my fingers curled into a fist.

"The Bazaar," Zaire continued, skirting over whatever he had almost said, "is in danger. Human souls fuel the very thing that grants our immortality, but there are enemies that work to attain my power. Cassian is no better than them, staging a coup to take my throne and seize eternal life for only himself." He spat at him and dug the blades harder under his jaw.

"That is a lie!" Cassian growled, the words coming out harsh and strained. But Zaire's silvery speech had already struck a chord with the Bazaar's subjects. A nervous whisper flooded the throne room.

"I only acted to save Hazel. I will not let you subject her to an eternity of pain and—" A hard punch from Zaire left Cassian breathless and doubled over. I bit my fist to keep from crying out.

"Betrayal is the most serious sin in my kingdom." Zaire lifted the scimitar above his head, poised to strike. "You will suffer for what you have done."

I moved without thinking, ignoring Saskia's shout of surprise and the fact that I had no plan. "Stop!" I shouldered my way through the crowd lingering near the throne and threw myself in front of Cassian.

Zaire blinked in surprise.

That was all it took for Saskia to burst from her hiding spot and move with the power of a lioness, cutting down any guard in her path. Before my eyes could register her movements, the guards holding Cassian slumped over, dead. Bronze throwing knives burst between their ribs like gruesome budding flowers.

The crowd screamed, merchants falling backwards as they scrambled for the large doors that led into the night. They clambered away from the sharp knives and vicious grace of the swift siren, united by their fear of death.

Zaire stumbled back, his face a mask of rage. He lifted his sword, aiming for Saskia, but she was too quick. She danced out of the way, faster than my human eyes could follow. In one graceful bound, she sliced through the chains binding Cassian. Metal hissed and melted, pooling at the king's feet. Zaire jerked back.

I dove for Cassian, catching him as he fell to his side. Pushing his hair back, I checked his eyes. They were rolled back in his head and the fresh cut on his cheek burned angrily.

Zaire roared, his steely eyes squarely on the siren. "Kill her!" he shouted to the guards spilling into the throne room like an army of bronze statues.

A beautiful sound, a song so mournful it made me want to weep, washed over the crowd. I swayed, and so did everyone else. The air grew thick. Time seemed to slow. Eyelids grew heavy and at once every guard and citizen slumped over in a rattle of armor and thud of limbs.

Saskia was singing. The magic in the song was so powerful it simmered in my bones. Even Zaire looked affected, his hands clumsy around the hilt of his swords. He stumbled off the platform of his throne, cursing as he fell over the body of a guard.

I fought through the fog, ignoring the desire to close my eyes and sink into oblivion. I hooked my arms under Cassian's and yanked him to the shadow of one of the great columns. He staggered a little, eyes fluttering. But then he sat up, reaching for my arm.

"Hazel?" he rasped.

I thanked the gods, the Fates, anything that I could that he was alive.

"Are you okay?" I cupped his face, turning it to inspect the damage.

He wiped at the blood under his nose and nodded, though his eyes darkened. The jagged cut on his face made my heart clench.

"I told you to leave," he said, his voice cracking. "*Why* did you come back?"

"I couldn't leave you to die," I whispered.

"He wouldn't have killed me. He wouldn't give me that escape. You shouldn't have come," Cassian murmured, his thumb caressing my cheek.

The clang of metal as Zaire and Saskia battled rang through the air. He looked over my shoulder and assessed the almost silent throne room.

"What happened?" he demanded, face pale.

I adjusted my grip on Saskia's golden dagger, my palm sweaty. "We're here to rescue you."

His strangled laugh sent a thrill through me. Cassian got to his feet and reached for a guard, digging through his pockets. He pulled out a familiar looking vial, a healing potion, and downed it.

Instantly he looked better, healthier. His nose straightened with a pop. The cut below his eye and across his cheek faded to a white scar and would not disappear. I clenched my teeth, grinding them to dust. Zaire had marked him as a coward, but he could not be further from the truth.

I wanted to say something, to tell him that—I didn't know. That I couldn't leave him? That the thought of him dying was worse than my own death? But I didn't get the chance.

"You insufferable siren!" Zaire screamed.

Saskia and Zaire locked in a deadly dance of blades. She was quicker than he was, moving around faster than he could turn. But she was also weaker. Her skin was sallow, sweat shone on her forehead. The magic behind her song had taken too much out of her.

"I should have killed you centuries ago when I had the chance. You have been nothing but a thorn in my side for years! Rescuing those pathetic mortal pets of yours and keeping me from reaping their souls."

"And you should have died eons ago," Saskia countered, digging her knife into his thigh as she rolled away. Zaire howled and clutched his leg. His eyes glowed silver, and he slashed at her.

"You will not take her from me," Zaire snarled.

Saskia grunted; her eyes bright as the sun. "You will never be a god, only a charlatan masquerading as a king."

Cassian stiffened at my side just as Saskia gasped, crumpling. I blinked, clutching his arm tight. A blur and then another choking gasp.

Zaire stood over the siren while she coughed and clutched at her stomach, where a ragged, gaping wound leaked blood much too fast.

Everything went silent.

The king looked utterly inhuman, more savage than anything I had ever seen. He leaned over the fallen siren as her skin faded to an ashy grey. "I will be a god," he hissed. "And I will be greater than any who have come before, and last ages after humanity has withered."

Zaire yanked his scimitar free.

Saskia let out a terrible groan of pain.

"We have to go." Cassian's voice tore. His strong hands pulled me away. But it was too late. Zaire was no longer under the influence of Saskia's song. He moved across the room like a lightning bolt, so fast I didn't have time to strike with my dagger.

"I am glad you have returned, my love." Zaire smirked, leveling his bloody scimitar at Cassian's throat. "I was afraid you would miss the show."

TWENTY-FOUR

Baltazar, that hateful guard, ripped Cassian from my side so quickly it hurt. Four soldiers leveled blades against Cassian's almost bare chest while Zaire clamped one arm around my shoulders and dragged me towards the throne.

I screamed and thrashed and stomped at his feet wildly, desperate to get to Saskia, to see if she was alive. But Zaire was immovable, made of steel and stone. To anyone from afar, it might look as if we were in an embrace, like courting lovers. The thought only made my grief and anger swirl brighter. I fought him the whole way up the raised platform and to the empty throne.

He dumped me on the ground at the base of the seat. My head knocked against the armrest, blood crusting in my hair. I snarled at him, trying to crawl away. But he grabbed my ankles and pulled me back. My skin scraped against the stone floor.

"Look at what you've done," he purred, motioning to the quiet throne room. Many of his subjects were still passed out, the power of Saskia's song lingering like a drug in the air. Only a few guards, the ones who held Cassian at bay, were awake.

"Let me go," I screamed, my hair wild around my face, my heart somewhere in my throat.

Zaire knelt before me, leaning so close his lips brushed my hair. "You never fail to surprise me, my love." One hand held my shoulder against the cold marble of his throne. The other lifted, trailing down my neck. I knocked his hand away and raised my fist. He seized my wrist before I could connect with his skin.

"I wouldn't do that if I were you."

"I am not afraid of you!" I screamed. My voice was ragged with unshed tears. "Kill me if you like. But if you harm Cassian, or anyone else, I will never be your queen."

"Oh, I am sure I can convince you. Even after Cassian's little trick with the necklace, I have another way. You must know, Hazel, that I always get what I want."

I struggled against his grip. "You will not have me." His eyes flashed like he enjoyed my pain. "I'd sooner kill myself than let you use me in whatever foolish plan you've concocted to be like the gods!"

His expression darkened but his smile remained, cold and predatory. "Guards, why don't you show our future queen the surprise I have been keeping for her."

Even when two of his conscious guards slipped away into a hallway of the palace, I couldn't bring myself to look away from Saskia. Her body was limp, her once golden eyes shut. I wanted to scream, to pummel Zaire into a bloody pulp. But his hold on me was stronger than iron bands.

How could she be gone? Dead. Because of me.

"You should know better than to cross me, my dear." Zaire curled his fingers under my chin, nails biting into my cheeks, forcing me to look at him. "Give in, become my immortal queen, and I vow no more harm will come to those you love."

I would have spat in his face if I could. But my mouth was dry and my chest ached like he had ripped my heart from its place amongst my ribs. His cold gaze penetrated deep into my eyes, and I did not believe him.

The two guards returned before I could say anything that could further anger him. For a moment I didn't even bother to look at the new prisoner they held between them. It was just another person who had wronged the vengeful immortal. But then I heard a voice that sent a thousand cold needles into my skin.

"Hazel?" the prisoner rasped, sounding dazed and slurred. "Where am I? What's going on?"

I wrenched my face from Zaire's hands, twisting in his grip to face the young woman shackled in heavy iron chains. Leaves and grass stuck wildly in her hair. Her dress was tattered at the hem, her bare feet caked in dirt and covered in cuts and bruises.

I gasped, the air burning my lungs like poison. "Adelaide?"

At that moment, the unconscious citizens of the Bazaar stirred, rousing from the sleep induced by Saskia. Adelaide's bright blue eyes were wide with horror. She took in the monsters and creatures littered at her feet and the dead siren. Stared at blood seeping into the stone beneath her body.

I grit my teeth, biting back a howl of anger. "What did you do to her?"

Zaire's lips curled in a feral grin and he fisted my hair. Pain radiated through my scalp as he heaved me to my feet, twisting my head so I had no choice but to stare at my frightened sister. Cassian shouted something, but Baltazar kicked him in the stomach, a look of relish on his cruel face.

"I only did what I had to," Zaire hummed, releasing my hair. I screamed and shoved away from him, running to my sister. The guards did nothing as I collided with her, holding her shoulders. I hugged Adelaide fiercely, tears stinging my eyes. But she did not move.

"Are you alright? What did he do to you?" Her arms didn't lift to embrace me back. I pulled away, searching her eyes. They were cloudy and unfocused, as if she were seeing through a thick mist. *Gods, no.*

"I knew the moment you returned from the Underworld you had a spirit that would not be easily broken," Zaire spoke, his voice smooth and sharp all at once. "You have a strength I've not seen in a mortal since I counted myself among your pitiful kind. But you have a weakness, a fatal flaw that I immediately saw, just as any other with half a mind could."

"Let her go!" I snapped, turning from my disoriented sister long enough to bare my teeth at Zaire. "Now, before I rip your heart out myself."

"Hazel," Cassian spoke, his voice tense with a warning. "Don't let him—"

A guard cut him off, jamming a gag into his mouth and tying it roughly behind his head. Cassian growled and the muscles in his arms and chest strained as he thrashed against Baltazar.

"You are so desperate to be loved that you would sacrifice your own life to save those you care for, even if they feel nothing for you in return," Zaire said. The hairs on my arms prickled at his assessment.

"How did you get her here? Let her go!" I demanded. But it was useless. I knew that. No one could force Zaire to do anything he did not wish to. My stomach curdled at the sight of Adelaide before me, there but not.

"Your dear, beautiful half-sister was easy to trick. A few whispers in the night and she wandered into the Bazaar like any other mortal. She was far easier to capture than you," Zaire sighed. He left his raised dais and circled Adelaide and me like a hungry shark. "I knew you would not forget her or your life back on your pitiful island. So, I will make a bargain with you."

"A bargain?" I laughed once, derisively, angling my body between my listless sister and the prowling monster. "I will never agree. You have broken your word too many times."

Zaire's expression slipped for a second, blazing with bright indignation before it fell back into place. "I have allowed you to get what you seek, have I not?" He nodded towards the pocket of my dress. I set my hand against the cold container of spring water. He knew.

"I don't want it for myself."

Zaire laughed, a low, abrasive sound. "I know. But there *is* something you want, and I can offer it to you."

I glared at him, summoning every ounce of venom and anger I could into my voice. "You don't know anything about love. You're a monster. I would rather be alone, hated, and forgotten than be with you."

Zaire's face went slack. Cassian tried to say something, but his words were muffled by the gag and strangled by the sword tips the guards placed at his throat. All around us, creatures stumbled to their feet or sat heavily on the ground, looking dazed.

The King of the Bazaar gritted his teeth and stepped forward. I flinched instinctively, but he wasn't going for me. One moment Adelaide was behind me and the next Zaire had her by the throat and dragged her to the raised platform.

"Adelaide!" I gasped, my hands reaching blindly. Zaire held her against his chest, his fingers pressed to her lips. She struggled, her cloudy eyes and muddled brain making her struggles slow and sloppy.

Even with the gag in his mouth Cassian gasped, his eyes wide. I couldn't process what was happening. Zaire snarled at me, his hands pushing something delicate and bright white towards my sister's lips. The blood drained from my face and my hands went ice cold.

"Wait." My voice was small. "Don't, please!" I lurched forward, but apparently, the effects of Saskia's siren song faded completely because the rest of the guards stood at attention, blocking me from the throne. Adelaide's hands swatted at her mouth, trying to push the white flower away.

"Agree to be my queen," Zaire demanded, his voice sharp and commanding, "or I will feed her the lotus flower and she will be damned. Another shade lost in the Underworld's maze for all eternity."

The blood in my veins froze, pooling in my heart. I thought of the monsters I had seen in the Underworld, the lotus-eaters who searched endlessly for the pleasure the flower offered until they lost their minds and souls for all time. That fate for Adelaide, pale and inhuman, devouring helpless mortals, was a knife to my chest.

My eyes remained trained on the flower crushed against my sister's lips. *Don't open your mouth,* I prayed silently and lifted my hands to show Zaire I was unarmed. He remained impassive, as still as a statue. My thoughts raced. I looked once at Cassian, who shook his head vigorously, pleading with me not to give in to his cousin's demands.

My shoulders drooped, and a prickling chill crept across my skin. Something cold and lifeless fell into place around my heart. "Please," I licked my lips, "I will agree if you let her and Cassian go. I will do whatever you want."

I didn't recognize the sound of my voice. Small and timid. A broken thing once more. It was the voice that belong to who I had been on Veara island, a time that felt so impossibly long ago.

Zaire grinned.

Cassian struggled against his captors, but more guards closed in, their sword points leveling with his heart. Zaire lifted his hand absently, like it was a trifle.

"Let Cassian go. I can do worse than death, which I know you have craved for centuries." Zaire's lips tilted in a wicked smile. "Instead, I will keep your enchantment in place. You will be cursed to be an immortal in the human world. You will wander for eternity, alone and surrounded by death but unable to follow."

Cassian's face paled and for a moment I thought he might faint. The guards lowered their weapons slowly like there was nothing they wanted more than to run their former captain through.

Zaire turned to me and an eerie silence fell over the crowd in the packed throne room, heavy and oppressive. He passed a guard the lotus flower and unlocked Adelaide's shackles. Part of me was shocked Zaire followed his word without digging for another loophole or caveat. The other part of me felt dead and cold, knowing soon I would be a monster. Just like him.

"Take them to the gates. If Cassian tries to do anything," Zaire shot his cousin with a look of pure hatred, "feed the girl the flower."

"No!" I protested, but Zaire ignored me. The guard nodded and took hold of one of Adelaide's arms. He pulled her away, and another pair of sentries pushed Cassian towards the exit.

I pitched after them, what little of my heart remained twisting to shreds. "Wait, please. At least let me say goodbye," I begged.

Zaire's eyes glittered with a victorious light. He was reveling in my anguish, my pain. And he no doubt enjoyed showing his subjects just how ruthless he could be. He considered for a moment. Maybe he saw the brokenness in my eyes. Relished it.

"Let them say their goodbyes. She will forget them soon enough." Zaire nodded towards the doors that led into the hallway. The guards drove Adelaide and Cassian forward. I kept my eyes trained on the one who held the lotus flower, petals crushed in his vice-like grip.

Zaire took my elbow, and I didn't fight him this time. I let him guide me into the cool air of the hall. Beyond us, the lights of the Bazaar glittered through the large windows like a sea of stars.

My blood rushed past my ears and my breath grew shallower with each step. I would never see my sister again. I would never escape with Cassian. I doomed him to wander the earth forever, immortal and totally alone.

"Unbind my cousin. If he values my queen's life or that of her sister, he will do nothing stupid," Zaire ordered, his voice languid. The guards untied Cassian and took out the gag. A harsh, angry line of red cut across his cheeks. His brown eyes were almost black in the darkness as he cast his eyes between me and Zaire.

I reeled forward, hardly feeling anything until I fell into Cassian's embrace. Zaire let me go and stood by his guards at the wide-open doors. Close enough to hear anything we said. My spirit shriveled a little more.

"Hazel, you don't understand what you're doing. You don't know what a curse it is to live forever," Cassian said urgently, his voice low and desperate. "It won't be like the other creatures here. You will never be able to die unless Zaire does it by his own hand!"

I glanced over my shoulder. Zaire gazed at us, his mouth quivering with a self-satisfied smile. "I can't let him hurt Adelaide. Look what he did to Saskia," I said, my voice ragged. My sister stood, listless and confused, near the windows looking over a strange, foreign land. "And I couldn't let him use you just to get to me."

Cassian gripped my arms, dragging me closer. I tried to ignore how badly it hurt to let him touch me, knowing soon I would never feel his warmth again. Never feel *anything* again.

"I don't care what happens to me! Zaire won't give you the diluted elixir he gives his subjects. Nothing will kill you. No wound, no fall, no amount of torture. Everyone you know and love will grow old and die while you stand there, unchanged. There is no worse fate you could imagine."

His face was completely unmasked. He spoke from experience, from centuries of wishing he could finally fade away.

"I have to do this. There is no other way." I tried to keep myself from breaking down in front of him, but with Adelaide right there, lost and frightened and confused, I couldn't keep a tear from staining my cheek.

He reached out, his thumb deftly wiping away the errant tear. I gazed up at him and something in my chest tightened. I didn't want him to leave me here to become a monster.

Forever, an eternity, alone.

"There has to be something," he murmured, his voice dropping. "We can fight him. We can get Adelaide and ourselves out of the Bazaar."

I shook my head firmly, the very thought sending a quiver of panic across my spine. "No, he'll kill you and force Adelaide to become a lotus-eater. There isn't time. Take my sister. Promise... promise you'll take care of her. Keep her safe for me." My voice broke, a crack I couldn't hide.

His face, healed but marked by his cousin's brutality, twisted with pain. "How can you ask me to leave you here with him? I—" he cut himself off like was afraid to finish whatever he was trying to say.

I tried to think of something brave, anything that could provide some level of comfort. But suddenly his hands were in my hair and he tugged me forward, crushing me to his chest as his mouth dipped down and captured mine. For a moment, I stood there, stunned. But then I felt the scratch of his short beard against my skin, smelled his distinct oiled-wood scent, and heard him breathe in sharply when I let my hands pull him closer.

His lips scraped against my jaw, trailing a line until he met my mouth again. His hands fisted in my dress, dragging me closer. I pressed against him, wishing we could melt into the stars and be like this forever.

His kiss was far different from the ones I'd experienced. With Linus, it had been about him and always on his terms. I felt like I was being rewarded when he paid me any attention. But Cassian's kiss was desperate and fiery. It was like if he took his hands from me, I'd disappear. It was an intoxicating feeling, simply being wanted.

"That's enough," a guard barked, breaking the dizzying spell.

All too soon, Cassian pulled away, his breath coming in quick gasps. I blinked back the stars that had burst behind my eyelids. Carefully, he unwound his hands from my hair and waist. I kept my fingers curled in his shirt.

It wasn't supposed to be like this.

Zaire appeared at my side, shoving Cassian aside. "Take the traitor and the girl to the gates. Now!" he snarled, his eyes wild and furious.

Baltazar and another guard snatched Cassian and Adelaide by the collars, shoving them towards the grand entrance of the palace, the Bazaar, and the closing gates. Cassian dug his heels in, trying to face us.

I touched my lips, another slice of my heart tearing to bits.

"Hazel, the berries, if you can—" he tried desperately to speak, but Baltazar silenced him, one hand around his throat. Before I could do anything, they pushed Adelaide and Cassian out of the palace.

The doors slammed shut with a thunderous crack, and then I was alone with Zaire.

Twenty-Five

I didn't speak when Zaire pulled me back into the throne room. He sat on the stone monument and I remained at his side. Minutes dragged by as he completed giving the elixir to all of his subjects. I wondered if they knew he diluted it, that he kept complete and utter immortality only for himself.

When the last vial was handed out and the last terrible creature had greedily downed the potion, he stood from his lavish throne.

"Come, my queen," he said, his words clipped. His fists had been clenched at his sides since Cassian kissed me. I wondered if he was truly jealous or simply angry that his power had been undermined, yet again, by the one he used to trust.

I found I didn't care.

Zaire led me through the palace, past grand chambers and elaborate decorations. I didn't protest or try to run. What would be the point? We walked by the half-destroyed ballroom. Guards and maids were busy cleaning up after the attack. I wasn't sure what happened to the body of the winged serpent.

I only wished it had killed me.

Soon, Zaire and I were completely alone. He led me through a portion of the palace that looked somehow older than the rest. The walls were made of carved sandstone, a burnt orange color. Large brass sconces held flaming torches. There weren't many windows, but the floors were covered with plush rugs. My skirts whispered over them, absorbing the sound of my footsteps.

"You will be officially crowned tomorrow as Queen of the Bazaar. It will be a lavish affair. I have been planning it since the moment I learned of your presence," Zaire said as if the words were a compliment.

I barely kept myself from sneering. "You may have forced me to be your queen, but that does not mean you need to pretend to be civil. You forget I know who you truly are."

Zaire's eyes flickered with annoyance. But then he stopped in front of a set of large wooden doors enforced with heavy iron hinges. He swung them open to reveal a lush set of rooms.

It looked like a palace that had risen from the sands of the desert kingdoms thousands of years ago. I wondered if this was what Cassian had experienced as a mortal. But then I felt a stab of pain at the reminder I would never get to ask.

"You may know who I once was," he said, voice tight, "but that does not mean you understand who I am now. I am beyond petty mortal squabbles."

I snorted.

Irritation once again blazed in his silver eyes before he shut the door behind us, sliding a large lock into place. Immediately, a cold sweat gathered at the nape of my neck. Despite knowing it was futile, I looked around the room for escapes.

The windows were impossible. We were at the top of the palace, at least eight floors above the ground. Outside, the entire Bazaar spread before us, including the faint blue lines of the gates. They were so close to sliding shut I could hardly see a slice of darkness separating them. My heart twisted at the thought of Cassian and Adelaide escaping through those same gates, returning to the mortal world.

I tore my eyes away, a lump lodging in my throat. The Bazaar would not appear for another thirty years. By then, Adelaide would be well into her fifties. She would have children—a family. As for Cassian, who knew what would become of him?

I had a terrible feeling I would never see him again. He would easily forget about the stupid mortal girl he had known for a handful of days.

"I wish I could say I expected Cassian's betrayal." Zaire's jaw tightened. "But then again, my cousin has always been unsatisfied with his lot."

He threw open a set of glass doors that spilled out onto a long balcony. It overlooked the sheer cliff that fell into the mist and then the rest of the Bazaar. Warm lamplight glowed, shining onto a brass platter with two large goblets. Even from afar, I could see the clear water glittering in the cups.

"I told you when we first met that I understood you better than anyone, and most assuredly, better than Cassian ever could," Zaire said. I wanted to roll my eyes. But even that movement felt like too much effort. I was silent.

It took a moment, but he breathed deeply and rearranged his face into that familiar mask of serene displeasure. "Come now, my love. No need to be so morose over someone you never knew. Not truly."

"You understand nothing," I said, my voice thick.

"You act as though you know everything about my mortal life, simply because you heard a tiny sliver of it. Then again, maybe you know more than I give credit for." He stepped closer, his eyes bright as the stars. "No one has ever understood what it is to be rejected by their own family, their entire kingdom, even. Beaten and bruised and tormented. Not until you."

"We are not the same," I said, wrapping my arms around my middle. Zaire didn't react. He simply lifted the two goblets and returned to where I stood, pressed against a wall near a set of cushions on the floor.

"You may try to convince yourself of that, but it will never be true." Zaire set the goblets down on a low table beside me.

I kept my eyes trained on the horizon, trying to prolong the last few seconds of my mortality. Would I still be able to feel pain or pleasure? Would I become so intoxicated with the promise of more that I would forget what it was like to be real and fragile?

"Cassian was always the lucky one. While my wicked father beat me daily, he ignored it. He lavished in my father and uncle's praise while they trained him to rule the kingdom. He had endless servants, respect, wealth, and yes—even women." Zaire seemed to grin at the ache that caused me. "But he was also foolish. I may have been as lowly and despised as you, but I was cunning. Now, look where I am and look where he is."

Tearing my eyes from the slowly closing gates, I studied Zaire's face, the sharp planes, and the ethereal yet wild beauty. I tried to imagine him as a human man, one without magic and power. Even though he claimed to be above the pettiness of mortality, I saw the wrath bubbling below his calm facade. Anger and revenge were the only things he seemed to know.

I curled my lip and faced away again. "Cassian has honor. That is far more than I can say for you, *my king*."

I flinched when one of his fingers trailed down my arm. My skin crawled at the thought of him touching me again. Would I be able to fight him? Would I even want to once he forced that water down my throat?

A thousand impossible questions swirled through my head. The goblets sat on the table, looking up at me with the promise of cool, crisp eternity. I felt the heavy metal canister in my pocket, weighing against the outside of my thigh.

I winced at the reminder that I had not only failed Adelaide and Cassian, but Niklaus, too. What would become of his wife now that I had taken away her only chance? But I felt Zaire would never have let me leave his Bazaar with the water. Everything had been planned since I'd set foot in this wicked place.

"You must understand something," Zaire said, moving to stare out the windows and the faint blue of the gates. He clasped his hands behind his back thoughtfully. "You may curse me and long to be rid of me, but once you understand what I can give you, what we can do for one another, you will thank me for this gift."

"I have already done your bidding in the Underworld. What else could I be useful for?" I crossed my arms, the metal canister growing colder and colder against my skin through the thin tulle.

"You know how rare a soul like yours is. Complete, without blemish. I myself lost a portion of my soul in my first foray into the Bazaar, before I understood how it worked and what it could do for me. Cassian as well. But you, you were not tempted so easily."

"What does it matter to be missing a piece of a soul or twenty?" I didn't feel like talking. I wanted to forget, to wipe everything that had happened from my memory. Saskia's death, Linus' betrayal, the Citadel, and losing Adelaide and Cassian. It felt like too much for one person to carry. I didn't care what Zaire said, it felt like my soul was shattered into a thousand tiny pieces.

The scar on his face looked paler and the stars above seemed to gleam brighter, glaring down at the usurper below. His face was wicked and devious like I had asked the right question for once.

"You act so superior to me, to everyone in the Bazaar, but you don't know its history." Zaire turned from the balcony and came to sit next to the goblets, his eyes snapping with silver fire. He looked like a madman.

"Where we stand used to be the gods' domain. They existed between worlds, just like I do now. They ruled this plane and the mortal world. But they lost power as more mortals defied their reign. It was easy enough to sway their subjects to my cause. The gods were overthrown, banished to the stars as punishment for their greed and dominion over man and monster."

"I know the gods faded. They tell it to us as children to frighten us into behaving," I snapped.

Zaire smiled coolly before continuing. "If I had not come and ruled, monsters would have ravaged the world as they did in the past. Gods would have played with humans like toys. I can control these creatures, use them for my own purposes. I gift them immortality as a reward. I am not selfish in my generosity, Hazel." His purring voice took on a sultry tone, and I grimaced. "All this the gods must watch. But if I do not gain the full powers of the gods for myself, they will break out of their cells soon enough."

"You're saying the gods could actually escape after so long?" I asked incredulously. Arae and Saskia's warnings scratched at my memory.

"Indeed. They watch me from their prison above, waiting to be set free and regain hold of their old kingdom. I have been the king for over a thousand years. Humans have prospered and been shielded from the horrors of the old world. So has the Bazaar."

"You take human souls!" I countered. "How is it prospering when you take people's lives to extend your own?"

"I do what I must. The gods are stirring once more. They wish to regain their physical forms. If I cannot keep them at bay, the gods will simply use broken humans that litter my land as vessels and regain a hold on the world. A human missing part of a soul is easy prey for a god."

"You are no better than they are," I said, pouring every ounce of disdain I had for him into my words. "Aren't you doing the same thing?"

Zaire breathed out sharply, like I was too stupid to get the point. "On the contrary, my queen. I am a merciful ruler. I strengthened the borders of the Bazaar to restrain monsters and mythical creatures that harm and use humans for nothing more than a meal and entertainment. I keep the Bazaar from appearing for as long as I am able before I must collect more human souls that power my magic. Without me, the world would be overrun. I am better than the old gods ever were."

"You're masking your hunger for power under the guise of charity. You are just worried if the Bazaar was more accessible to humans, they would overthrow you, just as you did to the gods."

For a moment I regretted the fire in my words. Zaire's face hardened into stone and his eyes turned into pools of quicksilver, dangerous and deadly. He stood slowly, gathering himself to his full height, inch by inch, until he towered over me. I felt power radiating from him, something raw and unmistakable. He could blast me into smithereens with a single look. Something held him back and always had. I just didn't know what it was.

"You idolize Cassian for his betrayal of me. You think he did something honorable. He wanted to take you from me, leave me open and vulnerable to attack from my enemies. But he is no better than I. He has harvested human souls for much longer than you have existed. Don't let something as foolish as affection cloud that truth."

I kept my mouth shut, partially out of fear and partly from my anger. My teeth clenched so hard I tasted blood. Zaire stepped back and lifted the goblet, sweeping it up into his palm with long, elegant fingers.

"You wonder why I chose you, why I have spared your life and aided you in such a menial task. The answer is simple, Hazel. You are not wholly human. You are something else entirely."

"What do you mean?" I scoffed, wiping at my cheeks. "I am as human as you used to be."

Zaire shook his head, his teeth baring in a wolfish grin. "Don't you wonder why you can withstand the temptations my Bazaar offers? Do you not think it odd that you can endure intense enchantments? How you can travel to the Underworld when no mortal has ever done so and returned with your mind undamaged?"

"You said it was because I had an intact soul." Even as I spoke, my tongue felt heavy and blurred my words together. Blood rushed past my ears, making Zaire sound like he was far away.

"A normal human is so far beneath my notice that I hardly care when a new one wanders into my kingdom. But you were different. I felt a spark of power the moment the worlds began to merge. And when I sent you to the Underworld to retrieve my stolen items from Marcel, you returned unscathed and unharmed by the lotus-eaters."

"We were lucky," I protested, shaking my head vigorously. Another trick, another attempt to control my mind. "We got away because of Cassian, not me."

"That is where you're wrong, my dear. The only reason Cassian or Baltazar survived is because of the strength they have attained from the immortality I granted them. But you, and any regular mortal, would have withered and cowered and gone mad in an instant. The God of the Dead does not relinquish souls promised to him easily."

"So, you assume I'm not human? That's madness." I stepped away, gulping down air. It was too hot in the room. The braziers and sconces burned too brightly. Sweat clung to my chest, making my dress sticky and uncomfortable.

"Why would I care about you if you were human?" His tone was acidic and sharp. "I tested you, watched you, and sent Cassian to collect information. I knew almost immediately you were something I had been searching for centuries."

"Stop." I could only whisper.

Zaire advanced on me, prowling like a tiger. "Don't you wonder why your mother went mad after your birth? Don't you find it odd you were so hated and reviled, almost as if you carried an aura of otherness with you? And haven't you ever wondered why you never knew who your father was?"

"Enough!" I shouted, holding my hand up to keep him at bay. "My father was a nameless sailor, nothing more. I am just human."

"Deny all you want, Hazel, but deep down you know the truth. You have withstood far more than any human is capable of. You hear certain objects calling to you. You sense the presence of the gods in their old domain at every turn. You are sensitive to this world for a reason."

"No." The protest was a pitiful whisper.

Zaire's nostrils flared and power rolled off of him in waves, bright white light filling the room as if he were trying to consume it. "You have felt something stirring since you entered the Bazaar. You are not merely mortal, Hazel. You are half-god."

I wanted to laugh, but instead, a strangled choking sound scraped its way out of my throat.

Zaire grinned, passing his fingers across the backs of my shoulders. "Don't fret. I have chosen you for this reason, Hazel. You are part of both worlds. You are the only half-god in a thousand years, a way for a foolish escaped god to control me. But I will not let him win. With your strength, we can keep the others at bay and their cruelty from the world forever."

I blanched at his words, a terrible feeling of realization creeping through my gut. "I don't understand."

"Drink this, and you will," Zaire promised, his voice dropping into the low melodic tone he used when trying to manipulate others. I hated that I swayed on my feet, that my eyes traced the rim of the goblet he extended. "The gates will close soon. You must sever your ties with your human half and embrace the other. Together, we can root out the gods once and for all."

"I can't." I tried to push it away. "My family—"

"Cares nothing for you. Your father is an escaped god that created you only to abandon you. Adelaide, your dear sister, was relieved when you disappeared. She has endured the burden of your existence her entire life, borne the shame of it. You have ruined her prospects for years. You are the reason your mother is dead." Zaire's words stung, but his voice was thick and sweet as honey. "They will not care if you do not return. Linus is already in the arms of Veronica. Cassian will forget about you, just a mortal girl he met on the endless line of his immortality. Be with me and you become a goddess. Be with me and become free."

A part of me broke like it did when the necklaces tempted me. This time the water called, begging to run through my veins and burn away this weak human shell and replace my blood with golden ichor. To claim the power that was rightfully mine.

Zaire walked behind me, going in a slow circle. I felt the magic in his words, lulling me into a stupor. Even while I watched the gates inch closer and closer together, my willpower faded. How many times did I have to be reminded that no one, not even my family, cared for me until I finally understood it?

His words echoed in my brain, reverberating through my skull. *Burden. Shame. Forgotten.*

He was right. I had always been a blight. What did one satchel of gold do to a ruined reputation? Would anything change if I had Niklaus' money? I didn't know if Linus would change his mind or if I even wanted him to. Then I thought of Cassian. What were a few days with me compared to a lifetime of experience and power?

My circumstances would never change. But I could become someone, *something* else entirely.

"Join me, Hazel. Together we can discover the secrets of the gods. We will destroy them, eliminate their threat forever. We will start a new age and everyone will fall to their knees and worship you. They will speak your name like ambrosia on their tongues. You will be the greatest goddess to have ever existed. You can find your father and have a new home in a new world."

Zaire extended the second goblet to me. My fingers moved numbly, clumsily clasping around the stem. The metal was cool. I saw myself reflected in the rippling surface. It was so clear, like looking into nothingness. I could almost taste it. Almost feel it spill across my tongue and burn down my throat, changing me from the inside out. I would finally be respected. Mortals would adore me.

They would *love* me.

Zaire fed me images of humans bowing before us, throwing rose petals on the ground so my feet would not touch the earth. I looked powerful. My hair glimmered bronze, my eyes were a brilliant silver and my skin was a flawless olive. I looked taller, lither, and agile. My eyes snapped with power. I was beautiful and dangerous and forbidding.

I wanted that vision so badly. Zaire was preying on my weaknesses again, using them against me. I strained and tried to surface in my mind.

What had I come here for? I was missing someone... someone I had feelings for. Who were they? The thoughts of protest grew dimmer and dimmer as I lifted the goblet to my lips, moving to cup it with one hand.

I imagined my mysterious father, an escaped god wandering with broken power in the mortal world. I had so many questions. Did he want me? Did he mean to have a half-human child? Where did I belong?

The questions hurt so badly I shied away from them, from the fear that always dominated my thoughts. If I drank the water, I would become a veritable goddess, not a mere attempt like Zaire was. I could have everything, *be* everything.

The scent of the water filled the room. Crisp liquid and endless eternity. I lifted my other hand, ready to cup the goblet and drink, when I brushed the pocket of my dress, skirting over the light tulle. Something sharp, like the prick of a thorn, grazed my thumb. I yelped and dropped the goblet, spilling the potion all over the floor, splashing Zaire's polished boots. He cursed and jumped away, dabbing at his pant legs.

He kept his voice calm, but there was a bite behind his words. "I will call a maid to bring us more." He ducked out of the heavy wooden doors.

Once he was gone, I took in a deep, shaking breath. I reached into my pocket and felt the little bundle of pomegranate buds I had wrapped in tulle. I unwound the strips of fabric and studied them. Tiny thorns, ones that were not natural for the fruit, clung to the green vine, as dark purple as the waxy rinds. A bead of bright red blood smeared my thumb, still stinging.

I stared at the skin of the purple fruit, so smooth and tempting. So otherworldly. Then I sucked in a hard breath, almost choking on it. The pomegranates, there was something important about them. Something

I hadn't figured out before. But staring at them, resting in my palm, something clicked.

Marcel begging Zaire. *I didn't mean to take the fruit.*

Saskia glaring at the vials with distaste. *He dilutes the potion.*

Cassian stooping to collect red fruit in the Underworld. His eyes wide as he is torn from my side. *The berries! Hazel, if you can—*

A thousand instances and images flashed through my mind. I stumbled back, my knees hitting the low couch. I fell into the seat, my vision spinning and my stomach lurching with fierce, sickening hope.

The tint of the elixir that Zaire handed out to his subjects had been a soft purple. It had been diluted with something. Something that kept them bound to Zaire, immortal only to an extent. Could it be...

Zaire entered the room, an elaborate pitcher in hand that glowed with a soft white light. I swallowed hard and tucked the pomegranate buds into my palm and stood, doing my best to keep my voice and chin from trembling.

"I have considered your offer," I said, forcing a shy smile to my lips. "Perhaps you are right. I will show my family, my island, everyone, that they were wrong about me. They will fear me. Respect me."

"You see, then, the appeal of what I am offering." Zaire grinned, swiping the two goblets from the low table and setting them in front of us. "As a goddess and my queen, we will finally have the power to rule both worlds together and crush the old gods for good."

"I do." I let myself sway, like his magic was still weaving through my mind. I lowered my lashes and looked up at him through them. "I am sure there are many... advantages to being your queen."

I trailed my hand down his arm, lifting the goblets from him. His grin turned wolfish and hungry as he let his gaze rove my figure. I held my hand out to the pitcher and slowly filled the cups, my pulse pounding in my ears.

"Do you promise, once I am immortal, that we will get revenge on those who wronged me?" I set the pitcher down and adjusted the cups, one of the pomegranate bulbs tucked beneath my curled pinky and ring finger. I had to distract him somehow, keep him from tracking my movements.

"With your powers, we will roam wherever we wish, whenever we wish. We will raze that island to the ground," Zaire swore, his breath fanning across my face. He reached up and pushed my hair back, tucking it behind my ear, leaving a freezing trail of barely suppressed revulsion across my cheek. "And once you are immortal, we will destroy the gods and anyone who dares challenge us. Together."

He leaned forward, capturing my lips in a frenzied kiss. His mouth was cold and hard, the cruel slant of his lips on mine bruising and unforgiving. He let his hands wander my sides, drift over my body like he was imaging every way he could own it.

Finally, he broke away, eyes heated. I forced myself to look dazed instead of revolted. My mouth hurt, matching the thrum in my chest.

"Let us drink," I whispered, forcing a husky tone to my words. Zaire's eyes flashed with approval.

I pushed his cup towards him, squeezing lightly on the soft, unripe bud. A warm drip of liquid slipped between my knuckles and I pulled my hand away, folding it on my lap while I scooped up my goblet. My eyes tracked the dark purple drop slowly slipping over the rim.

Zaire tipped his head back and downed the elixir like it was a fine wine. I held my breath and pretended to take a sip, hesitating like I was afraid of the taste. The King of the Bazaar grinned and my heart stuttered to a stop.

His dazzling white teeth, sharp and cruel, were stained a soft pink. His face fell.

"What—"

He stood, hand outstretched to seize my throat, but immediately doubled over as if someone had struck him. I screamed and jumped away, my glass spilling over the rich carpets. Zaire let out a howl of agony and staggered forward, reaching for me with his hands curled into claws. I tripped on my skirts and scrambled over the back of the low couch.

Something was wrong.

The stench of burning flesh filled the air. Zaire's skin rippled and bubbled, and an animalistic growl ripped through his teeth. He fell onto his side. His hands scraped wildly at his chest and he made a terrible gurgling sound, like his throat had been slashed.

Steam curled from his skin, leeching away the radiant glow until he looked ashen and almost grey. His hair lost its luster, no longer a glossy black. Bit by bit he was reduced from a glimmering star to a burned-out comet. He writhed on the floor, cursing and spitting and gasping.

"What have you done?" he shouted so loud I feared the guards would be on me in an instant.

The steam and reek from his burning skin faded slowly. His fingers inched towards his scimitars, fallen from his scabbard in his agony. I leaped forward, snatching them away. My heart thundered like the waves of the raging North Sea. He looked small and wounded, the scar on his face an angry red. His eyes were no longer silver, but a dull brown.

"I've made you what you fear most," I spat, leaning over him as he coughed and sputtered and groaned in pain. "You're mortal, without an intact soul. I doubt you'll make it far in the Bazaar without losing the rest of it or being killed by those who you have tortured for so long."

I turned away, ready to flee from the palace and make a break for the gates. I still had some time. If I hurried, I could make it.

"Foolish girl!" Zaire's strangled, choking laugh froze my feet to the floor, just a step away from the exit. Everything in me screamed to run, to get out as fast as I could before it was too late. But Zaire's bloodied, broken form on the ground rooted me in place. "You don't know what you've done!"

"I've stopped you," I said, trying to keep my voice hard. "You won't harm another human again."

Zaire coughed. A terrible rattling sound deep in his chest. Sweat slicked his ashen skin. "The fruit does not merely put a check on immortality, it can burn it away completely! I was the only thing keeping the gods at bay! Now you've opened their gate yourself. You've fallen right into their plan."

"You're lying. The gods are locked away, you said so yourself." I put my hand on the door and yanked it open. For a moment the world was still, like a long breath being held. And then I rocked sideways as the whole palace pitched on a rolling, roaring earthquake.

My head knocked against a flying chair leg, leaving me dazed. A high-pitched sound split my skull. I blinked away the spots gathering behind my eyelids. The earth continued to shake, but not so violently as before. I stumbled to my feet, tripping over fallen furniture and heavy decorations.

"They have awoken," Zaire cursed, and spat blood from his mouth. He lay crushed under a heavy table rimmed with bronze trim. "Without me to keep their powers at bay, they will find their freedom. It is only a matter of time. Any pathetic human in this Bazaar could be their next vessel."

"How could turning you mortal do that?" I threw back at him, fighting the urge to free him from the heavy wooden table. He was a monster, he deserved this. He would wrap his fingers around my throat and snuff out my life in an instant.

"Your father," he coughed. "He knew one day you'd be drawn into the Bazaar and that I would want you for myself. You have done exactly as he expected. I was the god's jailer, Hazel. Without a pure immortal to rule the Bazaar, magic will seek an equilibrium. My power kept them locked in their prison. Now there is no one strong enough to hold back the imbalance!" Zaire howled, red-stained spit flying from his teeth.

I fell back a step. The world careened to the side again as thunder and lightning cracked across the sky. Sandstone bricks fell, careening from the ceiling. A tremendous gust of wind buffeted the palace and burst through the windows, sending shards of glass raining down.

The faint blue lines against the sky were so close I couldn't tell if they had met. I cast my eyes between Zaire and the trembling castle before I cursed and threw my shoulder against the table. It was unbearably heavy, and the constant trembling of the earth and sway of the collapsing building didn't help.

I took a deep breath, braced my legs against the sandstone floor, and shoved with all my might. The table slid off of Zaire. He rolled away, reaching for the scimitars I had dropped at the first shake of the earth. I dove over him and grabbed the heavy hilts, my skirts tangling around my legs.

"I hope you always remember this, Zaire," I said, while he crawled towards anything he could use as a weapon. "That a mortal saved you."

Then I turned and ran as thunder and earthquakes split the world.

TWENTY-SIX

For the first time since I had been in the Bazaar, there was no warm lamplight. The roads, once speckled with light shining through multi-colored lanterns, were dark. But they were not empty.

The palace rocked and quaked behind me when I left it, and Zaire, behind. The halls had been abandoned and lay in ruins. I bolted down the main road, my eyes trained on the gates and my hand fisted around Cassian's charm.

Another massive earthquake roared through the Bazaar. All around me, the world was crumbling to dust and chaos. Creatures clawed from the ground like the living dead. Mortals with glassy eyes were taken and snatched up by any being with teeth and talons.

I tightened my grip on the scimitars, the heavy golden hilts awkward in my too-small hands. A large bird-headed man in a tunic lunged at me, clacking his beak and aiming to rip off my arm. I screamed, falling to the earth. A few panicked naiads trampled over me, one of their silk slippers connecting with my cheek.

Blood filled my mouth. But I didn't have time to shake myself out of my stupor or crawl to my feet. I rolled onto my back just as the bird-headed man charged for me again, eyes wild. His beak stopped just short of my neck. Warm blood, sticky and pungent, dripped down my arm and over the blade of the scimitar I had buried deep in his chest. I yelped and pushed the creature away.

I fought a sickening surge of nausea and pulled the sword free. Screams filled the air, and I crawled away from the sticky blood. Pulling myself up, I continued running, pushing past the panicked crowds of crazed mortals and living myths. Bricks and roofs tumbled down, crashing into the ground with groaning wails.

I staggered, coughing as dust and grime pushed past my tongue. Lightning cracked overhead, briefly illuminating the grisly scene. A ghostly being with sallow grey skin and stringy black hair crouched over a mortal woman who didn't move. Its jaw was covered in slick red.

The lightning faded, the bluish light seeping out of the sky and plummeting the world into darkness again. I reeled away, pushing my legs as hard as I could. The Bazaar did not move, did not change paths, or close off tunnels. It seemed cold and dead.

Thunder ravaged the sky. I staggered through the broken streets and passed by the Citadel—only it looked different. While the rest of the Bazaar turned to ash and dust, the Citadel pulled itself back together. The broken roofs re-tiled themselves. The cracked columns rejoined. A wicked red light burned in the braziers in the courtyard of the grand temple.

I sucked in a panicked breath and kept moving, even though my lungs hurt and dread pricked at my skin.

The gates. I had to get to the gates. There were no more spare seconds, no minutes left to pause. Time was liquid slipping between my fingers, painting my heart in a million shades of bright red fear. The blue lines reaching high into the heavens flickered.

Crowds of panicked creatures and reveling monsters parted, and I saw the courtyard with the massive fountain, the one I had first entered when I came to the Bazaar. The basin lay broken, cracked like a large boulder or club had smashed it.

No people danced in the streets. No magical goblets of lotus-wine passed from hand to greedy hand. There was nothing. No one. A sense of wrongness curdled my stomach. And beyond the fountain, right between two half-collapsed villas, stood the gates.

They had looked blue against the sky, but up close I could see they were gossamer silver. They stretched up high, shimmering and delicate, almost like they were made of mist. Howls of strange creatures sliced the air and for the first time, I entertained the thought of what it might be like if I were sealed in the Bazaar for the next thirty years. Trapped in the chaos and hell that I had created.

I broke into a run. My feet stung in my shredded slippers as I ran over the uneven stones and rubble. A sliver remained between the gates, a breath of space.

The cackles of monsters, the screams of dazed mortals pricked at my skin. I had done this. I had made Zaire mortal and doomed them to ruin. Perhaps he was right. Maybe I had made a mistake in taking it upon myself to decide his fate.

Though guilt and shame burned a hole in my chest, I lurched through the tiny opening in the gates, pulling myself through the two shafts of searing, feverish light.

I fell until there was nothing but immeasurable cold and a sinking feeling that I might be just as terrible as Zaire.

TWENTY-SEVEN

As a girl growing up in the wilds of the North Sea, I had gotten used to the bitter cold. Winters were fierce on Veara Island and the surrounding archipelago and fjords. Ice always grew thick around the boats in the harbor and the snowfall was continually heavy, wet, and miserable.

I had always admired the cold and its harsh resilience. Marveled at the way it could grow and change and overtake life and land. It was hard and unmoving, confident in its yearly unwelcome reign.

But the moment I opened my eyes, I held no respect for winter. For its cold and calculating force. It was too much like Zaire. Like me.

The black, rocky beach cut at my bare arm and snagged on my dress. I laid on my side, the lighthouse on the headland casting a sharp beam through the bitter air. It was the deepest part of the night, cold and windy. My skin felt numb and red. Frost coated my eyelashes and ice clung to my ragged dress.

For a blessed moment, I thought everything had been a dream brought on by severe cold. But then I saw two figures down the beach, hunched against the wind, looking lost and half dead, and I remembered.

"Adelaide?" I called into the wind.

Dragging myself to my feet, teeth clacking with cold, I tried to walk. My shoe clattered against something metal. Zaire's scimitars. Staggering, I picked up the freezing metal and promptly recoiled. The handles shifted beneath my frozen fingers, changing and moving like liquid until the curved blades shrank to two small daggers with ornate golden handles and a looping metal belt. I didn't have time to marvel. It was hardly the most magical thing I'd seen.

I strapped them and their strange belt over my hips and lurched over the beach.

The two figures didn't move. The absence of the warmth that had radiated everywhere in the Bazaar hit my skin with a slap. I wobbled over sharp rocks, slipping on frozen sea ice. My lips and cheeks ached with cold. The wind struck my bare skin, and for a moment, I welcomed the burn of cold. The dark end it could give.

The light in the tower circled again, casting a shaft of orange on the two kneeling figures. My misery faded the moment I saw Cassian stooping near the edge of the beach. In his lap was the limp form of my sister. Wind howled from the sea and I stumbled forward, collapsing on the rocky shore.

"Hazel!" Cassian's head whipped up, eyes wide and unblinking. I crawled forward, my chest caving in. He eased Adelaide onto the grass before he leapt to his feet, sweeping me against his chest. "What happened? How did you get away?"

I wanted nothing more than to sink into his arms. His skin still felt warm, and he smelled of incense and spice and sweet smoke. I curled my frozen fingers around the collar of his torn shirt, pulling him in tightly. His hands cupped my face, traced my jaw. A sob lodged in my throat.

How could I tell him what I had done?

"Zaire — I got away," I stammered, my teeth clicking too hard to form the words. To tell him the disaster of my choices. Of my birth.

His brown eyes softened as the wind tangled his dark hair. He dug his fingers into my side and pulled me to his chest. For a moment, the freezing air was gone. I smelled incense and oil and beautiful things again. I clutched onto him fiercely, a strange mixture of relief and guilt bubbling in my chest. I took a gasp of air before I released him again, my heart beating fast.

Adelaide made a low keening sound as she shivered violently, chasing away any more thoughts of Cassian.

"What happened to her?" I shouted over the roar of the sea and the whipping of the wind. Cassian swallowed hard, his eyes studying my face like he wasn't sure if I was real or not. His thumb traced my cheek, but my skin was so numb I couldn't feel it.

His own face looked to be slowly freezing and his fingers were clumsy. I didn't know how long they had been out in the cold.

"I think she will be alright if we get her somewhere warm," he said, his body wracked with shivers. "Some of the lotus flower got into her mouth."

If it were even possible, my blood ran colder. "Is she... will she be like those things in the Underworld?"

Cassian shook his head, his dark hair wet and slick from the icy ocean spray. "I don't think so. She only ingested a small amount. She might have trouble remembering what happened to her for a long time. Maybe forever."

I winced, and Cassian gave me a heartbreaking look of pity. Getting to my tattered feet, I let go of his hand, wishing that I could say more, put into words how much he had helped me. How thankful I was that he had left everything he had known behind, just for me and my sister.

But I settled for, "We have to go somewhere dry."

He struggled to nod, his warm bronze skin looking far too grey. He pulled Adelaide into his arms like she was nothing more than a sack of flour. I held my shaking fingers to my mouth and bent to study her face. She was pale; her lips were tinged blue, matching the hint on her fingertips.

"The inn," I said, my voice quavering. "We need to get to the inn in town."

The struggle up the hill and across the rocky coast to town was arduous and slow. It felt like my first night in the Bazaar, when I had tried so hard to make progress but got nowhere at all.

Finally, we abandoned sand for the cobblestone of the main road. It was deserted. Most people were still too afraid to come outside. The Alignment had not yet truly ended, and the seven planets remained clustered together in a bright line of light. The islanders did not want to be spirited away and consumed by monsters.

For once, I didn't think the superstition was foolish.

Though I had been in the same building only a few days ago, the inn looked foreign now. The roof was bent, warped by time and salt. The windows were dirty and dim, and the swinging sign cracked and peeling. No hint of bright colors or exotic spices.

Cassian and I held Adelaide up, looping her arms over our necks. He kicked open the door, sending a swirl of snow over the rough floor. The blistering heat of the fireplace stung my skin. We set Adelaide down as the innkeeper, a man with a bald head and a red nose, lumbered up to us by the fire.

"Just what do you think you're doing here?" he demanded, eyes flickering over our shoulders at the howling night.

"She's ill. Can't you see she needs a place to rest?" Cassian growled.

"I can't let you in here lookin' like that," the innkeeper said gruffly, jerking his chin towards me. "You'll scare away good paying customers."

I glanced at my dress. It was tattered and no longer beautiful. Dirt, grime, and streaks of sand stained the once pristine tulle. The sage green looked no better than a waterlogged leaf. I opened my mouth to protest, to let out a string of angry curses, but someone spoke before I could.

A heavily accented voice cut in, "I'll be paying for her care, if you don't mind."

Cassian and I turned at the same time. Niklaus. He looked the same as before in his grey suit and hat pulled a little low over his eyes. I don't know why I expected everything to be different just because I no longer recognized myself.

"Of course, sir, as you wish," the innkeeper bumbled, bowing and scraping and offering anything under the sun to Niklaus.

"Have her brought to a room and send for the doctor immediately," Niklaus said, tossing a small purse of coins at the innkeeper. The innkeeper's mustache bobbed as he nodded, eyes hungrily staring down at the money. He disappeared upstairs after waving two maids forward to carry Adelaide.

My throat tightened. "Wait. Don't take her." I moved to block them from where Adelaide slumped on a chair, pale and still.

"It's all right, Hazel. She will be well cared for. Once she is strong enough, you can take her back home," Niklaus spoke in a soothing voice.

I hesitated. The maids stood behind me, fidgeting. Cassian glared at Niklaus and the maids like they were enemies to hack apart. Adelaide groaned, sweat on her pale, ashen brow. I shut my eyes. Memories of Zaire clutching her to his chest, the lotus flower at her lips. I grit my teeth, fighting the wave of guilt and helpless fury.

Sniffing, I tucked Adelaide's hair behind her ear and rubbed her fingers, trying to coax warmth into them again.

"Be careful with her," I told the maids, my voice cracking.

"It will be alright, Hazel. Let them care for her tonight. You need to rest." Niklaus set a gloved hand on my shoulder. "And we have business to discuss."

TWENTY-EIGHT

Cassian and I waited in a set of private apartments at the far end of the inn. Though Veara Island was not known for its luxuries, it was one of the nicest rooms I had seen outside of the Bazaar — a testament to Niklaus' wealth.

"This Niklaus," Cassian licked his lips and leaned his forearms on his knees, all restless energy, "he is the one who offered you money in exchange for medicine, yes?"

The room was empty, besides myself and Cassian, but still I looked around for any sign of eavesdroppers. Niklaus had disappeared a moment earlier to settle his tab with the innkeeper. I wasn't sure why that sent a jolt of coldness through me. Of course Niklaus wanted to leave now that he had what he came for. He would want to return to his wife.

"He found me in this same inn after my aunt's party," I said, rubbing at my frozen fingers. I noticed that the band around my tongue, the enchantment Niklaus had over my words, was gone. "He offered to pay me if I went to the Bazaar in his stead."

Cassian grunted in acknowledgement, but his face twisted in thought. "I remember following you here, knowing you were close to entering the Bazaar, but I do not recall sensing him. Even now, I struggle to locate him. It is as if his essence is deliberately weak."

"What do you mean?" I adjusted in my seat, scooting closer to the low flame burning the coals in the hearth. My thoughts swirled around Adelaide and how pale her face looked. How weak and confused she was.

Cassian reached out to touch my knee and flashed a tired smile, but it didn't reach his eyes. "I am sure it is nothing. Tell me more about your benefactor. How does Niklaus know of the Bazaar and the medicines Zaire hides in the palace? That was a closely guarded secret that very few mortals ever discovered."

I studied his face for a moment. Cassian looked earnest, with an undercurrent of unabashed curiosity burning below. I shrugged, testing the freedom to speak of what happened the night at the inn on the eve of the Alignment.

As I told him about Niklaus' offer, and of his mention of his own time in the Bazaar three decades earlier, Cassian's shoulders tensed.

"That cannot be right." He shook his head and clasped my hand tightly. "Think, Hazel. Did he say he wanted any kind of medicine at all from the palace or something specific?"

"Specific," I stuttered, surprised at the intensity in Cassian's eyes. "I couldn't tell you in the Bazaar, but he wanted something very specific. Water from a spring in the palace."

His gaze dropped to my pocket and his nostrils flared, as if he could smell the water in the small flask at my side. "The water from the fountain?" Cassian clipped each word at the end.

A sickening rush of dread washed over me, draining my fingers of blood. I held onto Cassian tighter, tethering myself to him. I'd forgotten my questions about Nicklaus and his knowledge of the water. So much had happened.

Before I could say anything else, Niklaus strode into the room, his gait graceful despite his age. With a flourish, he took a seat in a plush, high-backed chair opposite Cassian and me.

It looked a little like a throne.

"I apologize for making you wait, Hazel. I know you are tired and worried about your sister. Shall we conclude our business together and part ways?" Niklaus' voice was like velvet across my skin, a familiar sensation, and one that made my stomach curdle.

Cassian straightened and watched the other man with narrowed eyes. I felt each of his muscles coil as he leaned back in his chair, trying to look casual and relaxed. But I couldn't force myself to move, to blink, or even breath.

Arae and Zaire's words crashed through my mind as Niklaus reached into a trunk at his side, withdrawing several purses of heavy coins. He opened the mouth of one bag, even as everything inside of me frayed at a terrible realization.

Water and berries and secrets and gods.

"I hope this does not feel too much. Believe me, it is the very least I could do," Niklaus said, nodding towards the heavy purse bursting with bills and precious coins and jewels. My mouth went dry at the sight, but I had seen enough glittering treasures for a lifetime. They held no appeal to me now.

Cassian smiled tightly, but his fingers tapped nervously on his thigh and I knew he had reached the same conclusion as I had. When Niklaus met my eyes, the truth hit me in the gut. They were a silvery purple, and despite the lines marking his face, I felt a twinge of recognition as he finally looked at me square on.

Seconds skittered past in silence.

"Ah." Niklaus sat back and slowly crossed one ankle over the other leg, the picture of calm. "It appears you have discovered my little secret."

"You wanted the water because you knew what it was," I said softly, not trusting my voice. "You knew it would grant immortality. You don't want it for your wife, you want it for yourself."

It had always been the water, never an elixir or potion.

Cassian went rigid at my side, his fingers searching for his empty scabbard. Vaguely, the metal daggers at my belt burned through the fabric of my dress, straight to my skin. Cassian's eyes flicked to them, a fierce surge of determination stealing over his features. But I couldn't move. I felt heavy and leaden.

"I do not need the water to live forever like Zaire. I already have immortality," Niklaus snarled, his vicious tone so startling that my tongue stuck to the roof of my mouth. "I can take any vessel I wish. This one has served me since I escaped the Bazaar during the last Alignment. Now that you are here, I do not need to find another."

Cassian's nostrils flared, and he leapt to his feet. "You're the escaped god Zaire has been so afraid of. Irra, isn't it? You sensed Hazel. You knew she could enter the Bazaar and that Zaire would use her."

Niklaus—Irra—flicked a disapproving glare at Cassian. My stomach twisted, and the world spun. I cursed my stupid, trusting self. Why would anyone offer a sobbing young woman, with a stained family name, endless money? I was nothing. Always nothing.

"You're a clever one, aren't you? But not clever enough. I didn't simply sense Hazel. I always knew she was here. It was by my design, after all." Irra stood languidly, a strange power radiating from his skin. Cassian staggered a little, sensing it too.

The god continued, "This man's name was, in fact, Niklaus and he was the governor's brother. Such a shame what happened to him and his party in the Bazaar those years ago." He grinned sickeningly. "I have no qualms about shedding blood, especially to get what I wish. Once his soul was tattered and missing a few pieces, I lured him easily enough. But once I fled the Bazaar, I realized I had no way of returning to search for my fellow god's prisons without the keys, my scimitars. I have been trying to find a way back but have had no luck. So, I made my own luck."

He looked at me squarely.

"You used me, because you knew I was half-god. You couldn't break Zaire's enchantments on the prisons without your full powers," I said emotionlessly. Irra grinned before he extended his hand, as if offering to lead me in a dance.

"Yes," he answered simply. That response shouldn't have hurt me. I knew it was coming. I had been used by everyone I had met in the past week for powers I didn't understand and blood I didn't want.

"Hazel," Cassian's voice was full of warning, "come and stand behind me. We're leaving with Adelaide. Now."

Irra's eyes darkened and, in a flash, he stood before me, his hand clamped around my jaw. I jerked back in surprise, planting my foot against his stomach as he leaned over me, his other hand braced against the back of my chair. He didn't budge, no matter how hard I pushed.

A heavy thud echoed on the floorboards and Cassian groaned, as if in pain.

"Stay back," Irra snarled. I strained against the god's grip, my eyes searching for bronzed skin. Cassian lay sprawled on the ground.

"Don't touch her!" Cassian gasped; his face twisted in agony.

Irra scoffed. "As if I would harm my own daughter."

Daughter.

I widened my eyes, breath catching as I struggled. Though the vessel he possessed looked nothing like me, there was something in his air that felt familiar. He had made his own luck. *Made* it. With me. He had created me, seduced my mother, and left me here to use when the next Alignment came. The revelation sat in my gut like a rock.

I wasn't merely a bastard. I was the daughter of chaos and ruin.

"Get off of me," I cried, grinding my heel into his stomach. But the god leaned closer, his breath sweet and ashy.

"Give me what you swore. You are still under oath to fulfill your promise."

"I'm not giving you anything! What did you do to him?" I struggled against his hand, but he was incredibly strong for a man of his age. I couldn't turn my head, but from the corner of my eye, I saw Cassian. The only sign he was still alive were the whites of his eyes flashing as he thrashed against his invisible bonds.

"You have already given me so much," Irra murmured, and suddenly I felt the cold bite of metal trace my jaw. He held one dagger in his hand. The scimitars. I gagged as a now familiar scent burned my nose. His flesh was burning away.

"You should know not to bargain with a god. Your word, once freely given, is unbreakable. Make this easy on both of us and hand over the water. I will be benevolent and let your little guardian friend live. Perhaps."

Charred flesh. I smelled it pungent and strong. My stomach heaved, and I choked on a cough. Irra's hand smoked wherever it touched the blade. Zaire's blades... the ones he had stolen from a god. This god.

"It is a pleasure to hold my weapon of power in my hands again. They are the keys to many prisons, you know. But I am free now, and with them I will regain my hold on—"

Blood bubbled from his mouth just as his features rearranged into shock. The second dagger, the one I'd had at my belt, wedged behind my back and the couch lodged deep in his chest, clasped in my fist. I pulled it back roughly, ignoring the urge to vomit, and kicked hard.

Irra stumbled, gasping and grabbing at his chest, blood spilling between his fingers. He didn't drop the other dagger.

I wasted no time. I had to leave, had to get Cassian and Adelaide safe. Tripping from the god, I ignored the smell of charring flesh and the sound of my father choking on his own blood.

Cassian groaned, but he moved. I breathed a sigh of relief and helped him to his feet even as Irra cursed and twisted on the ground, hand reaching after us, his tenuous power broken for a moment.

"We have to go! If he gets the water now that he has his weapons, he will regain his full godly form," Cassian said.

"We need to get Adelaide," I protested as Cassian grabbed my arm and yanked me from the inn and into the cold night once more. The door banged against the wall and glass shattered. Irra was coming after us, knife wound or not.

"There isn't time! Where is the water? We have to get rid of it!" Cassian's voice was frantic with fear and I felt it leach into my mind. Cold panic gripped me as we stumbled from the inn and towards the empty beaches in the frigid night.

I forced my legs to run, to move. Cassian held my hand, pulling me along, but Irra was gaining. I could feel his presence at the back of my neck. It was now or never. We reached the edge of the cliffs where the sea churned below, angry and hungry.

My fingers fumbled at my pocket as I drew out the flask of water. It burned hot to the touch, a harsh contrast to the bitter air. Why hadn't I kept the other berries? Would they even work on a god?

Cassian took the other dagger from me as I struggled to open the flask.

"Hurry! I can try to hold him off," Cassian urged, his voice ragged and uncertain. He stepped forward just as the burning god collided with his chest. They tumbled in the winter-brown grass.

My fingers were clumsy with panic, and I cursed. I dropped to my knees, using the hem of my skirt to open the lid of the canister. Cassian cried out, an unmistakable sound of pain and my heart squeezed tight. Irra stood, his chest heaving, as he wiped blood off of his blades. He had both of them.

"No," I whispered. Cassian writhed on the ground and in the dim moonlight I saw red pooling on his chest and stomach.

Irra, the god, my father, met my eyes. My stomach heaved, my teeth clenching over a scream. The elixir Zaire used for his own immortality was not a potion to be mixed and created. It was pure water, straight from the very spring Niklaus had tricked me into finding.

Curling my lip, I tipped the flask over and let the water fall to the grass at my knees.

Irra roared with anger, his hand flicking to the side. I soared violently through the air, an unseen force tearing my neck to the side. I tumbled through the grass, rolling twice, my skirts tangling around my legs.

My vision swam, the world spinning. Irra stood over the flask, silver and gleaming under the stars. He dropped to his knees, the daggers lying at his side, stained with Cassian's blood.

"Hazel!" Cassian cried out, a wet cough wracking his body a moment later. I heard the warning in his voice too late. The god held the flask to his lips and I knew I had made a mistake. Why hadn't I dumped it into the sea, flask and all? A single drop of water from the fountain would be enough, Niklaus had told me so himself that night when it all began.

I had failed Cassian. Adelaide. Everyone.

Irra stood slowly, flexing his fingers like they were brand new. His skin bubbled and smoked, burning away completely. It was finished. First the scimitars, his old weapons of power, and now the water from the Spring of Immortality. I had handed this god everything he wanted on a silver platter. I'd never made the damning connection.

A terrible smell coated my tongue as Irra's skin burned so brightly I had to look away. His graying hair disappeared, next his wrinkled skin and grey suit. He screamed, an unearthly sound. In a flash, poor Niklaus was gone, changed into something sinister and deadly.

A god, unmistakably so, stood before me, slowly working out each muscle. Dark golden skin, glowing with power, rippled over marble-like muscle. Deep brown hair spilled over his shoulders, coming to a prominent widow's peak at his brow. A blood red robe swathed his body, towering and fierce. A cruel face, sharp and ageless, tipped towards the seven planets burning in the sky.

The Alignment was almost over. He would enter the Bazaar and free the others. I had done this.

Cassian groaned, pulling me from my muddled thoughts, sharpening my vision. He rolled to his side, clawing his way towards the god. The sight of him, bruised and bloodied and ragged, broke something deep inside.

I couldn't let him sacrifice everything for me, only to fail.

The seven points of light burned brighter, a rush of energy spilling across the sea and colliding with the island. The planets shifted, their neat line burning with multicolored light, bathing the sky in color.

No. I couldn't just lie there, paralyzed by fear. Not anymore. Ignoring the pain in each limb, I pulled myself to my feet. One of the golden daggers glimmered a few yards from the god. I dove for it, pulling my arm back, before I thrust it with all my weight into the Irra's back.

Surprise rippled across my father's face as he twisted. The dagger shifted in my grip, growing and changing until I held a full scimitar once more. The metal hummed, happy to be touching its old master in his true form. The edge barely sank into Irra's skin. A bead of golden blood slithered down the blade and stained the god's chest.

I yanked it free.

"Foolish child," Irra snarled, flicking his hand like swatting a gnat. I soared through the air again, my body totally at his mercy as I rolled and tumbled, my back shredded by the black rocks of the coast. "You think you can harm me in this form? You think you can trick me and free yourself of an oath you made with the God of Chaos?"

He stormed towards me, the grass at his feet withering and dying. I blinked, my head aching, and then he loomed over me. I felt a spray of salt water against my cheek as stones slid and shifted. The edge of the cliff bit into my shoulder.

"Time's up," I whispered as I let go of the scimitar and heard it tumble down the cliff and into the water. The coppery taste of blood filled my mouth as his invisible powers gripped my throat. "The Bazaar is closed for another thirty years."

"I have my weapons," Irra snarled. "I can open the gates anytime I wish."

"If you can find them," I said, distantly aware I was smiling. "I'm sure that won't be a bother, having only one key."

Another ripple of pure energy slammed into the island. The seven plants continued to break apart and Irra glowered at me, even as I felt time slow to a crawl. I saw the decision in his silver eyes. He cursed and dove for his other scimitar lying in the grass near Cassian's still body.

Faster than my eyes could track, he slashed the air, tearing it apart with his sword. Rich spices, smoke, and incense filled my nose as the god straightened and stepped through the gates and into the Bazaar.

Irra turned, his body blurring as he glared, his face filled with such rage it tore the breath from my lungs. And then the rift closed as the planets tore themselves apart.

TWENTY-NINE

Warm hands cupped my cheeks. The tang of metal hung in the air and the waves and wind were nearly silent. Slowly, I opened my eyes. Cassian, his dark hair plastered to his face, leaned over me, my head cradled in his lap.

"You're alive," I croaked, visions of blood spilling from his chest streaking through my thoughts.

"I'm immortal, remember?" Cassian laughed a little, even as his mouth trembled and he smoothed my wild hair back. "And I wouldn't dare die on you. I'm sure you'd just find a way to bring me back."

"But the scimitars, he stabbed you—" I bolted upright. My lungs were too tight. I couldn't breathe. Saskia's golden eyes fading played in my memories.

I twisted, my fingers tearing apart his ruined and bloodied shirt. But his bronze skin was flawless. Not a single cut marred the sculpted muscles of his chest and stomach. My cheeks burned at the realization that I was touching his naked skin.

Cassian captured my hands with one of his. "Only Zaire can ever kill me. I can be injured, but I'll heal. I'm fine, I promise." He lifted my hands to his lips and pressed a reverent kiss to my knuckles.

I cringed at his affection, shame hitting me like a boulder. "This is all my fault. Irra got his powers back because of me. What I did."

His eyebrows pulled together. "His plan has been decades in the making. You couldn't have known and there was no way for me to ask you in the Bazaar. Not when both of us had been bound by oaths."

"No, you don't understand. I didn't just get away from Zaire. I took his immortality with the fruit from the fountain. He's mortal again. Probably dead." I shook my head, looking away from his surprised expression. "The Bazaar, and everyone in it, is suffering now because I thought what I was doing was right. But now the gods can be freed. Irra has no one to challenge him."

Cassian turned my face towards his. "Listen to me. Irra would have overrun the Bazaar if Zaire was there or not. His plan was impossible to truly predict."

I tugged my face away, a sob burning my throat. "Irra has one of his scimitars and his powers back, Cassian. I took Zaire's immortality and doomed all those people. I ruined everything."

"It's not your fault," Cassian shushed me, ignoring my protests and pulling me to his chest. "Zaire and those in the Bazaar made their choices long ago. You had no way of knowing what would happen or who Niklaus really was. We were all fooled."

Hot tears trailed down my cheeks and I shut my eyes, imagining all the terrible things Irra would do once he released the other gods. "What are we going to do? I let him and Zaire manipulate me, and everyone is paying the price. Saskia, Adelaide, and now the Bazaar."

Cassian pulled away until I could see the unbridled determination in his expression. "Zaire had to be stopped, no matter the outcome. And this isn't the end. Irra will need time to come into his full powers with such a small dose of the water. The palace will be in ruins and the fountain hidden, maybe even destroyed. He has only one scimitar, only one key. You bought us time. We will stop him. I know we will."

My heart squeezed at his brutal defense. I didn't deserve it. I was a monster, driven by my selfishness, and look what it had gotten me. Each time I blinked, flashes of monsters dragging mortals through the dim streets of the Bazaar surfaced. Glassy eyes and blood. There was so much pain. So much cruelty.

I thought I would drown in it.

Cassian's warm fingers gathered me close until I was practically in his lap. He smoothed my hair back, tipping my chin up once more until I had to look at him. Swimming in the depths of his deep brown eyes, I saw flashes of the Bazaar. The lovely, beautiful things.

"I know you don't see it, but I do," he whispered, his words smooth and deep. "I am not a good man." I opened my mouth to protest, but he shook his head.

"There is no use denying it. I have done terrible things in the name of Zaire. I wallowed in my anger and guilt until you came. You trusted me after everything I helped Zaire do. After my past. Love is not a weakness, Hazel. If I have to spend the next thousand years proving that you are enough, for me, for yourself, then I'll gladly do so."

And then Cassian kissed me. It felt like it did in the Bazaar, but infinitely brighter. No monsters lurked. For the moment, there was no threat of imminent death and plotting. But his lips were still urgent and pleading against mine, like there wasn't enough time to savor this. Never enough time to bask in the strange feeling twisting deep in my belly. He pulled me against his chest, his arms crushing me to his bare skin. His lips were soft and warm and tasted of spice and incense.

The knot in my chest slowly loosened. The memories of the past week faded to dust. Despite the fear that I had doomed the both of us, warmth flooded through me, like it always did when he touched me. Maybe he was right. Zaire had to be stopped, despite the consequences.

I let my muscles loosen and threaded my fingers through his hair, wishing I had somehow met Cassian before. Because if this is what... *love* truly felt like, despite the pain and the anger and the lies, I would trade every second I had of this life, every wasted moment on Linus, and fall into Cassian forever.

THIRTY

It took a fair bit of convincing on Cassian's part to persuade the innkeeper not to call the constable and have us arrested. In the end, a few gold coins from the bags Niklaus—*Irra* — had given me, sent him on his way.

We had scoured the rocky shore for an hour in the freezing cold for the other scimitar and found it washed up near a shallow cave on the cliff side. Cassian kept it in his scabbard, our only hope of finding some way to stop Irra. Half a key to the prison of the gods.

Adelaide slept safely in an upstairs room with a roaring fire. The doctor said she was fine, only that she looked exhausted and needed rest. But he didn't know what I did.

Cassian sat next to me on a cozy couch by the fire in Adelaide's room. The night faded into morning. His hand rested on my back and I fought the desire to lean completely against him. To let myself feel for him like I did for Linus. So I stared hard at Adelaide's still body.

Cassian's fingers moved to the base of my throat, tracing the necklace that hung against my skin and pulling me from my thoughts. "I like this charm better than that ring," he rumbled in my ear, large fingers tracing the double crescent moons against my sternum.

"Don't think I didn't notice you threw it away." I narrow my eyes at him, but a shiver rippled over my skin.

"I'm sure I don't know what you're getting at." He made a mock sound of outrage and pulled me closer.

I rolled my eyes, but my voice softened. "Thank you. For giving it to me. For helping me and proving I could trust you."

His eyes burned a deep amber. "Anything for you, Hazel. I would do anything, *give* anything to help you."

"How does it work?" I asked, ignoring the way my heart flipped at the earnestness in his voice. "Is it like your tattoo?"

Adelaide shifted in her bed, sweat sticking to her skin. Cassian frowned and reached for a fresh towel, dunking it in icy water before placing it over my sister's brow. My heart squeezed again as he shifted, sitting back down beside me.

"My tattoo is more of a brand." He touched his cheek, where a new scar, pale and jagged, ran beneath his eye. "It was the mark Zaire gave me to seal our bond. It kept me at his side, kept me from leaving the Bazaar. But it also gave me access to its secrets. The mark holds part of Arae's innate power over darkness and mysteries. Secrets and paths. I made that pendant using a sliver of that power. For you."

I smiled, touching the token and studying the dark mark on the back of his hand. A piece of him rested against my skin. It felt more intimate, more permanent than Linus' paltry glass ring.

My good mood faded. "Will Irra be able to open some of the prisons?" I asked.

"Not right away with one key. He will find another way to open the doors, I'm sure. Even so, Irra will need to unearth the fountain or find an older way to return the gods to their true forms. It will take time, but once the gods have their powers fully restored and have burned away their vessels," Cassian swallowed, "it will be worse than it was before. They will want vengeance on the mortals who have long forgotten them, who helped imprison and erase them from the world."

"How can we stop it?" I sat up, my eyes tracing Adelaide's sleeping face. Her brow furrowed and her lips trembled. I wondered if, even in her dreams, she was trying to remember.

Cassian rubbed his eyes. Even with the evidence of battle and the dungeons still on him, he looked radiant. I couldn't help but feel a dagger in my heart at the thought of Zaire's curse, branded into Cassian's skin. How he would walk among the world as an immortal, alone, and forgotten to time. Lost to me. I couldn't think of that, or it would tear me apart.

"I'm not sure, but we will find a way. Zaire wanted to use you in his battle against the gods. I fear our answers are tied to your blood."

I swallowed and looked away from Adelaide. I had seen how immortals treated humans. What could a useless half-god like me do to protect them? My powers, whatever they were, had only ever been used by others against me.

"But we have years until the gates open again, right? They will be contained for a while at least." I tried to keep the hope out of my voice.

Cassian grimaced and studied his hands. "I don't know," he said carefully. "With Zaire gone, there is no telling. There are no reigns holding back the power of the Citadel."

I stared out the window as the sun broke over the waves and spread across the island, coating the boiling sea in a watercolor of pinks, oranges, and reds. I imagined the sun as the old gods, tearing across the world.

Cassian shifted again, his arms wrapping around me as if he were afraid I'd disappear. His warmth radiating through my bones more than the fire. "I haven't seen a sunrise in a thousand years," he said, his voice breathy with wonder.

I turned to look at him, at a man who had sacrificed everything to help a girl he hardly knew. I wanted to tell him then that I loved him, despite everything. But I'd thought myself in love once before. And Cassian could break me far worse than Linus ever had.

If I had learned anything in my time in the Bazaar and with Zaire, it was that my greatest weakness was my desperate desire for love. I didn't know if Cassian was capable of feeling true love after all he had gone through over the centuries. Losing parts of his soul. Killing for Zaire.

I thought of my mother pining for a man she thought she had loved who turned out to be a wicked god.

Adelaide rolled over again; her brow tight. I tried to reign in my traitorous heart and focus on her. There was someone who I loved and loved me in return. Someone who needed me.

"We have to find a way to stop Irra," I said, mostly to myself. "There has to be something, some forgotten thing that can help us. I can't lose my sister again."

Cassian nodded grimly, his hands trailing down my arms and leaving fire in their wake. My heart tore a little as I fought against the words threatening to spill from my tongue.

"I think I know where we can find answers," he said, his eyes a million miles away. "A place I haven't seen since the gods walked the earth."

"Where?" I asked, chilled.

"Home." He stared down at me, apprehension and fear twisting his handsome features. "I have to go home."

EPILOGUE

Fire rained from the roofs of buildings and fell into the canals, illuminating the water that ran red with blood. The screams had long ago died away. The bodies of mortals with their glassy eyes lay strewn about the Bazaar, cold and lifeless.

Zaire cursed at the waste of souls.

His old guards were scattered, hunting for any remaining mortals to spirit away their souls to hoard for themselves. Or perhaps to gather vessels for their new masters, the gods. How easily they had turned on him.

Fools. Damn them all.

Irra had returned like a phoenix from the ashes, stirring the memories of the older creatures that had once happily served him and his kind. The King of the Bazaar's once-loyal army now served a god.

Irra had returned to the Citadel, a scimitar in his hand, and finally restored the old city of the gods. Red lights rained from the sky, Irra's power spreading and searching for signs of the other prisons hidden throughout the Bazaar.

Zaire growled and dragged himself further through the streets, his leg a tangled mess of broken bones behind him. For a thousand years he had ruled the Bazaar. He had brought peace and order to the lawless plane, granting his followers eternal life. He had been *better* than a god, stronger than one too.

At least the fountain was destroyed now beneath the ruins of his old home.

Zaire's leg caught on the mangled body of a dead naiad, and he bit back a series of curses. He dragged himself farther towards the endless river that toppled off the edge of the Bazaar and into nothingness.

Hazel had been clever, turning his immortality against him. But she was foolish and brash, just like her insufferable father. They may have thought they won, but Zaire was not done yet.

He waved his hand over a crystal half-submerged in the glittering water near the roaring waterfall. Nothing happened. He gritted his teeth, despising the feeling of being mortal and without magic once more.

Zaire wrapped his bloodied fingers around the crystal and pushed. It sank into the water, leaving swirling eddies in its wake. The rocks around him tumbled away, falling over the void to reveal a cave.

He had been wise enough to forge alliances with powerful beings, even with some of the few lesser gods he had allowed to remain. The yawning tunnel stretched before him, smelling of dankness, death, and decay. He still had power here.

Though most of his former subjects had abandoned him, there was at least one sniveling man he could rely on. Baltazar peered at him from within the tunnel, lips twisted down in fear. He knew the wrath of Zaire as a mortal as well as when he was king. His fear was well placed.

"My lord," he stammered, face pale, "I have done as you asked. They await you in the ancient lands."

A limp form rested in his soldier's arms. Dark skin, a filthy amber dress. Saskia groaned in pain, her slashed belly leaking blood. Zaire grinned through his own pain to see the haughty siren brought low.

"Will she live?" he asked.

Baltazar shifted, and Saskia whimpered again. "She will. I stole a vial from another soldier's body. Her powers will work shortly."

"Then bring her with us. We must get started." Zaire smiled and hoisted himself up, leaning against the obsidian sides of the tunnel. The once-powerful King of the Bazaar inched forward, clawing his way into the Underworld, and straight towards his passage to the world of the mortals.

Also by Catelyn Wilson

Beyond the Hawthorne Tree

About the Author

Catelyn writes Young and New Adult fantasy with mythological twists. She grew up traveling the world and enjoys sprinkling the culture and history of her homes throughout her novels.

Currently she lives in Texas with her husband where she writes and obsesses over her dog. One day she dreams of owning highland cattle and miniature donkeys.

Follow her to stay up to date on new releases, giveaways, and other announcements! She is most active on TikTok and Instagram and her handle for both is @Catelyn_Writes.

Acknowledgments

This book has been a whirlwind! I had the idea for a magical bazaar that appears once in a while sometime in 2020. Of course, we all know how that year went. I was just starting a new teaching job, had barely graduated college, and was extremely stressed out. So this poor book got written, neglected, re-written, neglected again, partially abandoned, and then re-written one more time. Yay.

Thank you to my wonderful editor and friend Katie Taylor. Not only are you a fantastic writer yourself, but you always make time for my books, ideas, and complaints. It's not fair that you live so far away.

To my sister, Camille, who painstakingly works with me to create fantastic character art, chapter headings, and anything else my non-artistic self begs her for. Your love of art and history is everywhere in this book.

To my sister, Courtney, who cheerleads me every step of the way. You rock, even if you pretend reading isn't your thing. We all know you're a little liar, you cross-fitting goddess.

Maddie, my book club member, neighbor, and fellow book addict: your help and support is so appreciated.

And finally to Mom, Dad, and Taylor—you always support my ideas and I'm glad you let me share them with you in my own time and my own way. I love you! (Please ignore the kissing scenes).